BROKEN SLATE

A SEAN COLEMAN THRILLER

JOHN A. DALY

BQB

Virginia

Published in the United States by BQB Publishing
(an imprint of Boutique of Quality Books Publishing, Inc.)
www.bqbpublishing.com

978-1-945448-08-9 (p)
978-1-945448-09-6 (e)

Library of Congress Control Number: 2017936395

Book design by Robin Krauss, www.bookformatters.com
Cover design by Ellis Dixon, www.ellisdixon.com
First editor: Kimberly Fout
Second Editor: Olivia Swenson

Also in the Sean Coleman Thriller series from John A. Daly

From a Dead Sleep
Blood Trade

Praise for John A. Daly
and *Broken Slate*

"John Daly has a magical writing style, and his books keep you up late at night turning pages. Sean, the protagonist, helps you see the world through his eyes in a total escape from daily life. You won't want to put it down."

— Dana Perino, Former White House Press Secretary

"Crackling with gunfire and suspense, the opening pages of BROKEN SLATE make clear that John A. Daly writes with assurance and style -- and without fear or political correctness. This third installment in the Sean Coleman series brings us an engrossing thriller, centered around a deeply flawed but compelling character: an antihero for the post-9/11 age."

— James Rosen, Fox News chief Washington correspondent
and author of *The Strong Man* and *Cheney One On One*

"What a great f***ing book. Seriously . . . Sean Coleman is the kind of character that pisses you off---he's emotionally broken, often thoughtless, and sometimes a jerk. He's also loyal, honorable, and anything but a super hero. In short, John Daly's Sean Coleman is a lot like you and me."

— Terry Schappert, U.S. Army Special Forces,
and host of *Warriors*, *Shark Attack Survival Guide*,
***Dude You're Screwed!*, and**
Hollywood Weapons: Fact or Fiction?

Praise for John A. Daly
and *From a Dead Sleep*

Some writers are thoughtful. Some have style. John Daly has both. When I read his work, it's time well spent.

— Bernard Goldberg,
New York Times **bestselling author of *Bias***

An epic thriller with a memorable, unorthodox main character . . . a riveting read . . .

— *Colorado Country Life Magazine*

A fast-reading suspense book that surprised me so much, I had to finish it in one sitting.

— Alice de Sturler
of the American Investigative Society of Cold Cases

A thriller that packs a punch! This was a very exciting debut novel from John A. Daly. This novel packs a lot of jaw-dropping action into its well-structured narrative—a narrative that gives life to the myriad of characters that inhabit its pages and provides plenty of plot twists and turns to keep you glued to the pages.

— Reading, Writing, and Riesling book blog

I loved this book. The suspense had me sitting on the edge of my seat . . . The author did a fabulous job with the setting details—I could picture every touch, smell, sight that the characters went through . . .

— Yawatta Hosby, author of the novel *One by One*

From a Dead Sleep is a page-turner, an exciting, well-written thriller with a solid back story and more than enough plot twists to keep you guessing.

— Marilyn Armstrong, Serendipity book blog

Praise for *Blood Trade*

"This book has so many twists, turns, mis-directions and layers of plot that I even forgot to eat where I was so involved. The characters are larger than life and when you think you know them there is another surprise just around the corner."

— Best Selling Crime Thrillers

5 stars. "Blood Trade is an awesome read that keeps you on your toes. You never know what is going to happen next and each new piece of the puzzle that is revealed is something you'd never expect. This is not one of those "guess who did it" thrillers. You honestly can't do that. You'll have the ah-ha moments when your realize who did something, but you'd never guess it was that person before-hand.

John A. Daly is masterful at writing a good thriller and I can't wait to read more thriller novels from him."

— The Goth Girl Reads

"This is the first book I've read from John Daly, it is not the first in the series but I was not confused. This book could be read as a stand alone. The main character Sean Coleman is not your typical Hot guy that can't do anything wrong. He has an alcoholic past, and the town where he lives doesn't take him serious, and is just a joke to them. Thus making a Believable character with flaws, that is more real."

— Vanessa Visagie, Vanessa Reviews

"The second in a series that will certainly continue, this book is a darned good read. The status of hero is shared by a super cop now living in a small community and his hapless (formerly) alcoholic brother-in-law. The main characters are well developed and the storyline good. This reader was torn between who to cheer for (the 'goodies' or the 'baddies') on several occasions and in many respects, the plot is quite unique.

An enjoyable read with characters that wouldn't fit in with either the 'gung ho' or the 'splendidly rich and beautiful' crowd that usually populate American action stories and all the better for it!

This is a stand alone book despite being the second in the series. My enjoyment wasn't marred by not having read the first and I will certainly go back and read the predecessor."

— Mary Edgley, Goodreads

To the loves of my life, Sarah, Chase, and Olivia.

To my parents, John ("Jack") and Barbara.

Chapter 1

J ack lost his balance, tumbling down the last half of the hardwood staircase. He crashed in a heap at the bottom, breathless and with blood in his mouth.

Sweat streamed from under his ski cap as his heart thudded in his chest. He'd likely broken a rib, but the adrenaline rushing through his aged body wouldn't let him feel it.

Get up! echoed through his skull. He scrambled to his hands and knees and spared a precious second to palm the outside of a vinyl duffle bag strapped over his shoulder. *It's still there.*

Teeth clenched, he climbed to his feet and scurried down the short hallway. He entered the living area he'd passed through on his way in, where a small Victorian lamp in the corner shaped shadows off the leather couches, large busts, and thick art that decorated the walls. The hands on the clock beside the lamp read four twenty-five.

The window he'd gained entry through was just around the corner. He was sure the others hadn't noticed it was open in the dark of night—if they had, they would have *all* been dead, not just Bobby and the woman.

The men were close behind him, their rapid footsteps on the staircase like an avalanche.

"Don't let him get away!" a frail voice wailed in panic—the man who'd been giving the orders upstairs.

Jack had nearly reached the window when he realized the heavy, stubborn pane had slid down, just far enough to make a quick escape through it difficult. Unfortunately, it was still his best alternative.

After the melee upstairs, there'd be no talking his way out of this, no debating. The men's opening argument would be a bullet through his head.

Taking a deep breath, he tucked the duffle bag under his arm and lowered his shoulder to smash into the pane. He crashed through the window, twisting his feet up as the noise echoed in the quiet night.

He fell a few feet amid splintered wood and shattered glass before hitting a large, metal air conditioning unit, not breaking its indifferent humming. His body teetered on the edge before toppling to the flagstone walkway. Sharp pain shot through his shin when his knee made contact with the rock.

Something punched through the remaining jagged glass of the window, spraying shards through the air. He heard no gun blast but knew the man with the silencer was shooting at him.

He wasn't going to make it over the eight-foot stone wall again— no time to search out a tree limb to climb across like before. His only hope was to get to the back end of the property along the beach. Jack got to his feet and hobbled alongside the house as best he could, glass sprinkling from the folds of his clothes. He reached the corner of the building and darted around it, out of the line of fire from the back windows.

He took a few deep breaths as he glanced up at four imposing white pillars that overlooked the wide, concrete patio spread out before him. The pillars stood on a porch just feet above him. Dim pool lights lit the surreally calm water of the large pool. Small lights hugged a footpath that cut through the yard toward the faint sound of breaking waves.

Knowing they'd be on him at any moment, he wiped the blood from his mouth with the back of his arm and bolted for the path. He stumbled between the wicker chairs beside a glass table, then skirted the covered hot tub. The moment he reached the grass, something struck him behind the top of his shoulder so hard that he nearly lost his balance, but he caught up with his own momentum and leveled out. A terrible pain burned his shoulder and Jack knew he'd been shot.

He kept his head low, a tear sliding from his eye as he staggered on and off the path through short shrubs and piles of mulch. Jack hoped his erratic movements would keep his pursuers from lining up a clean shot.

I should have brought a fucking gun. Bobby's drunken squawk about the house being empty all night should have made this a clean job—in and out. How could he have been so goddamned stupid? All of that blood. Those mangled bodies. The sickening sight filled Jack's mind. *No one deserves that. If I survive the night, this won't be over. None of this was worth it.*

A bullet whizzed past his head and he ducked off the path. He tore his way through some low-hanging tree limbs that smelled of nectar, and clawed spider webs from his face as he stumbled through a bed of large rocks, finally reaching a tall chain-link fence. Beyond it, the moon illuminated the ocean surf as it rushed in toward the shore.

The crack of a limb behind him commanded the turn of his head. A flashlight beam pierced the trees, and with a spark of hope, Jack saw it waver and shake uncertainly. They didn't know where he was.

He turned and scrambled along the fence, his hands carefully sliding across coarse metal until he found the gate—securely padlocked shut.

Hiding without a weapon and with at least three men covering the grounds was suicide. His best chance was to go up, even with his broken rib and injured shoulder. He bit his lip, leaped and grasped the fence, then gripped his way toward the sky. His ascension was clumsy—he was no longer a young man—and the metal stretched and wailed from his weight, but he kept going, holding his breath until he reached the top.

Swinging his legs in a summersault motion, he pulled forward. When he tried to drop to the other side, he discovered he was tethered to the fence by the duffle bag strap hooked under his arm. Twisting his body against the fence, he cursed God and kicked as he yanked the bag hard with both hands. Its strap gave way just as a spark from another shot flared off the metal post beside him.

He fell to the ground, landing hard on his butt, his aching leg pleading for mercy. Flipping onto his chest, he crawled across the sand. Wincing from the pain in his ribs and shoulder, he kept low until he managed to gain enough footing to stand.

With the duffle bag pinned to his stomach, Jack lumbered over a ridge of piled turf. The gentle breeze off of the ocean greeted him with a gust of sand. He spit it out along with bile and blood and suppressed a reflexive cough.

To the north, a tall, rippling barrier of walls and fences seemed to go on for an eternity, marking multiple sprawling properties edging the beach. In the distance was a row of street lamps that hovered above Pritchard Bridge. He dredged his way along clumps of sand toward it. If he could make it to the bridge, he'd at least stand a chance. He'd get away with his life—and the money.

The rocky landscape up to the road would be tough to negotiate, but the stretch of marsh below it was thick with tall grass and private piers. Coupled with the bridge's concrete piles leading all the way to the island, there'd be plenty of hiding spots. There, he could wait things out—even until daybreak if needed.

The chain-link fence rattled. *Someone's scaling it.* Jack boosted his pace, nearly crying out in pain with each step forward. Thoughts of his family and how long it had been since he'd seen them fluttered through his mind. For perhaps the first time, he wondered how they'd react to knowing what his life had become . . . this man, Jack Slate, who'd lost himself so long ago.

Crossing over another large grassy mound of sand, he suddenly felt a glass bottle shatter below his feet. He tripped and fell forward, landing across a large object that felt like neither sand nor rock.

"What . . . the fuck?" a groggy voice moaned from directly below him.

"Jesus!" Jack gasped.

The man beneath him squirmed, trying to roll over to his side, but Jack kept him pinned to his back. The smell of alcohol wafted over him before he covered the man's mouth with his hand.

"Shh!" Jack pled with wide eyes, knowing the man could not see how serious he was. "Hold still!"

The man pulled at Jack's hand, kicking weakly in the sand as he tried to shout. Jack held his hand tighter to the man's mouth.

When the beam of a flashlight crept over the mound of sand beside them, Jack lowered his body as best he could.

"Goddammit!" he whispered through clenched teeth, just inches from the man's face. "Stop moving and shut up or I'll fucking kill you!"

The threat proved fruitless. The man was so incoherent that Jack was convinced he hadn't the capacity to understand a word. He arched just high enough to deliver a wicked uppercut. The drunken man's head snapped to the sand and he stopped moving.

Jack fell flat to the man's chest, ignoring the pain in his ribs as the flashlight beam lit up the area just beyond them. His pursuer was close. At any second he would be right on top of them. Jack twisted his head to the side, searching for anything he could use as a weapon. No rock, no driftwood. A dark object lay just within reach—a surfboard about six and a half feet in length, with the telltale Harbour brand triangle logo in white print on its deck. Jack knew a little something about surfing.

The man he'd just cold-cocked was a surfer, probably having snuck onto the private beach to catch some early morning waves before any of the residents or crew showed up, but then getting carried away with the booze. Jack had fallen victim to the same habit a few times over the years.

The board was too big and heavy to use as an effective weapon, and the thought of pulling it over the top of their bodies to hide behind lasted only seconds.

The beam of light bounced off of something reflective just above the mound of sand providing Jack's only cover—another empty beer bottle. A small crab poked at its lip with its pincher.

When the light left the bottle, Jack grabbed its neck. When he sensed his pursuer was within a few feet, the man's trudging steps steady and unaware, he lunged to his knees with a snarl and threw the bottle like a battle-axe directly at the man's face.

The bottle exploded on impact and the flashlight fell to the ground. The man wobbled backwards, clutching his nose. Jack tackled him to the sand before he could get off a shot. He blindly punched the man's face and gouged what he thought were the man's eyes, and then kneed his groin. The man doubled over and Jack struck his head with fist after fist. The man became limp, sagging to the sand.

Jack's fingers traced the man's left arm up to his hand, then did the same with his right. The gun was in neither. He found the flashlight and lit up the small section of beach around his body, searching the sand. The gun was nowhere. "Shit!"

The slumped man's bloody face glistened under the beam. As Jack bent to search beneath the man for the gun, a loud voice sounded out from the gate. Another jostling flashlight beam approached from the south. Jack knew he didn't have time to search.

He straightened and looked between the approaching flashlight and the faraway lights of the bridge—a lifeline too far out of reach. He'd never make it, even without an injured leg. His eyes shifted to the surfboard a few yards away and then to the ocean's waves rolling ashore from the east.

Jack positioned the flashlight on the sand so it pointed in the direction of the man approaching him. He hoped its distracting glare was enough to earn him a few extra seconds. He grabbed the board with his good arm and limped into the waves. Once in thigh-deep, he laid out the board and dropped gently to his chest along its deck, letting his feet dangle behind him.

He swam forward, one arm hanging uselessly at his side, the

other clinging to the board, and his feet kicking steadily. For a brief moment, he felt almost completely free, as he had once as a child in a crisp mountain lake. He remembered watching his parents from the water that day as they argued loudly over God knew what in front of a campfire; they never needed an excuse to fight. They were oblivious to his whereabouts that day, as they often were, so he had swam even farther until he could no longer hear their angry voices. From the heart of the lake, he'd looked up at the clear blue sky and told himself he'd never again let others dictate his life.

That memory vanished as saltwater entered the hole in his shoulder. *Stings like a son of a bitch* screamed through his mind, and he fought back the urge to cry out in pain.

Both he and the board were dark, but it would only be a matter of time before the man ashore figured out where he was. Sure enough, a beam of light quickly spread out across the whitecaps. Jack was already submerging when it homed in on his board. He heard a shot go off before water covered his head.

Keeping one hand around the board, he kicked to put more distance between him and the shore. When he lifted his head out of the water, gasping, the lights along the beach looked like lightning bugs.

He grinned, spitting saltwater from his mouth. With a sharp wince, he climbed up on top of the board again. His heart steadied and the pain of his injuries strengthened as the adrenaline rush petered out. His shoulder throbbed and his swollen leg felt tight against the inside of his pants. He lay flat along the board with his duffle bag beside him, the bulge of what was likely $50,000 in cash pressing against his side. With his cheek plastered to the board's deck, he let himself drift for a few moments.

An intensely bright spotlight suddenly lit him up. He gasped and covered his face with his arm as his heart shot back into overdrive. After staring through slit eyes for several seconds, he finally made out the outline of a good-sized yacht whose broad deck hosted the light. He hadn't heard its approach, but it was very close—only a couple dozen yards out. It was stopping, its engine barely purring.

He couldn't fathom why such a boat would be there so early, right off the coast, without using its running lights. A concerned voice echoed out from behind the glare.

"Hey! Are you okay?"

Jack wasn't sure how to answer. He was far from okay, but having gotten away with his life and a big haul of cash, fresh attention wasn't something he wanted. He couldn't play himself off as drifting around in the ocean at night, fully-clothed, with a hole in his shoulder, simply for the sport of it. He had to let this man help him, and he needed a quick story that made sense.

Before he could speak, the abrupt blare of radio static poured out from the deck of the yacht, followed by an angry voice. "I said shoot him, goddammit, or it's yo' ass!"

Jack watched with bulging eyes and mouth agape as the silhouette of the man with thick, curly hair peered down at him.

The man trembled as he reached for something at his side. "I'm s-s-sorry," he wailed.

Jack flattened to his board again, arm and legs desperately paddling the water to escape the glare of the spotlight. He glanced back to the yacht. A flash and the roar of a gun met him. A forceful impact stunned him, and he heard something plop into the water. A chunk of the surfboard? When he reached to the top of his head, he felt his broken skull and what was likely brain tissue oozing out.

He collapsed to his board as his eyesight blurred. The sound of pulsating sirens echoed along the swaying water. The light fell away from his body and he was adrift again. Random images of children playing on a swing set and a scolding woman with wet, sunken eyes played through his broken mind. He felt no pain other than the torment of regret and it nudged him relentlessly until he succumbed to his body's defeat.

Chapter 2

The motor of the small wooden boat sputtered through mild waves as the stout man in his fifties sitting toward the front of its hull used his hairy arm to shield his eyes from the bright sunlight. A police shield was embroidered on his collared, short-sleeve shirt, and a black pistol holstered at his side gleamed as he motioned to the fisherman at the stern, whose help he'd commandeered, to ease back on the engine.

They glided forward, past a few more pillars, until they slid under the shade of the deck of the bridge that hovered above. There, the familiar smell of brine and decaying sea life reminded the lawman of the creamed corn he'd had with his dinner the night before. Above the sporadic fuss of automobiles crossing overhead were the shouts of two young voices.

"Over here!" one of them yelled.

The police chief looked up. Once the hot sun beat down on the boat again from the other side of the bridge, two pairs of thin arms waved from above, over the railing. The policeman's eyes met the adolescent faces of two boys above, and he wondered which one had phoned in the finding. They both pointed downward.

Where ocean waves met freshwater marsh lay a dark object. Part of it was submerged in the water, while the rest—three or four feet in length—was propped up against a cluster of cattails straining at an angle from its weight. A half dozen seagulls paraded around the scene. They took flight as the boat approached.

"Chief Quammen?" called the man working the motor, probing for instruction.

"Shut it off," the police chief replied in a New York accent. "And you may want to look away."

As the engine petered, Quammen leaned forward and wrapped a meaty hand around a bundle of cattails. He pulled them in close and glared at the body they revealed. It was face down, with what was left of its mutilated skull and its lower torso draped across a dark blue surfboard.

Quammen shook his head and took a deep breath. He leaned back on his heels, adjusted his belt, and raised his gaze back to the bridge. He spotted a young man—possibly a teenager—in a dark baseball cap and T-shirt, leaning across its railing about forty feet down from the boys. He had a thin build and a light complexion. With a fishing pole out over the banister, he was in the middle of adjusting his hat when he noticed Quammen staring up at him.

Quammen held the man's gaze for a moment before tightening his jaw and nodding in acknowledgement.

Strands of wavy red hair dangling from below the rim of his cap blew around his face as the young man nodded back.

Quammen turned his attention to the body in the cattails. The morning was going to be messy.

Chapter 3

"You ever seen a live grasshopper screwing a dead one on the sidewalk?"

The portly, fourteen-year-old boy's eyes bulged as the question caused him to choke on a swig of Wild Cherry flavored *Capri Sun*. "What?" he managed to gasp. His eyes glistened with moisture below his dark bangs.

Sean let the ends of his lips curl, his eyes still drawn across the clear, calm body of water that occupied Beggar's Basin, a sprawling reservoir that sat at the bottom of a Colorado mountain range. Majestic pines crowded all but the west end of the lake, seeming to jockey for position to be admired. Other than a young couple sitting in a slow-moving canoe a few hundred yards out and a half-dozen anglers staggered across the shore, he and the boy had the tranquil area to themselves.

Sean leaned back in the lawn chair, his nearly 240-pound, thirty-nine-year-old body forcing a loud creak from its rusted metal hinges. His shadow partially shaded the boy's smaller frame. "I said, have you ever seen a grasshopper—one that's alive—screwing a dead grasshopper on the sidewalk? You know, riding on its back."

The boy's face had turned beet red, either from the coughing fit or out of embarrassment. Clad in a striped yellow and brown T-shirt and dark jogging shorts, he leaned forward in his chair and let out a clearing cough without bothering to cover his mouth.

Sean enjoyed getting an animated reaction out of Toby. Over the past year, he'd found that it was a relatively easy thing to do. The two had grown close after the death of Sean's uncle, who'd died saving the boy's life from a madman. Sean felt he owed it to his uncle to continue looking after Toby, when the boy's mother would allow it, but the truth was that it wasn't much of a burden. Sean had come to enjoy serving as a bit of a father figure, having never had any children of his own.

The boy sank back into his seat, face still red. "You're asking me, Sean, if I've ever seen a grasshopper that's alive riding on the back of one that's dead?"

"Yeah. I think I was pretty clear."

"I . . . I don't know. I don't think so. Have you?"

Sean reached to his side and pulled an old, beat-up fishing rod from the center of the forked tree branch spiked into the ground. He sat up straight and his hand fumbled for his tackle box. Toby mimicked Sean's movements, reaching for his own tackle box. The late-morning sun forced them to squint. Sean felt its warmth along his scalp under his short, graying hair. It wasn't easy being the owner of a struggling security company, where he was the only guard— and only employee, for that matter. The work wasn't consistent and neither was the pay. But it did have a few perks. Being able to fish on a Thursday was one of them.

"Sure have, Toby," he told the boy. "Lots of times. When I was a kid, I used to see them all over the place on the other side of the reservoir, by the long grass."

"Are you talking about the bike trail? The paved one? I love that trail." Toby's eyes lit up. "Mom and I rode our bikes on it two months ago. I kept honking my horn because it made a cool echo sound off the rocks, but Mom told me to knock it off because it was annoying the people who were fishing. They never actually complained to her per se, but—"

"Yeah, the bike trail," Sean interrupted, knowing that the boy's account of the event could last the rest of the day if left to its own momentum. "In the fall, before the weather started turning cold, there'd always be a bunch of splattered grasshoppers littering the concrete. It still happens. People run over those things with their bicycles, more often than not doing it on purpose. Crunch! Flat as pancakes. Sometimes just half of their bodies, but enough to kill them either way. Even with guts hanging out of their mouths or asses, other grasshoppers will just jump right on their backs and start humping the hell out of them, or whatever they do. It's a sad, sad thing."

"Yuck," Toby said, cringing with widened nostrils. "Why would grasshoppers do that?"

Sean closed one eye and examined the hook at the end of his line. He rotated it in his large fingers. "Instinct. Pure instinct."

"Instinct?"

"It's what they're born to do, I guess. I'm no grasshopper zoologist, so I can't say for sure whether it's the scent that draws them in or what. I just know they can't help themselves. They have no choice in the matter."

Toby nodded his head, though Sean wasn't sure if the boy had understood his explanation.

"Sean?"

"What?"

"I don't think there's such a thing as a grasshopper zoologist," the boy said after a lengthy pause.

"I know."

"Sean?"

"What?"

Toby pulled his own fishing pole into his hands. "Why would someone do that on purpose? Run over grasshoppers on their bikes, I mean. It doesn't seem very nice."

"Well, I suppose there's something satisfying about crunching an insect like that, especially when you're riding fast and you've got only one shot at it. It's kind of like hunting. There's some sport to it. A feeling of power."

"Oh, I get it," said Toby. "Kind of like dry cereal."

Sean nodded absently. Then the boy's words sank in. "Wait. Cereal? What in the hell are you talking about?" He let the hook swing from his hand and glanced at the boy.

Toby's long eyelashes fluttered. A wide grin formed on his mouth when he met Sean's questioning look. "You know, like when you're eating cereal and a piece of it falls on the floor, and you know you should just pick it up, but you don't pick it up because you want to see what happens when you step on it. You think to yourself, *Can I turn that sucker into powder or will it break up into a few pieces?*"

Sean winced and shook his head. "No. Not like that at all. That's what you think about when you drop cereal on the floor?"

"Yes. Except for when I'm eating Lucky Charms. When a marshmallow hits the floor, I can't bring myself to step on it. They're soft, there aren't that many of them in the box, and that leprechaun on TV is right when he says they're magically delicious."

Sean's face further soured.

Toby continued. "Cocoa Puffs, on the other hand, may provide essential vitamins and minerals, but a good stomp will explode one of them into a kazillion pieces. Do you know what time it is?"

Sean glared at him. He'd gotten to know the boy well over the past year, but the awkwardness of his ramblings was something he had never quite gotten used to. Toby had Asperger's syndrome, a high-functioning form of autism. It supposedly contributed to the funny, irrational, and downright weird comments that sometimes fell from his mouth.

"Uh. The time, yeah . . . I'm guessing a little after ten," said Sean, remembering what the boy had asked him. "Late for a date or something?"

A high-pitched laugh exploded out of Toby's mouth, drawing looks from the couple across the water in the canoe. The boy hunched forward in his seat and capped his hand over his mouth for a second. "No, silly. I just can't fish for very long this morning. Mom and Ron

Oldhorse are taking me to the alpine slide over in Winter Park. I've never been there before and I've read that it's the largest in the state. It's over 3,000 feet long, Sean!"

Sean's eyebrows formed sharp arches, but not in reaction to the length of the slide. "Oldhorse is going? He's actually coming down off his mountain to sit his stiff ass on a ski lift and then slide down a hill on a plastic sled?" He shook his head. "I didn't think that guy mounted anything that didn't have hooves. Well, except for your mom." When Toby gave him a confused look, he added, "Never mind. We'll just write if off to true love."

The boy shrugged and focused back to his fishing pole and line, examining the hook in the same fashion he had witnessed Sean doing a minute earlier.

Oldhorse was a good man and had helped bring Sean's uncle's killer to justice. He was also an eccentric. Of Native American heritage, he lived in a secluded cabin in the mountains and resisted modern conveniences like automobiles and even electricity. His survivalist lifestyle seemed incompatible with that of Toby's mother, but somehow the two made their relationship work. The fact that Oldhorse was willing to accompany the family to a tourist trap in Winter Park suggested that acclimating to the twenty-first century wasn't out of the question.

"Make sure you get some sunscreen on those pasty white legs of yours before you get on that slide," Sean said. "Otherwise you'll be walking around like Matt Houston tomorrow."

"Matt Houston? Is he a friend of yours?"

"You don't know about Matt Houston? Oh, come on," Sean muttered, shaking his head in disappointment. "It's a detective show. On television. From back in the eighties. Lee Horsley played Matt Houston—some rich dick who walked around like he had a stick up his ass."

"Ugh," said Toby, his face wrinkling at the imagery.

"Some good plots though. Some good investigative tips."

Toby seemed to think this over for a moment. "Sean, why were you asking me if I'd ever seen live grasshoppers screwing dead ones?" He reduced his voice to a careful whisper when pronouncing the word "screwing."

Sean chuckled, scratching his unshaven face with the back of his hand. "Because when they're out of the grass, and they're mounting a dead friend, they're distracted. Easy pickins'."

He pulled a plastic margarine container from his tackle box and rested it on his lap. An "X" had been cut into the center of the lid. He carefully peeled back the lid and pulled from it a large, lively grasshopper. It squirmed wildly between his fingers, long antenna pointed up. Toby nearly fell out of his chair, his rod dropping to the ground as he leaped to his feet.

"Oh my gosh! What are you doing?" he breathlessly asked, taking some cautious steps backward along the gravely shore. His eyes were huge. By the time Sean answered, the boy was nearly standing in the water.

"Easy, Tobes. They make good bait. The fish like how animated they are." Sean pierced his hook through the side of the insect's crisp skin. The point came out the other end, along with some greenish, pus-like fluid. "Doesn't that look tasty?"

"Oh, that's nasty, Sean," said the boy, his face distorting into horror. He turned his head away.

"No worse than the worms you brought."

The distinct sound of the slam of a car door echoed its way across the water, drawing Sean's attention. In the distance, near the dirt parking lot where Sean had left his Nova, he saw the thin figure of a man in an olive-colored, long-sleeved dress shirt and tie and matching pants standing in front of what looked like a Jeep Cherokee. He was a short man with dark hair. He placed his hand to his forehead to block the sun as he carefully panned the area. Once his gaze stopped on Sean, the man lowered his hand.

Sean stood up.

"Is that Chief Lumbergh?" asked Toby, excitement in his voice. He mimicked Sean's narrow-eyed glare.

"Yeah."

"Did he come to fish with us?"

"No. I don't know why he's here. He should be working up in Winston, like every other day."

"Sean?"

"What?"

"Did you ever run over grasshoppers on your bike? You know, when you were a kid?"

Sean's dry expression didn't change as he answered. "Toby, I was the Saddam Hussein of grasshopper killers."

Sean watched Lumbergh slowly walk toward them along the wide perimeter of the reservoir. His shoulders rode low, and even from a distance Sean could tell that his demeanor was off. It wasn't that of the confident, spry man who had served and protected Sean's hometown of Winston in recent years as their police chief. An unmistakable sense of humility and altruism accompanied his stride, and Sean felt that whatever exchange was about to take place would somehow mark a new chapter in the pair's complicated history. That history included years of resentment over career-related jealousy and sacrifice, but Lumbergh wasn't there on official business. He appeared to be there as Sean's brother-in-law. Something was wrong.

Sean placed his pole on his chair, told Toby to stay put, and made his way toward Lumbergh. He mirrored the lawman's pace and closing the gap between them gave the anxious thoughts bouncing off the inside his skull time to tangle. He worried that there was something wrong with his sister, Diana, or their baby, but if that were the case, Lumbergh would be a mess. It had to be something else.

Not until Lumbergh was thirty yards out did Sean think of his mother, Dolores. She had suffered a crippling stroke a couple years back and had lived with the chief and Diana ever since. *Had she fallen? Had she passed on during the night?* The fear of never clearing the air between them began to swirl in Sean's gut. When he stepped on a patch of loose gravel, its crackle was deafening.

Lumbergh raised his hand in somber greeting as he drew close. The bright sun made his thinning hair nearly transparent, exposing his scalp beneath a subtle comb-over. A light breeze pressed his tie to his shirt. His Glock was visible, sticking out of a thin leather holster at his side.

"What is it, Gary?" Sean asked before Lumbergh could utter a word.

At six foot five, Sean towered over his brother-in-law, who stood at the inversed height of five foot six. Sean's imposing shadow nearly eclipsed the chief's entire body.

"Is it Mom?"

Lumbergh's unfocused gaze seemed to stare right through Sean. His mouth opened, but no words came out. It was as if whatever line he'd scripted in his mind on the walk over had suddenly been deemed a poor choice of words.

"Come on, Gary."

Lumbergh nodded his head as if to reassure himself before meeting Sean's stare. "It's not your mother, Sean. It's your father. He's dead."

Chapter 4

"How in the hell would they even know to call us?" Sean asked, rubbing his knuckles along his forehead as he gazed at his sister.

"The police in South Carolina?" replied Diana, her elbows resting on top of the wooden table in her small kitchen. When she lowered a large mug of coffee from her mouth, her red eyes wearily held his. She looked emotionally spent, likely not only from the morning's news of their father, but also from a sleepless night.

"Yeah. The Pawleys Island police. We haven't heard from *good old Dad* in decades—not since the prick left." Sean sighed. When they had tried finding him through public records a while back, they had come up empty-handed. "Absolutely nothing. Diddly shit! But the second he croaks, the cops are able to figure out who his family is and call us right up on the phone?"

The familiar whistling from the opening theme of the *Andy Griffith Show* floated its way into the kitchen from a television set in the adjoining living room. The tune felt eerie and awkward in the context of the weighty conversation.

"He changed *his* last name, too," answered Diana. "I'm not sure when. He was going by Jack *Slate*, not Jack Hansen. They got the information from some woman he was living with." She brushed her disheveled auburn hair from her face. Her dark eyes narrowed as they rose to meet his.

He glared at her for a moment before sneering and shaking his head. He turned away and rubbed his hand through his short hair.

"Jack Slate . . . It sounds like a cheesy character from one of the old detective shows I watch. And this woman," he sighed, "who is she? Does he have another family somewhere? Other kids?"

She set her mug down on the table, leaned her slender body back in her chair and adjusted her white blouse. She fought back a yawn of fatigue. "No. It sounds like she was just some girlfriend. They'd been together less than a year. We're the only kids he has, at least as far as anyone knows. We're his remaining family—his *next of kin*."

"Family," Sean scoffed. "That asshole stopped being a member of this family over thirty years ago. He probably didn't even know that his brother died last year. God, both of them murdered. How's that for a family legacy?"

As Diana nodded her head, staring off into space, Sean thought about their Uncle Zed. Since his death, a day hadn't gone by that one of his "quotes of wisdom" or just his kind smile and laugh hadn't flashed through Sean's mind. Sean missed him deeply. He was the closest thing he'd had to a father after his real one had left. It felt criminal that Zed's passing had gone unrecognized by his brother, whose slack he had done his best to pick up all of those years. Even Sean and Diana's mother hadn't appreciated Zed's role in her children's lives. The two rarely spoke when he was still alive, and when they did, she had treated him like dirt. Guilt by genetic association.

Sean peered into the small living room where their mother sat. All he could see of Dolores was the top of her head. Random threads of her white hair draped over the back of her firmly cushioned chair. Just like every day around this time, she was staring at the tube in a state of virtual hypnosis, watching old black-and-white comedies from the Golden Age of television. The glare of the sun through a nearby window lit up the tiny dust particles that hung in the air between her and Don Knotts.

"Did you tell her about Dad?" he asked Diana.

"I tried," she replied. "I don't know what makes it into her head anymore. It's tough to get any kind of reaction. I think she probably figured he'd died a long time ago, on some sidewalk with his hand wrapped around a bottle of booze in a paper bag."

He nodded. "Part of me figured that, too."

"Not me," she said, her eyes still in a glaze. "I knew he was alive."

He looked at her and read a peculiar sense of guilt, possibly conflict, in her demeanor. When her eyes lifted to meet his, the timid expression reminded him of the time, when they were children, she'd broken his record player and was afraid to tell him.

"What is it, D?"

She sighed and let her gaze fall to the table. "He called me. He called me three years ago."

His eyes bulged and posture shot upright. "What do you mean, he *called* you?"

"It was back when I was living in Chicago, before Mom's stroke. Just out of the blue he called me. I don't know how he got my number."

His mouth gaped open. He threw his hands up in the air. "And you're just now telling me this? Jesus, D! Why the hell wouldn't you tell me about something like that?"

She instinctively lifted her finger to her mouth. In her eyes, he read the worry that his raised voice would awaken her newborn baby, Ashley, who was finally asleep in another room. Her eyes moistened as she leaned forward in her chair and shook her head. "Because I didn't think you could handle it at the time, Sean. You were in a bad place—the drinking, the self-destructiveness—and I thought it would just make things worse."

"How could it have made things worse? Part of who I was back then . . . it was *because* I grew up without him!" His jaw tightened as he stood and paced to the other side of the room. He spun to face her. "I know that he wasn't a hell of a great father when he was here. I know that he often acted like he didn't give a shit when it came to us; I remember that better than you do. But Christ . . . I was *seven* when he left. And from that day, Mom always treated me like I was somehow to blame for it."

She opened her mouth to speak, but he cut her off.

"It never made any sense, but that was how it felt—that I had caused it. Jesus, I carried that guilt around for years. I *still* do." He took a breath before continuing. "Listen, I know I was being a dick when we were trying to track him down. I know I said I'd help you with it, and then acted like an obnoxious ass every step of the way. I was a bitter drunk. But how . . . how could you *not* tell me that he called?"

He was surprised with how freely the words flowed from his mouth. He'd never opened up before about the pain and torment his father's abandonment had brought him. It had always felt like *his* problem to deal with, and his alone. He had built up a dam over the years to keep those feelings trapped and hidden from others, but now the dam was cracking and the water was streaming out.

"I didn't tell you because he didn't want to talk to you, Sean!" Diana finally snapped back, clenching her fists. A tear rolled down her cheek.

In the two seconds it took for her to release those words, Sean felt his heart crash down to the pit of his stomach. He went silent.

"He was a son of a bitch, Sean!" she wailed before biting her lip. She continued, quiet and forceful. "He wasn't our father. He was just some asshole who got Mom pregnant! He didn't *deserve* us. He didn't deserve to be part of our lives!" More tears came, and she covered her face with her hands. "God, I can't deal with this right now."

He hated seeing his sister upset. She had always been the rock of their family. She was young enough when their father left not to miss him in same way that Sean did. She hadn't known him as well. Diana's youthful innocence had given their mother the strength Dolores so desperately needed to move on after being abandoned—though Sean knew that Diana, like him, had never *really* moved on.

Out in the living room, their mother hadn't so much as flinched in reaction to the raised voices behind her. Her attention remained glued to a weight-loss commercial with an annoying jingle. Even the baby in the other room hadn't stirred.

Sean took a breath and walked up behind his sister. He rested his hand on her shoulder, and she reached up and placed her hand over his. He shoved aside his bitterness at being left out of the conversation with their father. Diana had needed him to be strong, and he hadn't been there for her—he had been at the bottom of a bottle, where he had kept himself for a number of years.

"What did he say to you?" he asked in a softer voice.

She wiped her face with her free hand. "We only spoke for a minute. He told me that he'd thought of me over the years and that he hoped I was living a good life. Stuff like that. Stuff you'd expect him to say."

He nodded. "You said he didn't want to talk to me?"

She let out a deep breath and placed her hand to her forehead. "I tried to get him to call you, Sean. I even offered to set up a three-way conference. He said he didn't *need* to talk to you."

"He didn't *need* to? What the hell does that mean?" He pulled his hand away.

"I don't know, but that's exactly how he said it, as if he didn't owe you the courtesy of a call. Maybe because you're a man, he didn't think you needed any emotional handholding like I apparently did— as if a son somehow has it in him to deal with abandonment better than a daughter. Or maybe he just felt guilty. I'm telling you, Sean, we drew the motherlode of shitty dads. He probably only called *me* because he saw some sappy Hallmark commercial with a father and daughter, and he decided in a brief moment of sobriety to look up his *little girl*."

Sean let some breath escape his lungs. He narrowed his eyes and shook his head. "Did he say where he was?"

"No. A few minutes after the call, I thought to do a star-69. I found, when someone else picked up, that he'd called from a payphone at an Interstate rest area in Ohio. He'd been traveling, I guess."

A loud wail echoed down the hallway that led away from the living room.

"Dammit," Diana groaned, slumping forward in her chair. "She only slept two hours last night."

"Is she sick or something?"

"No. Ashley's just doing what babies do—cry. A lot." She pulled herself to her feet and rubbed her eyes with the palms of her hands. "I should rock and probably feed her. Can you stick around for a little bit? We need to talk some more."

Sean nodded.

Soon after Diana left the room, Ashley's crying dwindled down. Sean searched through the fridge, pushing a few bottles of beer aside to grab out a can of diet cola. He snapped it open and downed half of it in a single gulp. He watched his mother sitting lifelessly in her chair and wondered if she had nodded off. He thought of all of the friction that had divided them over the years: the constant arguing, back when she could still argue; the disappointment he'd always been to her. He'd probably reminded her of his father to some extent— the man whose surname she refused to let her children continue to grow up with, legally changing it to her maiden name of "Coleman" sometime in the 1970s. Still, the animosity she felt for Sean seemed to begin long before his drinking and all his other problems began. It started when he was young—possibly even before his father had walked out on them.

A screen door swung open at the front of the house and footsteps banged from down the hallway. Sean watched Lumbergh emerge from around the corner, adjusting his shirt from the car ride. He chomped on a piece of gum as he walked right past Sean's mother on his way to the kitchen, barely acknowledging her. To him, her presence was as familiar as the chair she sat in.

"Where's Diana?" he asked.

"Rocking Ashley." Sean crossed in front of him and leaned against the kitchen counter. "She woke up. Did you get Toby home all right?"

"Yes," Lumbergh said, a little out of breath. "And I heard everything I ever wanted to know and more about the alpine slide at Winter Park."

Sean smirked. Toby did ramble.

Lumbergh rifled through the fridge, grabbed a bottled water, and joined Sean. "It's getting hot out there. Contrary to popular belief, the summer is *not* over." He twisted off its cap after spitting the ball of gum like a blow-dart into the kitchen trashcan.

"Gary, what do they know about who shot my dad?" Sean bluntly asked. "You said you'd explain more later."

Lumbergh nodded as the swig of water slid down his throat. "The authorities don't have anyone in custody yet. No serious suspects either. But I talked to the local police chief and found out quite a bit."

"Like what?"

"I was getting there. They're going off of the theory that your dad, Jack *Slate*, had likely burglarized one of the expensive beach homes close to where his body was found. Slate, who'd had a couple of other burglary beefs, was found dressed in black. He had a large chunk of cash on him and some locksmith tools."

"A thief, huh?" Sean scoffed. "That figures."

Lumbergh continued, "Someone had also beaten up a teenager who'd been camping on the beach outside the housing community the night before Slate's body was discovered, soaked in saltwater. The kid's description of how the man was dressed matched the clothes Jack was found in."

"The kid wasn't any part of it?"

"No, just a random bystander, it seems. Sean, this is more information than a victim's family would normally receive so early in a case, but—"

"But you're the big-shot police chief of Winston, I get it. Professional courtesy and all of that."

"I wasn't fishing for accolades, Sean. I was just explaining how I know all of this."

"I know," Sean said, tamping down his reflexive sarcasm. "Shouldn't it be a pretty simple case to figure out? Whoever he robbed is the person who shot him."

"You'd think," said Lumbergh, taking another drink. "Of course, wouldn't they have taken their money back afterwards? Also, the police have talked to all homeowners in the area, and no one has reported a break-in. No one's reported *anything* stolen—let alone a stack of cash. Hell, no one even heard a gunshot that night."

Sean scowled. "What do you think that means?"

"That whoever he robbed might have been into something shady and doesn't want any attention coming back on them."

Sean's gaze drifted off in another direction as Lumbergh's words sank in.

"It'll play out though," Lumbergh added. "Don't worry. The guy in charge over there, Travis Quammen, seems to have his shit together. He promised to keep me in the loop. He's confident they'll figure out everything that happened and who did it."

Sean nodded. The tone of the conversation felt detached—hollow, as if the man being discussed was an unfamiliar name from a newspaper article. It was nothing short of surreal considering Sean couldn't remember a day going by in his life when he hadn't thought of his father at least once, if only briefly. The unanswered questions of where he had gone and why he had left felt like rusty anchors chained around his legs. Sean had never expected his father to return to Winston, but the hopelessness that had come from abandonment kept him from ever truly sailing on with life. Yet with this news, it felt as if those chains had never existed—and neither had his father.

The collection of forensic evidence from Sean's father's body had just about been completed, according to Chief Quammen. Lumbergh explained that because Sean and Diana were Slate's only remaining family, they were responsible for the body and what was to be done with it. The irony of the situation wasn't lost on Sean. In life, his father had relinquished all responsibilities for his children, yet in death he had become their burden.

"We should bury him here," Diana said from behind them.

When they turned their heads to meet her, they found her hesitant eyes shifting back and forth between them. She was holding baby Ashley in her arms, swaddled up in a pink blanket, her delicate eyes closed.

"What?" Sean demanded, his face contorted. "Why?"

"Because like it or not—and I *don't* like it—he is of our blood," she reminded. "Without him, there'd be no us. Plus, it's the decent thing to do."

"Oh Christ!" Sean shook his head. "Listen, if we need to take care of his burial, we'll take care of it. Fine. I'm sure it will cost a pretty penny, but we'll pay whoever we need to pay to put him in the ground out in South Carolina. Maybe we can get the chick he lived with to help us out. Whatever life he had wasn't here with us, D. It was out there."

"I'll take her," muttered Lumbergh, leaning in to carefully gather his daughter from his wife's arms. Ashley stirred a bit during the exchange, and Lumbergh shushed and rocked her once he had her cushioned against his chest. He then left the room, apparently content to let the siblings sort out the family business.

"Listen, Sean," Diana continued, pulling a damp burp cloth from her shoulder, "you're right. We don't know what his life was like out there. All we know is what his life was like here. His parents are buried here, and now so is Uncle Zed. He and Zed were once a big part of this town. You've seen the old newspaper clippings just like I have. They helped build churches and schools together. Both were star athletes—"

"Oh come on!" Sean interrupted with a raised voice, eyes rolling heavenward. "Are you honestly telling me you want this to happen for its *historical significance*?"

She lowered her head and let out a sigh. "No, it's not just that—"

"What else then? You yourself said no more than fifteen minutes ago that he wasn't really our father, that he didn't deserve to be part of our lives."

"Maybe it's because I'm a mother now. I don't know. Maybe it's because I see the big picture whenever I look into Ashley's eyes. I just feel like our family tree means something. Mom's the last of that generation. I want Ashley to one day know all about her family and to understand her roots. It'll mean more if she's able to visit the gravesites of the Colemans and Hansens who came before her."

He listened carefully, and though he couldn't bring himself to subscribe to the same rationale, he knew she was being sincere.

"I think it's something I want for me, too," she continued. "I'll never forget what he did to us, but I *do* believe that I'll one day be able to forgive him, and when that day comes, I don't want to regret having laid him to rest two thousand miles away because it was convenient at the time."

He watched another tear roll slowly down his sister's cheek. It left behind a glistening trail before disappearing under her jaw. It had been a long time since Sean had cried his own tears over his father—not since he was a child. Sadness had been replaced with bitterness over the years, and the interest Sean had in one day meeting him again was driven more by a need for an explanation and desire to punch him in the face than it was a longing to reconnect. He'd always suspected it was different for Diana. When she led the charge on trying to track him down years earlier, she had sometimes talked of him as if he were a lost dog who needed finding. It had angered Sean, but now, he better understood where she was coming from.

"Okay," he heard himself somberly say. "We'll bury him here."

She lunged forward and wrapped her arms around him. He awkwardly patted her on the back. The two hadn't shared many hugs over the years. Sean was never a touchy-feely kind of guy, but he did his best at that moment to comfort her.

They spent the next twenty minutes discussing what needed to be done. With Lumbergh's help, they decided someone needed to fly out to South Carolina to manage the process. It wasn't going to get done over the phone—signatures were required, transportation had to be coordinated, onsite decisions needed to be made. The only remaining question was who would go. Diana clearly couldn't. Ashley was too young to travel, and a sleep-deprived mother trying to juggle a newborn with a complicated management process was a nightmare waiting to happen. Lumbergh couldn't either. His sole officer, Jefferson, had just left on a Mexican vacation with his wife—a "second honeymoon," whatever that meant. No one else was qualified to handle the day-to-day department duties.

When their eyes fell on Sean, he knew instantly that he could offer no valid excuse to get out of it. His job was flexible, and he had no security work lined up until the following Wednesday.

It had to be him.

Chapter 5

S ean impatiently shuffled around a file of slow-moving, fellow passengers who were making their way up the humid terminal gateway. They were the type of people one would expect to find at the Myrtle Beach International Airport any given day around noon: well-off elderly folks with high waistlines, bright clothes, and lots of stories to tell. Sean couldn't step off the plane fast enough.

With Diana's help, he'd booked the last remaining spot on a flight out of Denver. It was a window seat, and for a man Sean's size, it had been a very uncomfortable ride. With his arms pinned to his sides and his head tipped at an angle because of a low ceiling, he'd been forced to endure the upbeat ramblings of a blue-haired elderly woman seated next to him.

The two had carried on a marathon conversation, or so the woman seemed to think; she apparently hadn't realized that Sean never actually participated in it. Instead he had just sat there, drowning on her strong scent of VapoRub as she aired anecdote after anecdote about her grandkids, European trips, and economic inflation. Every once in a while, she'd drift to sleep for a few minutes before sputtering back to life like a lawnmower choking on its last fumes of gasoline. It was during those elusive moments that Sean's thoughts had drifted to his father. They hadn't been particularly coherent thoughts of yearning or regret—just random flashes from his childhood.

He remembered a game called Cochise that he, his sister, and his father sometimes played. It wasn't so much a game, in the traditional sense, as it was a call to arms. When Sean or his father would discover a mischievous Diana trying to sneak up on one of them, the shouted word "Cochise!" would result in the two of them tag-teaming her and holding her down for some tickle treatment. Sean couldn't remember, or perhaps never knew, why the name of the famous Indian was used as their war cry. He just knew that it had made for a type of fun his family had rarely shared.

Sean had thought of the day when his father had taught him how to shoot the six-inch barreled Colt Python that Sean still owned. The two annihilated dozens of empty beer cans and paper targets that Saturday, less than a week before Sean's father left and never came back. Sean could still remember the scent of chewing tobacco that drifted off his father's shirt and the uncharacteristic soberness in his eyes when the two talked. In some ways, it was like he was looking at Sean for the very first time, examining him closely as if he were a faded picture that had lost its detail. Years later, Sean decided that his father had already known that day that he was going to leave. Why he left was still a mystery—one that Sean's mother, even before her stroke, refused to offer any insight into.

When Sean finally reached the terminal, he found an open spot and dropped his small, carry-on suitcase to his side. He then stretched out his arms and let a deep, trembling breath escape his lungs. A satisfying pop from somewhere in his lower back let him know that the ordeal was over.

Clad in a pair of jeans and an old, short-sleeved aloha shirt he'd discovered at the back of his closet, he raised his arm to the ceiling and gave his armpit a quick sniff before deciding that the deodorant stick in his carry-on could probably stay there until he got to his motel.

Sean noticed the wide eyes of a young boy in an over-sized, red baseball cap; the kid seemed to be reacting to the sight of Sean assessing his own body odor. Sean picked up his carry-on and made his way toward the terminal corridor, offering the child a fleeting scowl as he did. He followed the signs pointing to ground transportation.

Security was thick throughout the airport. Several armed guards walked among the travelers with hawkish eyes, just like he'd seen back in Denver. It was the first time he'd flown since the 9/11 attacks, and it was impossible not to notice how dramatically things had changed. The screening process for both passengers and luggage was exhaustive. He'd even had to remove his boots for a special trip through the x-ray machine, a policy put in place after an Islamic terrorist nearly ignited a shoe bomb on a flight back in December. Sean raised no ruckus over the inconvenience but had wished he'd owned a pair of socks without holes.

One welcome byproduct of the extra security measures was that non-ticketed individuals were no longer allowed inside the terminals at all, thus Sean didn't have to deal with loud families greeting each other, divvying up luggage, and otherwise getting in his way. With his father's death fresh on his mind, Sean was sure he'd have found them even more irritating than he usually did.

He whisked past a motley crew of chauffeurs ranging from clean-cut men in suits to a woman in a tank top and shorts with dreadlocks and tattooed arms. All held up signs with names. Sean glanced over them, instinctively looking for his own before scoffing at the notion that anyone would be waiting for him. He had only flown a handful of times in his life, but was certain he'd looked for the words "Sean Coleman" on a driver's card in each instance. It was a habit he'd picked up from old episodes of *Magnum P.I.*

Having grown up as a detective-show-loving couch potato in the slow-paced, simple mountain town of Winston, having his name turn up in such fashion would have served as the ultimate status symbol—irrefutable proof that one had truly made it in life.

After signing his name a dozen times at the car rental counter, Sean felt his chest tighten when the bill's total glared at him from a computer monitor. His focus shifted to the skinny kid with a pointed nose and short, oily hair who stood behind the register; he couldn't have been older than 20. The young employee's body tensed up when he read the seriousness in Sean's eyes. He nervously tugged at the red company vest that hung from his shoulders.

"That includes *everything*, with the taxes and the liability insurance," the kid said, offering an awkward, sympathetic grin.

"We're still talking about a Ford Escort, right?" Sean said, not subduing the agitation in his voice. "Not a Corvette?"

"Y-yes sir."

With a deadpan gaze, Sean dug his hand into his back pocket, whipped out his wallet, and pried a seldom-used credit card from one of its pockets. He slapped it down on the counter and bit his lip, tempering himself and affirming in his mind that he would be splitting all costs with his sister.

"I'm going to need a map of the area," Sean said.

"A map?"

"Yeah, one of those things with roads that tells you how to get places. Are you going to charge me for that too?" Sean leaned forward.

"Oh, no sir. Not at all," replied the kid, shaking his head. His tongue slid to the corner of his mouth as he rifled through a drawer somewhere below his keyboard. Within seconds, he presented a folded street map to Sean.

"Myrtle Beach and surrounding areas," Sean read aloud. "Does this cover Pawleys Island?"

"Yes sir. Definitely."

"Do you know if I would need to park somewhere and take a boat, or is there a ferry?"

"Sir?"

"A boat. To the island."

The employee politely laughed, apparently thinking Sean was joking. The annoyed gaze he received told him he wasn't.

"Oh. No sir. Pawleys Island is a town. It's not an actual island.

Well, I mean, technically it *is* an island—part of it, at least—but the mainland area beside it is considered Pawleys Island too. You can get to the island itself just by driving over one of two short bridges and…" The kid must have read confusion in Sean's face, because he cut himself short. "Let me just show you."

Sean let him take the map. The kid unfolded it across his counter and used the sides of his hands to steamroll it flat. His hand slid to a sectioned-off area in the lower right corner, and his finger traced a coastline at the edge of a long, thin section of land. It didn't so much resemble an island as it did a continuation of the mainland, divided by a narrow river—like the warped piece of a jigsaw puzzle that didn't quite fit.

Sean nodded his head and folded the map into quarters, ignoring its natural creases. "No boat then."

"No sir," the kid said, his voice now upbeat. "This roadmap will get you there . . . free of charge."

Sean's eyes darted back to the kid, who quickly offered him an apologetic wince. He directed Sean to an outside parking lot. Sean snagged the keys from the desk, grabbed his paperwork and luggage, and made for the doors.

The moment he stepped outside, the humidity struck him like a warm, wet blanket thrown in his face. Growing up in the dry Colorado climate, mugginess was something he wasn't used to. It felt restrictive, as if he were being interrogated by Mother Nature about an unknown crime. With the climate, however, came some intriguing plant life. Sean found himself captivated by a row of strategically planted palm trees that sprouted from behind thick ferns at the edge of the lot. Their broad leaves swayed softly in the light breeze above their sturdy, layered trunks. Sean realized it was the first time he'd actually seen a palm tree in person. What little traveling he'd done over the years had been limited to the northern states.

He followed the numbers stenciled by each parking space until he'd walked nearly the full length of the lot. The Escort was parked in the third from the last space. It was bright red. Sean cursed under his breath and unlocked the driver's side door, glancing at a couple of tiny lizards that scurried under a nearby SUV.

He tossed his suitcase inside the car and fought with an adjustment level under the seat until he'd given himself as much room as he could get. He then climbed inside, unsurprised to find himself feeling hot and crammed. He cranked the engine and turned the air conditioning to its max setting. New-car smell and warmth blew against his face. Within seconds the air started to cool.

He unzipped the outer pocket of his suitcase, and pulled out a thin notepad. Instructions and addresses in his sister's handwriting filled the first three pages; Diana had always been good at organizing things. He spent the next fifteen minutes or so coordinating the addresses with cross streets on the map, and adding his own notes using a promotional pen he'd found in the glove box. Georgetown County Coroner's Office would be the first stop.

His decades-old reunion with his father would be less than an hour's drive.

Chapter 6

The man was inconsolable, his loud sobbing echoing in the mostly empty waiting room. His wails were like those of a lonely basset hound. His face was planted in his trembling hands, his hair a disheveled mess. Sean could do little more than cringe at the pathetic display and hope that the receptionist who'd walked over to comfort the man would find whatever magic words were required to bring the scene to a close.

Instead, the man slid out of his chair and onto his knees on the linoleum floor, wrapping his arms around the receptionist's legs and hugging them for support. He was a large man in his forties, bottom-heavy and dressed in white overalls with paint stains. He looked like a polar bear trying to contain a fish he'd pulled onto shore. When his cries grew in volume, Sean fought back the urge to yank out his own hair.

The receptionist was a middle-aged woman with red-framed glasses and kind, empathetic eyes. She patted the man on the head, and turned to Sean who had strategically seated himself in the chair farthest away.

"Sir? Mr. Coleman?" she asked. "Would you mind bringing me a box of tissues from my desk?"

"Oh God," Sean muttered, reluctantly climbing to his feet. He took a breath and lumbered over to the front desk where he found a pink Kleenex box. He handed it to her, averting his eyes from the debacle playing out before him.

"Thank you," she said, taking the box.

"Do you want me to pry him off you, or . . . "

"No, I'm fine. Thank you. The coroner will be ready to show you your father in just a couple of minutes."

Sean nodded.

"You lost your father, too?" the man on the floor suddenly blathered out, swiveling his wet face upward to meet Sean's. The man's eyes were red and veiny, and his thin mustache was plastered across his upper lip from the tears. "Mine just died in a roofing accident."

"At least you're taking it well," Sean replied.

The receptionist gasped and glared at Sean, an expression of sheer appall suddenly etched across her face. The man crumbled back to the floor now covered with slobber and disintegrated into a new flurry of bawling.

Sean held the receptionist's scowl for a moment before returning to his chair.

That really was an asshole thing to say, he thought. Had he had a relationship with his own father, he was certain the words would have never left his mouth. The truth was that a small part of Sean envied a man whose father had carved such a deep connection with his son that his death could draw such raw emotion. At the same time, he could have never envisioned himself clinging to a stranger's ankles for comfort.

The moment Sean sat down, he heard another man's voice call out his name. A round-faced gentleman, mostly bald with a little bit of gray hair above his ears, had poked the top half of his body though a pair of metal doors. He wore a white lab coat and thin-framed glasses. His face serious, he motioned Sean over with two fingers.

Sean grunted and rose to his feet, making his way back past the man on the floor and the receptionist. He stopped for a moment, took a breath, and gently placed his hand on the man's shoulder. "I'm sorry about your dad," he muttered.

The man in the lab coat led Sean into a wide hallway that smelled of solvents. He offered his hand and introduced himself as Malcolm Warner, the country coroner. Sean's curled lips didn't go unnoticed as the two men shook hands.

"Yes, like from the Cosby Show," the coroner said. "Only there's no Jamal and I have no idea what Rudy's up to these days." The line would have been humorous had he not delivered it in a tone void of levity. Sean could tell the fifty-something professional had grown tired of reciting the quip over the years.

The two made their way through a corridor with bare walls other than some fire extinguishers and odd-shaped electrical outlets. There were several sets of steel doors, but no activity. Sean heard no voices other than faint, monotonous dialogue that crept out from round speakers in the ceiling—likely from a local talk-radio show. Each step the men took across the linoleum sounded inordinately loud, heightened by the eeriness of the kind of work that routinely took place in the building.

"I just got off the phone with Chief Quammen," said Warner, scratching the top of his ear. "He wanted me to call him when you came to sign for the body."

"Why?"

"I think he just wants to introduce himself and probably talk to you about the case. He'll be over in a few minutes. He's in the area."

"What can *you* tell me about the case?" Sean asked.

"Well, as far as the investigation goes, I probably know less than you," replied Warner with half a chuckle. "I examine the bodies—perform autopsies. I give the police some pieces, and they use them to put the puzzle together."

When they reached an imposing double-door with a sign that read "Examination" above it, Warner stopped and turned to Sean. He opened his mouth to speak, but Sean cut him off.

"So what pieces can you slide into place for me?"

Warner's eyes narrowed. "Like I said, Quammen will be here in a few minutes."

Sean was getting frustrated at the man's side-stepping. "I know what you said, and I'm asking: What can *you* tell me?"

"Mr. Coleman, It's not really my place, nor is it appropriate—"

Sean interrupted again. "Listen, Warner, I'm in law enforcement myself, and I haven't seen the man in that room behind you in the last thirty years. We had no relationship. I promise you that there's nothing you could tell me that's going to set me off or send me to the floor in a pool of my own tears like that poor sap up front. I'm just asking you for a little professional courtesy."

Professional courtesy. It was a term Sean had sometimes heard his brother-in-law use when trying to dig information out of fellow peace officers. He'd also heard it on a number of episodes of *NYPD Blue*.

Warner's lips curled a bit and he nodded, seeming to admire Sean's straightforwardness. "Okay," he said, taking a step back and crossing his arms in front of his chest. "He was shot twice—once in the shoulder and once through the head."

"Was he shot at close range?"

"No. In fact, I suspect he was running from the shooter. The first bullet entered the back of his shoulder, not the front. The final one—the kill shot—came when he was in the water."

"The water?"

"Yes, he was found in the freshwater inlet that meets with the ocean in between the island and the mainland. His body washed up under a bridge on a surfboard. You didn't know that?"

Sean placed his hands on his hips. "I knew his body had washed up on shore. I didn't know anything about a surfboard or how he was shot."

Warner shrugged his shoulders. "It's probably not the type of information thought to be particularly relevant to a victim's family."

"Why do you think he was on a surfboard?"

"I couldn't tell you. Maybe just to stay afloat. It's not my job to figure out the series of events that led to one's death. I just determine what killed them."

"And what did kill him?"

"Excuse me?"

"What kind of gun was he shot with? What kind of bullets?"

Warner's face froze before he dropped his eyes to the ground uncomfortably. "I can't talk about that, Mr. Coleman. It's part of the police investigation. It's not public information at this point."

Sean's eyebrows raised in disbelief. "You can't tell me what he was shot with?"

"No. I can't. There's a method to all of this. It's the police's responsibility to decide what information gets put out and when." Warner tugged at his collar. "I've probably already said more than I should have, as a show of that *professional courtesy* you asked for."

Sean grumbled under his breath.

"What division of law enforcement are you with, anyway?" asked Warner.

"Security."

"Security?"

Sean pursed his lips and shook his head. "Private. Mainly property and protective services."

"Oh Jesus," Warner said, his shoulders deflating. "You're just a security guard?"

"Just a," affirmed Sean. "Is my father through here?" He pointed toward the set of doors beside them.

Warner glared at Sean in displeasure over being duped. He then sighed and muttered, "Come with me," before pushing open the doors and leading him inside the examination room.

The room was long and almost entirely white from the ceiling to the cement floor. It was noticeably colder than the rest of the building. Three steel tables with wheels, each about eight feet in length and four feet wide, were fastened to large metal sinks with arched faucets. Above each table, an adjustable arm held a large lamp with six embedded lights. Two hovered, unlit, above white blankets that covered the shapes of human bodies.

Sean felt his chest tighten. A chill that had little to do with the room's temperature brought goose bumps to his arms. He thought he had mentally prepared himself for this moment, but his body suddenly seemed to be calling the shots over his will. He forced himself to breathe as Warren strolled to the far side of the first table and peered up at Sean through the glare of his glasses.

"I realize that you haven't seen your father in quite some time," Warren said in a thoughtful tone, pulling some surgical gloves from his jacket and working them over his hands. "You're not here to identify him—that's already been done. You just need to sign that you've seen the body before we can release him to you and get the rest of the process rolling. It's policy."

Sean nodded. Warren flipped on the lamp above. It was on a dim setting that kept the presentation from being needlessly graphic.

"Okay. I'm going to pull the blanket off of his head. Keep in mind that that's where he was shot, so it's not going to be particularly pretty, though I did my best. Just nod at me when you're ready for me to place the blanket back over him."

Sean squared his jaw and nodded his head.

Warner carefully lifted the blanket off of the head of the body, keeping his eyes glued at Sean, whose own eyes quickly widened in disbelief.

"Is this a joke?" Sean snapped angrily.

Warner's eyes narrowed, and then he glanced down at the table. He flinched, his face paling before turning a deep red.

Lying before them was a life-sized, green-skinned mannequin—Dr. Frankenstein's monster. But how had this Halloween prop gotten in here?

"Son of a bitch!" Warner snarled, his teeth visible below his flared nostrils. He whipped the blanket off the mannequin. "Jordan!"

"What the hell kind of operation are you running here, Warner?"

Warner apologized profusely until a young man entered the room.

"Goddammit, Jordan!" Warner snarled, interrupting himself and turning on the man.

He was more of a kid than a man, no older than twenty, with a thin frame and thick, curly, bleached-blond hair. His skin was tan, and he wore an over-sized, wrinkled lab coat that covered most of a neon-green shirt and long shorts. He was carrying two cardboard boxes, one on top of the other, and his eyes were wide and baffled as they took in the scene.

"You still think this is all one big joke!" Warner hissed. "I could have given this internship to a long list of people, and—"

"Whoa, whoa, whoa!" cried the kid—Jordan. "Chill out for a sec." Jordan's eyes searched his surroundings for a moment before he found a small, metal table against the wall to set his boxes on.

"It's absolutely vital in this line of work that we show respect for the dead!" Warner sputtered, continuing the assault. "Why can't you get that through that sun-dried brain of yours?"

His arms now free, Jordan reached to his ears and pried some small, white ear buds from them; they appeared to be plugged into a small media player hidden inside the front pocket of his lab coat. Loud music poured out of them. "What now?" Jordan asked with raised eyebrows, turning his attention back to Warner.

Warner was livid, realizing the intern hadn't heard a word of his opening diatribe. "Come here!" he growled, grabbing Jordan by the arm and yanking him through the same double-doors he had just entered through.

Sean didn't know what to make of the exchange. His eyes fell back to Frankenstein, whose hollow shoulders seemed as if they were shrugging, imitating Sean's puzzlement.

The men's loud voices echoed down the hallway and filtered in through the closed doors. Sean could only decipher bits and pieces of the heated debate, but he gathered that the Frankenstein stunt was part of a practical joke the intern had intended solely for his boss.

"*Slate on table one* is what I told you!" Sean heard Warner shout. "Table one!"

"You said two! You said table two!" the kid shouted back in defiance.

Sean's head swiveled to meet the second covered body lying on the table just a few feet away. It sat in the shadows of the light above the first one. He slowly walked over to it, stepping around the crumpled up blanket Warner had dropped and a small metal drain in the floor. When he pressed his hand against what would have been the chest of the body, it was hard, solid, and cold—definitely not a Halloween decoration. He fiddled with the lamp above the body until he felt a switch. When he flipped it on, the light was blinding. He couldn't figure out how to dim it to the empathetic level of the first one but wasted no more than three seconds on the effort. His personal sensitivities didn't require appeasement.

He peeled off the blanket from the head to reveal gray, combed hair, and then a forehead with wrinkled skin. The flesh was so pale that each freckle and blemish appeared as if it had been applied with the tip of black or brown marker. At first, he didn't see the head wound Warner had described and thought for a moment that the clueless intern had screwed up for a second time. Then he realized that the flatness at the top of the skull behind the hairline wasn't an optical illusion from the positioning of the body. Part of his father's scalp was missing. Warner had just combed the hair in a way to partially conceal the wound for presentation—a kind gesture.

"Damn," Sean whispered, brushing away the curiosity of taking a closer look at what lay beyond the hair.

He took a breath and pulled the blanket under his father's chin. With the face fully exposed, he stepped back to take in the big picture. The eyebrows were marginally darker than the hair on the head, and the strong nose and chin that weren't so different from his uncle's. The right side of the face was a range of colors from purple to nearly black, and ended where his whiskers did, at the cheekbone. Bruising, Sean supposed.

Sean searched for some resemblance to how his father looked as a young man, even though faded memories and a couple of photographs were all he had to go on. He didn't immediately find it. Still, he felt a familiar presence laying there, the closed, fragile eyes so sentient that he half-expected them to open at any moment and unspool a lifetime of confessions. And if that sense alone wasn't enough to provide proper confirmation, Sean knew what would.

He circled over to the opposite side of the body and lifted the blanket off its right shoulder. There, behind a patch of wiry hair, he found what he was looking for: the head of a bald eagle below an arch of four stars. The word "Liberty" was barely legible below it, the tattoo having worn down significantly over the years. His father had gotten it while serving in the US Army around 1960. The same one had decorated the arm of his Uncle Zed, who also served.

As a child, Sean had sometimes stared at that tattoo as his father sat back in an old, beat-up recliner in their family's living room, drinking a beer and watching a game on television in an undershirt and boxers. Sean remembered wanting a tattoo of his own one day. When he had told his father, his father shook his head. "You need to *earn* this kind of ink, boy. This here means you did something with your life." Sean never did get a tattoo.

Up until the day he was abandoned, Sean had always wanted to be his father. He'd dreamed of growing up to achieve things and build things, whether it be in sports, serving the country, or laying the foundation for a church or school. Though he'd never presumed to understand the thoughts that were floating around in his father's mind back then, he did know that the man had built himself a legacy. And when he gave up that legacy by running away from his life, Sean gave up wanting to be him.

Sean had felt like he had been left adrift, later surviving on bitterness and booze-fueled instincts with no drive to achieve, and no will to better himself. For years he'd held the past in such contempt that he wound up inheriting all of the worst traits of the man whose shadow he'd so desperately wanted to escape. Sean was in a better place now, but the animosity still burned.

He pressed the tips of his fingers to the tattoo. When he felt his father's cold, coarse flesh, a chill raced through his spine, and he removed his hand. He let his eyes slide from the tattoo to the sutured skin above it. The coroner had fastened a large section of his father's shoulder back together, just beside the trapezius. The original laceration had to have been caused by the first bullet his father had taken, but the sutured area seemed much too large to have been caused by a single entry.

"Oh Jesus, I'm sorry," Warner said, reentering the room. His eyes shifted back and forth from Sean to his father's exposed body. "My intern has a stupid sense of humor. He's been giving me problems all summer."

"Your son?" Sean asked.

Warner let some air escape his lungs and shook his head. "My nephew. The one that belongs to my least favorite sister."

Sean nodded. "Good help is hard to find. I guess it's not like *Quincy M.E.* in the smaller towns."

Warner's eyebrows lowered at the reference.

"It was an old television show . . . about a medical examiner," Sean added. "He solved mysteries."

"Oh, I know," replied Warner with a wry smile. "I used to watch it. Hell, I still watch the reruns. I just don't hear it brought up all that often. Great show."

Sean nodded.

When the doors behind Warner sprung open again, the coroner immediately spun around and snarled, "I said to work on the trash!" He raised his hands in apology once he realized it wasn't his intern who'd entered. "Oh, I'm sorry, Chief."

Standing in the doorway was a short, bulky man in his early or mid-fifties. His wide eyes, full face, and loose jowls resembled those of a bulldog. Out of breath, he even appeared to be panting.

"Sean Coleman," the man said in a single gulp, looking past Warner. "Glad I caught you. I'm Travis Quammen . . . Pawleys Island's chief of police." His accent was that of a New Yorker.

Quammen had a dense salt-and-pepper mane that was parted so definitively at its center that the prophet Moses would have been impressed. Below his circular red nose hung a thick mustache that was darker than his hair.

Clad in a white polo shirt, dark pleated pants, and a holstered pistol hugging his side, Quammen thumped across the room and nodded a subtle greeting to Warner. Sean met the chief at the foot of the table and accepted his extended hand. It was wet with sweat.

"I'm sorry about your father," Quammen said, looking Sean in the eye.

"Thanks," answered Sean. "Any news on who killed him?"

Quammen's eyes widened. He released Sean's hand. "You really cut to the chase, don't you? Your brother-in-law said that about you."

Sean forced his breath out through his nose. "Oh yeah? Did Gary give you any other warnings?"

Quammen smirked. "Just that you got a little bit of a history with getting involved in police matters."

Sean shook his head. "Only when the *public servants* aren't getting the job done."

Quammen leveled his gaze as if deciding whether Sean's words were designed to be as confrontational as they sounded.

Sean's eyes fell to the chest of Quammen's shirt, where far-stretching wet spots rested below the armpits. To the right of the curly gray hair that popped out from his collar was an embroidered police shield. Sean was amused by its novelty.

Real policemen wear badges was what Sean wanted to say; instead came the words, "Don't worry, Chief. I won't step on your toes. I just want to be kept in the loop. My job is to get Jack Slate's body back to Colorado. That's all."

Quammen nodded, some suspicion still lingering in his eyes.

"Warner won't tell me what my father was shot with," Sean added. "Is there a reason for that?"

"Why don't we go out into the hallway and talk about the case?" Quammen said. "We'll let Mr. Warner wrap things up in here."

Warner fiddled with the overhead lamp and finally dimmed it. "When you're done, Mr. Coleman," he began, "we'll need to talk about having your father's body embalmed in order for him to be shipped by air. There's a funeral home just three blocks away that can take care of it, and they can also coordinate with your local funeral home on the transportation details."

"Yeah, your secretary filled me in on that. Adamson's is my next stop."

"Very good." Warner reached for the blanket to pull it back up over the body.

Sean quickly grabbed his wrist. "What's that?" he asked, pointing to his father's right hand. There were dark bruises and lacerations across his father's knuckles, just above his fingers.

"His hand connected hard with something," said Warner. "I took a close look at it. There was no debris other than some sand lodged in there."

Sean leaned in closer, squinting. "Those look kind of like teeth." He pointed to a dark row of what looked like small, uneven squares.

Warner suppressed a sigh, seemingly discarding the novice remark, as he leaned in to examine the hand. His face then tightened into a thoughtful frown. "Hmm."

"Come on, Sean" said Quammen. "Let's let Warner finish things up."

Quammen led Sean out of the room and back into the empty corridor that smelled of strong chemicals. There, he ran down the same explanation as Warner had about why some of the case's details needed to be kept under wraps. Sean barely listened to him, instead fixating on the lawman's accent.

Sean had envisioned the chief speaking with the deep Southern drawl prominent in films and television shows that take place in the South. It suddenly occurred to him that he hadn't once heard that famed accent since touching down in the state. The realization made him question his conventional couch-potato wisdom.

"The fewer details people know," Quammen continued, "the easier it is to wade through false leads. It also keeps the press from identifying and publicizing possible suspects before they're apprehended."

Sean had watched plenty of television police dramas in his time to understand that what Quammen was saying was true. Still, he stewed over not knowing all there was to know. He didn't consider *himself* to be a potential liability to the case, and he knew he definitely wouldn't be talking to the press. Sean began to wonder if Quammen's concerns were less about the press and more about Sean overstepping bounds. Lumbergh may have warned Quammen to be uncharitable with the information around Sean based on past experiences.

"Do you have any suspects yet?" Sean asked.

Quammen shook his head. "Unfortunately, no. A county investigator, Detective Rick Seedorf, is now heading up the case. I'm working with him on it, but he's the lead guy. His attention is solely devoted to it. He's working the angle that your father's death was the result of a burglary gone wrong. I'm assuming your brother-in-law told you that."

Sean nodded, reaching into his pants pocket for his notepad to write down the name of the detective.

Quammen continued. "The cash found on the body couldn't be traced. The saltwater pretty much took care of any chance of getting some prints off it. There weren't reports of break-ins along the coast, or in the neighboring areas. We did some outside inspections of the homes of residents who had already left for the season. We found nothing there either."

"The teenager on the beach—the one that my dad beat up," began Sean. "Is that 'the coast' you're talking about?"

"We gave that area the closest look," said Quammen. "Unfortunately, that kid let two days pass before coming forward. He didn't want his parents to know that he'd been drinking on the beach that night instead of sleeping over at a friend's house. In that time, the tide had pretty well scrubbed away at the beach in the spot where he *thinks* he was assaulted. Other than a vague description of your father, he wasn't of much use."

"My father's girlfriend. Did she know anything?"

"She didn't even know he had a police record," Quammen said. "And I tend to believe her. I think she thought he just cleaned pools."

"Cleaned pools?"

"Oh, I thought you knew. He was a pool cleaner."

"As in *swimming* pools?"

"Yes. There are sure as hell a lot of them here. That was his job. Self-employed. Did someone tell you differently?"

"No." Sean's eyes drifted to the floor. "I just didn't know . . . and didn't think to ask about it. Once I heard he was a thief, I guess it didn't occur to me that he could have also had a real job."

Quammen nodded, a hint of sympathy in his gaze.

Sean dug into his back pocket and pulled out the map from the car rental office. He unfolded it and held it up to the wall beside him. "Without compromising the investigation, can you at least show me where his body was found?"

"Yes. It's no secret." Quammen pulled out a pen that was clipped to the inside of his side pocket and clicked it open. "Why do you want to know?"

"Oh, I don't know. Is it odd for a son to want to know where his dead father was found?"

Quammen nodded slowly, the suspicion returning to his eyes. "I suppose not." He leaned forward and drew a small circle across the farthest south bridge that connected the island to the mainland.

"How about the beach, too?" Sean asked before Quammen could return the pen to his pocket.

"The beach?"

"Where the kid was beat up. Is *that* a secret?"

"We haven't released that information to the public. The kid's a minor. His parents want him left out of things."

"I'm not asking for his name. I just want the spot."

Quammen sighed and placed an X on a spot along the coastline, south of the bridge.

"Okay, so that's where my father stole the boy's surfboard."

The police chief's eyes widened. The pen fell from his hand and skittered along the floor. "How in the hell did you know that?"

"I didn't—until now. It *was* a hunch."

Quammen said nothing, instead measuring Sean with a gruff glare.

Sean continued. "Why else would a thief beat up some drunk kid on a beach unless he needed something of his, right? My father was found on a surfboard. It's not exactly brain science."

The policeman's face went deadpan. He was clearly unamused. "I think we're done here," he said, retrieving his pen from the floor and cramming it back in his pocket. "If you want to give me your motel info, I'll let you know if we get any new information that we can pass along."

Chapter 7

S ean took care of things at the funeral home and got back on the
highway. With the steering wheel in one hand and his crumpled
map in the other, he squinted at the small lettering on street signs,
pumping his brakes when the names were hard to make out. This
prompted the honks of horns behind him, which Sean merely swore
off.

By the time he found what he was looking for, the sun had descended below a string of impending rain clouds and was beginning
to disappear behind the uneven tips of an impenetrable wall of pine
trees that stood to the west. The tilted sign was short, sun-faded, and
partially concealed by some overgrown shrubs. Still, he might have
noticed it the first time he'd passed by if he had been looking for the
right community name. The sign didn't read "Paradise Acres," but
"Pair-a-dice Acres," and it displayed the image of two game-playing
dice below the slogan: "A lucky place to live!"

"You've got to be shitting me," Sean muttered, scoffing at the
cheesy play on words. He flipped on his turn signal and swung the
car through the narrow entrance beside the sign.

The road was paved but looked to have gone without maintenance
for several years. Large cracks splintered across the asphalt, making
it look like it had been cobbled together from thousands of smaller
sections. From the rifts rose raggedy weeds and some small trees.
The edges of the road were strangled with overgrowth. Even with his
windows rolled up and the air conditioning on, Sean could hear the

crackle beneath his tires. He felt as if he were tearing the road apart simply by driving on it.

The street turned to dirt after a hundred yards, and when Sean emerged from around the mesh of a chain-link fence, rows of single-level, long buildings came into clearer view. Most were light in color, but weathered and grimy. It took a moment for him to realize that they were mobile homes because of how high they stood. They were stilted up on cinderblocks—a precaution against the threat of floods during hurricane season.

A couple of young kids with dirty faces and tattered clothes ignored him as they kicked a deflated tetherball across the road. Sean saw no hint of amusement in their faces, only boredom. He braked long enough for them to pass. He then idled through the middle of the park, his eyes panning the numbers that hung above each front door. He pulled over to the side when he spotted the number twelve.

The siding on the home was pale blue. It might have been darker once, but the sun had bleached away its character. A wooden porch with short steps led to an aluminum screen door with a large dent at its base. The porch needed staining and was missing some of its railing. Sean's father clearly hadn't been as handy and attentive to maintenance work as Sean had remembered him being. An early 1990s lime green Datsun was parked in front of the home. The paint job wasn't factory.

Sean parked behind the Datsun. When he climbed out, he noticed some bed sheets dangling from a long clothesline tied from the corner of the home to a nearby tree. They swayed in the light wind as if they were sails. A large black bird dropped out of the air and landed on the line just long enough to let out an eerie cry, defecate on the sheet, and take flight again.

"A lucky place to live, my ass," Sean muttered.

The Datsun's engine ticked from recent use. Anxiety began to stew in his gut as he made his way up the short staircase. Its tired boards creaked from his weight. He tried to envision his father walking up and down those same steps every day while his forgotten family trudged through their lives a couple thousand miles away, haunted by his ghost.

He wasn't sure why he had expected to feel anything other than awkwardness at being there. Maybe he'd hoped that walking a short path in his father's shoes would present a coherent explanation—an answer to the elusive question of why he had chosen to live the life he had. Maybe it would advance pieces of the unfinished drawing that Sean had sketched in his mind. What he felt, however, wasn't clarity. It was silent renunciation for coming there—that was until he knocked on the screen door.

"Come on in!" a woman's loud, gravelly voice rang out almost instantly.

The screen door was closed, but the main door wasn't. Through the mesh, he saw a shag rug on a linoleum floor in a small entranceway. An unlit brass floor lamp stood on one side, and the sharp corner of what looked like a dining room set was visible on the other. The rest of the room was too dim to decipher due to the disappearing sun. The strong stench of cigarette smoke lingered in the air.

"Hello?" Sean said loudly, assuming the tenant inside was expecting someone else. "My name is Sean Coleman!"

"Come on in, Sean Coleman!" the gruff voice answered.

"Uh, okay." He pried open the door and let himself inside.

To his left was a small kitchen. A pile of unwashed bowls, cups, and plates filled the sink, accompanied by the reek of spoiled milk. To the right was a narrow dining room where numerous cardboard boxes of various sizes sat in disarray on the table he had seen from the outside.

Sitting on top of several of the boxes and scattered across the tiny bar in the kitchen sat an odd display of colorful balloon animals—elephants, giraffes, monkeys, and more. As Sean's eyes adjusted to the darkness, more latex figures came into view. They were everywhere, dangling from the chandelier above the table, hanging on décor along the walls, and standing on top of each other in pyramids. The spectacle bordered on the perverse.

His gaze followed a column of climbing monkeys attached with tape to the corner of a wall. At the top, they pointed to something that stole his breath. Mounted across the upper wall, just below the popcorn ceiling, was a row of evenly spaced plates—commemorative plates with colorful, detailed drawings of Elvis Presley, James Dean, Marilyn Monroe, Marlon Brando, and other celebrity icons from the same era.

The plates had once hung above the dining room of the house he'd grown up in, and now they were even positioned in exactly the same order. He recalled his father often gazing up at them with pride during dinner as the family ate in relative silence, rarely sharing or asking each other about what they had done during the day. His father's mind was often focused elsewhere—possibly clinging to earlier days of independence and glory. Maybe he had been wishing to be somewhere else.

Sean had assumed these were the plates his mother had angrily shattered against the wall the morning his father had left. He remembered the terrible clamor of that day as he and his sister huddled together in a corner of the room. The sound still echoed through his nightmares.

It seemed now that his father had taken the plates with him— either that or he'd picked up replacements at some point. It would have been easy enough. For years, the collection had been sold on late-night infomercials. Regardless, the plates were now smirking down at him. His father had apparently valued them more than his family.

Sean's hands tightened into fists. He wanted to leap up into the air like a crazed gorilla and rip them all down.

"You're Jack's boy, ain't ya?" called out the woman, snapping Sean out of his spell. "I could use your help, ya know!"

The voice had come from a hallway leading out of the dining

room. The uneven corridor creaked with each step. A mural painted across the wall displayed an obscure pattern of small lizards walking single file into the open mouth of a larger lizard. Sean followed the runts toward the cannibal. The stink of cigarettes grew stronger, and Sean soon saw smoke floating aimlessly in the open space of a bright room ahead.

When he entered the room, he saw more boxes on top of a low-lying queen-sized bed covered by a flowery comforter. A balloon rhinoceros hung off the edge of an open box. Beyond the pile, on the opposite side of the bed, a woman knelt on the floor. She had her back to him as she lowered an armful of mystery-genre paperback books into a box. She was thin—almost too thin—with dark, sun-dried skin. A spider tattoo on the back of her left shoulder peeked out from beneath the strap of a red tank top. Her artificially black hair stood high above her head as if it had been propped up with half a can of hairspray. The rest flowed down to her shoulders. It reminded Sean of the style teenage girls used to wear in Denver shopping malls back in the eighties. A small ashtray sat on a wooden chair beside her, hosting a half-spent butt.

"Are you Claudia?" he asked, expecting the answer to be no.

"Sure am," the woman said. She dropped the books into the box and turned her head toward him.

She wore no makeup. Her skin was loose, her lips were chapped, and crow's feet jetted out from her dark, Latino eyes. She'd spent much of her life under the sun. He guessed she was in her late fifties or early sixties. He had trouble visualizing the woman who knelt before him as his father's type, but he instantly realized how ridiculous that thought was. He didn't have a clue what his father's type was.

Claudia's eyes widened and her thin brows pointed to the ceiling as she appraised Sean. A smile formed on her face, displaying a set of yellowed but well-aligned teeth. She spun on the floor into a sitting position facing him, her dark legs sprouting out of short denim shorts. Sean imagined she was probably attractive in her earlier years, back around the time her hairdo was popular.

"Ya kinda look like him," she said in a coarse breath. "I mean, you're bigger and taller, and of course you're younger, but ya kinda look like him."

"Lucky me," he replied apathetically.

"Ya came for his things, didn't ya?" she said, climbing to her feet. "I thought ya would. I've been packing 'em up."

"No, actually," he said. "I don't care about any of that. You can give it all to Goodwill or whoever."

Her face soured. "Well why'd ya come then?"

He stared at her, uncertain of the answer himself. "I don't know," he mumbled. "I guess I was just curious."

"'Bout me?"

"About him." He took a deep breath. "You know. Where he lived. What he did. It's been years—decades . . ." He shook his head and let his tongue slide to the side of his mouth.

"I know," Claudia said. "I mean, I didn't know until after he died, but I know now." She shook her head. "There's a lot I didn't know about him. He didn't talk 'bout his past much. All I knew was that his name wasn't always Slate."

His eyes narrowed. "How did you know that?"

"He told me once. He was drunk one night and his eyes were all glazed over, and he was in one of them sappy moods of his. He said he'd changed his name a few years back. He liked the name Slate 'cause it was supposed to be like a 'clean slate'—him starting over and whatnot." She reached for her dwindling cigarette.

Sean snorted and shook his head. "Well, that's what he did all right. Started over. A wife and couple of little kids be damned."

She took a long drag, his remark seeming not to faze her.

"You said you didn't know about his family until after he died," he said. "What changed?"

She nodded and turned away from him to blow smoke from her

mouth. "I found some stuff—personal stuff in an old trunk he kept in a storage locker we shared. There were papers in it—papers that led me back to you guys."

He nodded. "What other *personal stuff?*"

"I'm having it brought over. You're welcome to go through it unless ya want it all sent to Goodwill, too."

He shrugged his shoulders. After a moment, he said, "I don't know."

She took a breath and asked, "Have you talked to the police? Have they found out anything new on the case?"

Sean filled her in on everything Chief Quammen had told him.

"Did you know he was a thief?" he asked, studying Claudia's face for a reaction.

She sneered. "If he was, he sucked at it. I'm not sayin' I'd have put it past him, but if he was stealin' shit, he sure as hell didn't reap any rewards. In case ya missed it, this place ain't exactly the Ritz. As far as I know, any money he had was from cleanin' pools. He had plenty of that work keepin' him busy."

He nodded. He'd only known Claudia for a few minutes, but she struck him as a straight shooter—a lot like his late uncle. He believed she was telling him the truth.

"Worked a lot of hours, did he?" he said, scratching the back of his head. "Where did he do most of his work? Around here?"

"Nah," she said, letting out a cough. "He was all spread out. Most of his work was up north, closer to Myrtle. He did a few homes down this way—along King's River, Beach Bridge, and Hagley—usually at the beginning of the week. He liked to sleep in on Mondays."

His face tightened. "Beach Bridge? Are you talking about Beach Bridge Road?"

She nodded as she sucked on her cigarette.

"Did you tell the police that?"

"No. Why? Is it important?"

He explained that the altercation his father had had with the surfer the night he was killed happened on a beach just behind Beach Bridge Road.

She shrugged. "He wouldn't have been working that late."

"But he's familiar with that area, right? From what I saw on a map, it's not a long road."

"It sure as hell ain't," she said. "It's really just an access road to the beach and no more than twenty homes. Big ones, though. I met him over there once when he ran out of chemicals. Dropped off a bucket for him. First and last reason I ever had to be there. Ya can get depressed, ya know, spending too much time around the South Carolina elite. They have a way of reminding ya of every one of your failings."

He understood what she meant. As a security guard, he'd sometimes be stationed outside of places he couldn't afford to step into, let alone mingle with the people who could. He'd watch them from his position out in the cold and snow as they wore thousand-dollar suits and dresses, sipped on wine, and exchanged plastic smiles. He'd always told himself that he wouldn't trade places with them in a million years—not those phony socialites. He knew deep down, though, that it was only because he couldn't.

"How many houses over there did he work at—on Beach Bridge?" Sean asked.

"I think just the one."

"Do you remember the address?"

"Why?"

The moment Sean opened his mouth to answer, a deafening pop burst directly behind his head. A jolt of adrenaline shot through his body and he quickly spun around, eyes bulging and heart racing, to find a stocky man with a round face and a larger-than-life smile staring back at him.

He was a young guy, probably around twenty, with a dark mop of hair and a pencil-thin mustache. He held the torn and shriveled remnants of a red balloon in his chubby fingers and erupted into obnoxious, almost hideous laughter that came from the very depths of his stomach. His bewildering amusement seemed to be at Sean's expense.

It pissed Sean off. His hand reflexively shot up under the man's multiple chins and clenched his throat. With a squared jaw and steam nearly blowing out his nose, he squeezed the man's neck until his eyes bulged and his laughter ceased.

"Wait, wait, wait!" Sean heard Claudia plead from behind him.

He pinned the offender against a tall dresser, tipping it back against the wall. Trinkets fell from its top and crashed to the floor.

"What the hell are you doing?" Sean snarled, ignoring the man's hands feebly tugging at his arm.

"Stop! He lives here!" Claudia shouted. "That's Dusty!"

"Dusty?" Sean's head pivoted toward her.

"He's my son. He's just . . . he has a different sense of humor than most people. He didn't mean any harm," she said. "He's one of them balloon enthusiasts, ya know? He gets carried away sometimes."

"A balloon *what*?" Sean softened his grip only a little.

"A balloon enthusiast." She spoke faster now, almost frantic. "People hire him for birthday parties and other shit. He makes animals, hats, and other things. Just stop it, okay? I think you're hurting him."

He turned his attention back to Dusty. The young man mirrored his mother's Hispanic-looking ethnicity, and he was clad in a white, sleeveless shirt that didn't quite contain his large gut. Stretched around his waist was a pair of uncomfortably snug denim shorts that were inexplicably similar to his mother's. With a panicked, reddened face, Dusty shoved his hand into the front pocket of his shorts. He retrieved a slip of paper from it, and with a shaking arm, began to tuck the paper in Sean's shirt pocket.

Sean let go of his neck and latched onto his wrist, allowing Dusty to suck down air before erupting into a wild coughing fit and nearly falling to his knees. Sean pried the paper from his hand. It was a business card. "Looney Ballooney, LLC" it read above a graphic of multicolored balloons. "Dustin Bouche, CEO" was also listed, along with a phone number.

He let go of Dusty's wrist and backed away from him. He glared at the strange man in utter disbelief. *Did this guy try to solicit my business while being choked out?* He couldn't find the words.

Claudia skirted toward her son, her cigarette nearly falling from her mouth. She scolded Dusty with her finger, pressing it into his bloated chest, and ordering him to apologize.

"Sorry," Dusty muttered with a raspy voice and a cough. His shoulders bowed and he stared at the floor, looking like an eight-year-old who'd been reprimanded by an adult.

Sean took a breath, trying to calm his racing heart. "What kind of asshole sneaks up behind someone they've never met, pops a balloon in their ear, and then laughs his ass off about it? People hire you for that shit?"

Dusty winced from the volume of Sean's voice. His lips pursed and his eyes flickered back and the forth from Sean's to the floor before they began to well up. He put his hand to his face as if he were about to cry—only it seemed phony, everything too exaggerated.

Sean cringed.

"My son is what some people might call a little socially awkward," Claudia explained.

Sean guessed it wasn't the first time the mother had had to apologize for her son's conduct.

She turned to Dusty. "Can you stop the mime shit and just make it right?"

The young man lifted his head, lips overly pouty. It reminded Sean of the Larry Mondello character from *Leave it to Beaver*. The man abruptly raised the palm of his hand in front of his own face. When he removed it a second later, the sad expression had been replaced with a bright smile.

"Jesus," Sean whispered under his breath.

Dusty reached around his mother, nearly shoving her to the side, and retrieved the business card from Sean's hand. He pulled a blue Sharpie marker from his back pocket, twisted off the plastic cap, and wrote something on the back of the card. With the smile still adorning his face, he handed it back to Sean, who reluctantly took it. Dusty then turned his back to the two, puffed his chest out in front of him, and left the room—head held high as if the whole exchange had been normal.

"One free event," Sean read from the card. He didn't know what to make of it, and he asked Claudia if her son was being a wise ass, but she insisted it wasn't his intent.

"He just gets into character sometimes, and he just can't help himself."

"Oh, is he . . ." Sean began, unsure of how to phrase the rest of his question on his mind.

"Is he what?"

"You know . . . specially educated or whatever?"

"Retarded?" she demanded, crossing her arms in front of her. Her eyes were wide, her teeth bared. "Ya think my son's *retarded*?"

"I . . . I don't know."

"He's a *performer*, Mr. Sean Coleman! He's eccentric, that's all. He's like that David Copperfield guy, and that other fella with the mallet and the watermelons. He's an entertainer!"

Sean's eyes stung from Claudia's smoky breath. He raised his hand to his forehead, trying to rub some sanity back into his skull. "The address of the place on Beach Bridge, where you brought my dad the chemicals. Do you remember it?"

She glared at him for another moment before swiping away the business card he still held in his hand. She walked over to the dresser, pulled a pencil from its top drawer, and scribbled down a number on the card. When she held it back out for Sean, she couldn't bring herself to look him in the eyes.

"Thanks," he said before taking it.

Sean stepped outside and off the front porch to the dirt. The sun had set, and a yellow Toyota pickup truck with a white shell was just pulling up beside his car. Its headlights went dim, and a young woman in her early twenties with long, dark hair climbed out. She wore a black, sleeveless shirt, and a pair of red athletic shorts hugged her trim waist. She seemed to be in a hurry, quickly exiting the truck and slamming its door shut. When she looked up and noticed Sean, she stopped in her tracks.

"Are you Sean?" she asked, out of breath.

He nodded.

She jogged over to him and wrapped her bronze, slender arms around his body, burying the side of her face against his chest. Sean was left confused and speechless, his arms limply hanging at his sides as her citrusy perfume overpowered him. He wondered if the whole trailer park was full of crazies.

"I'm so sorry," she told him, her voice careful and sincere. "I didn't know Jack had kids. He never talked about them. We always joked that he was a big kid himself."

"Okay," he grumbled. "Who are you?"

"I'm sorry," she giggled with a sniff, releasing her grip and taking a step back. Large hoops dangled from her ears. She wiped away a tear. "I'm Maria Ortíz. I'm Claudia's daughter. Did you already meet Claudia?"

He nodded, taking notice of a small stud in her nose. "Yeah. I was just leaving. Do you live here?"

"No. I'm just bringing some things over for my mother, from her storage locker," she explained. "She can't drive, you know. She was stupid enough to earn herself a DUI a few months ago."

His eyes narrowed. He glanced at the green Datsun parked next to them. Its engine was still ticking intermittently. "Well *someone's* been driving that car," he said, his investigative instincts kicking in.

"That's Dusty's car."

Sean's face twisted in disbelief. "Dusty can drive a car? He's allowed to? Legally?"

"Of course. What do you mean?"

He shook his head, deciding the question wasn't worth answering. He elected instead to pursue a more consequential one. "If you're Claudia's daughter, that means you're Dusty's . . . sister?" He braced for impact.

Maria's nose wrinkled. "Well, he's actually my half-brother."

"I'm half relieved."

"What?"

"Never mind. Did you bring my father's trunk over from the storage locker? Is that what you were getting?" His stomach growled as he spoke. He hadn't eaten since a quick bite at the Denver airport that morning.

"Yes, it's in the bed of my truck."

They walked to the back and Maria popped open the rear window and tailgate. Inside, under a dim dome light, sat a large hardwood chest with metal trim. It was beat up and dirty, and far longer and taller than he'd envisioned—at least six by three feet. There was clearly no way it would fit in his rental car. He couldn't have taken it with him even if he had wanted to. Still, the mention of *personal* items intrigued Sean. If Claudia had found information inside the trunk to link his father back to the children he had left more than thirty years ago, there might be enough left to piece together his father's entire life after leaving Winston. Sean hated that he cared about that part of his father's life, but he *did* care—enough to drive in the dark to a destitute trailer park merely because his father had lived there.

"Are you staying at a hotel?" Maria asked

"A Motel 6 along Highway 17. I still need to check in."

"I can follow you back there in my truck and drop off the trunk," she offered.

"Really?" he asked, digesting her words. "You sure it won't keep you from anything? It looked like you were in a hurry when you pulled up." His stomach grumbled again, and he was sure she heard it.

"No," she said with a relaxed smile. "I just didn't want to spend a lot of time over here tonight."

"Oh, because of Dusty?"

She gave him a strange look. "No. I went to the locker for my mother right after work, and she was just anxious to get this thing dropped off. I was going to chill at home for a bit before starting a shift at my other job. I'm picking up some extra hours because they're short-staffed."

He nodded. His stomach spoke for a third time. The growl might have even been a carry-over from the second.

"Why don't we grab a bite to eat after the motel?" she posed. "My treat. I'll tell you about your dad."

Chapter 8

O ff the beaten path east of Highway 17 sat a small, secluded seafood shack called the Wicked Scallop. Set in the center of a small sand parking lot blanketed with thousands of shattered seashells, the building's rippled tin roof stood above wood-planked walls and a slanted sign bragging, "Our *catch of the day* was swimming this morning."

Large, mossy trees and thick overgrowth along the property's outer rim served as a natural barrier between local patronage and out-of-town visitors. Only a few cars were parked out front as Sean pulled up behind Maria's truck. The bed of the vehicle rode much higher now that his father's trunk was sitting in his motel room. Sean, even with his size and strength, had had difficulty dragging it inside. Maria told him that it had taken two professional movers, who were loading up a neighboring locker, to get it inside her truck in the first place.

Sean was curious about what sat in its hull that made it so heavy, but he was also famished, and the young woman's offer to provide some insight on his father intrigued him. Plus, she wasn't bad company considering the rest of her family lineage—and the fact that she was buying. The trunk could wait until later.

He climbed out of his car and smelled salt in the breeze that slapped against his face. He could neither see nor hear the ocean, but he sensed it was close by. Also in the air was a whiff of rain. More clouds had rolled in, looking as though they could begin spitting at any moment.

He met Maria at the front of her truck under drooping palm leaves that swayed in the wind. She slipped the thin strap of a small purse over her shoulder, and they made their way up a short flight of wooden stairs. Its handrail was decorated with a couple strands of white Christmas lights that Sean guessed stayed up year-round. He held open the screen door at the side of the building. Maria slid in front of him, offering a polite grin as she stepped inside.

A loud harmonica solo in the middle of a winding southern rock song belted out from a couple of overhead speakers. The sound system hung above a well-stocked bar where an overweight, grinning man with a colorful shirt and a nametag reading "Al" mixed a drink for a thin, pale woman with frazzled hair and a ratty tank-top. Al was a black man, so the sight of him pouring booze in front of the Confederate flag that proudly hung on the wall behind him struck Sean as strange. It seemed even stranger after a closer look at Al's nametag revealed him to be the owner of the restaurant. Sean wrote the oddity off to "Southern culture"—something he knew little about.

Sean and Maria received a quick greeting from a young, friendly waitress with blonde hair and braces. She led them into a small dining room where only three tables were occupied. Sean was glad the place wasn't busy, remembering Maria said she had to work later that night. They passed by an open kitchen door where pots and pans clanged together, along with some employee chatter. Something sizzled on a grill from inside. Its spicy smell consumed the air, drawing more sounds from Sean's stomach.

The glossy wood paneling was barely visible behind a dense décor of mounted fish, nautical instruments, and ocean maps. The waitress seated Sean and Maria at a window between a pair of old kayak oars and a wide-eyed sailfish with its long, sharp nose pointed toward the ceiling. The window overlooked the dark parking lot a story below, but all Sean could see was his own reflection in the glass. A few drops of water had just landed on the other side of the window pane. He patted down some stray hair that had sprouted up in a curl on the top of his head, thanks to the South Carolina humidity.

"Your dad liked this place," Maria said as she scooted her chair and settled in. "He usually ordered the Shoo Mercy Shrimp and Grits."

"He was more of a steak and potatoes guy when I knew him," said Sean.

Though the restaurant wasn't well lit, a modified boat lantern that dangled above the table gave Sean a clear view of Maria's face. No longer hindered by dusk's dying sunlight and the shadows of buildings at night, he realized that she was very attractive. Her face was thin with delicate features, high cheekbones, and naturally full lips. Her silky olive skin, from her face to her bare shoulders, revealed no blemishes. The stud on her nose wasn't a simple diamond, as he first believed, but rather a tiny butterfly with fragile wings.

He skimmed his menu but felt a sudden urge to ask Maria a question he'd been thinking about ever since he had met his father's other family. "Was he good to you? To you and your family?"

Taken off guard by the question, she lowered her menu and took a moment to glance out the window before meeting his gaze. "Yeah," she answered, nodding her head a little. "He was all right. He was a pretty independent guy, you know."

"No. I don't know," he replied with a sigh.

She apologized with her eyes. "I suppose you don't. I just mean that he was a private person. Though he and my mother were in a relationship, it sometimes felt like they were more like roommates than anything. Just two people using each other to split the rent and feeling a little less lonely at night. I never saw love in their eyes when they looked at each other. He had his world and she had hers."

He listened intently as she continued.

"But he *was* good to her, as in he treated her with respect. They didn't argue much. He'd get a little fed up with Dusty sometimes, but everyone does."

He beat back a smirk, thinking at least some small punishment had been doled out to his father for leaving his Colorado family. Actually, living with Dusty could have been considered a *large* punishment. The waitress dropped off some water at their table. Maria ordered an iced tea and Sean a Diet Coke.

"You know, I wasn't surprised when I found out he had a family," Maria said.

His face tightened. "No? Why not?"

"It was in the way he looked at me sometimes." Her eyes shifted to the ceiling as she recalled a memory. "It was the same way my own father looks at me from time to time—that sadness in his face for not always having been there when I was growing up, yearning to be able to go back in time and help shape the person that I'd become. It was as if I somehow reminded your father of his past, and the things he regretted from it—you know, his former life."

He said nothing, letting the words stir in his stomach along with his hunger. When the waitress returned with the drinks, he ordered a burger, which immediately drew a scoff from Maria.

"Oh, come on, Sean," she protested. "You can't come to the Wicked Scallop and order a burger! This place has the best seafood in town! As fresh as it gets. Don't tell me that you can get food like this in Colorado?" A grin rode her face.

"I've eaten at Red Lobster before," he replied dryly.

An abrupt cackle slipped from the waitress. It probably came out louder than she had intended, turning the heads of every other customer in the room. Each bracket of her braces gleamed through the center of her broad smile. She clearly thought Sean had made a joke, though he hadn't.

Uncomfortable with the attention drawn to his table, Sean skimmed the menu and read out the first item under ten dollars.

"Scallops. Seared scallops." It was their special—listed in boldface font.

He immediately questioned his choice, unable to remember if

he had ever tried scallops. He nearly recanted, but the waitress had already written down his order and was on to Maria.

"I'll just take a burger," Maria said casually, her eyes glued to her menu.

His face contorted in disbelief. "What? But you . . . "

Maria lifted her eyes to meet his. There was a mischievousness in her expression, and she let out an endearing giggle. "Just kidding! I'll take the coconut shrimp."

Though he fought it, the young woman managed to melt a smile out of him. It evolved into a chuckle. "Very funny."

While they waited for their dinner, raindrops tapped the window beside them. Maria told Sean of how his father had liked to go deep sea fishing from time to time. With pride, she explained how he had once caught a 400-pound blue marlin that resembled the one mounted on a nearby wall as part of the décor. She also told him that Jack sometimes went surfing—usually by himself—never caring if he was the oldest man out there, riding the waves.

"He loved the water," she said, gazing out through the glistening window. "He even worked on a crabbing boat years ago, up in Alaska. He had a lot of funny stories from those days that he liked to tell— most of them about the guys he worked with. Real characters."

Though enlightening, the conversation felt increasingly off-kilter and uncomfortable. For every anecdote Maria described that matched Sean's memories of his father, there were three that didn't fit. He had never known his father to be fond of the ocean. In fact, he remembered his father once joking that he joined the Army instead of the Navy "back in the day" because he didn't have sea legs. He did recall that his father liked to fish. There were a few times that he had taken Sean and his sister to a nearby river to drop some lines in the water. They rarely caught anything. Jack's brother, Zed, was really the one who took the hobby seriously, and eventually it was Uncle Zed who got Sean interested in the pastime.

Sean had to keep reminding himself that a lot of things can

change in thirty years. In a brief moment of self-reflection, he realized that he himself had gone through quite a transition in just two years' time—from a good-for-nothing drunk with a chip on his shoulder to a sober business owner with responsibilities. Thus, the father who Sean remembered from his youth may have ceased to exist the moment he left Winston.

When the food arrived, his eyes widened at the size of the scallops that commandeered his plate. Each was three or four inches in diameter. "These are scallops?" he asked. "Christ. They're the size of pork chops."

"That's what makes them *wicked*!" the waitress joked, reciting a line she'd probably regurgitated a few hundred times. Her permanently affixed smile finally dwindled into a judgmental grimace when Sean asked for ketchup.

He poked one of the oversized scallops with a fork. It didn't resemble the mere morsels he'd sometimes noticed decorating pasta dishes in restaurant posters back in Colorado casinos. The ones in front of him filled his entire plate over a bed of rice.

His reaction seemed to amuse Maria, her nose crinkling as she grinned. Her eyes widened when he tore into the scallops armed only with a fork, halving them with the side of it, before sliding each chunk through a pool of ketchup on its way to his mouth. He then shoveled in rice by the spoonful, loading up his neglected stomach in record-breaking time. He was finished with his meal before Maria had even picked up her second piece of shrimp.

"Yeah. That was good," he said.

After adjusting himself in his chair, he brought up the investigation into his father's death and filled in Maria on everything Chief Quammen had told him. Much of the information had already been relayed to her family, but to his surprise, she knew some things that he hadn't heard. She told him about a police detective who had come to her mother's trailer two days after Jack's death—a Detective Prevenas. The information struck Sean as odd because Quammen had told him that the county investigator in his father's case had a last name of Seedorf. Sean quickly whipped out his notepad and confirmed that he had remembered the name correctly.

Prevenas had told Maria and her mother that Jack had been suspected of an earlier home burglary in Myrtle Beach that had occurred a week before his death. The detective had apologized for his timing, but asked Claudia if he could search their trailer for the items that had been reported stolen. Claudia had agreed. Prevenas had found nothing.

"He must be assigned out of Myrtle, working a separate case," he suggested. "I guess Jack stole until his luck ran out. Did Prevenas say if anyone thought the earlier burglary was connected to my father's death?"

She answered no and noted that Prevenas had specifically stated that the police had no reason to believe that. "Was it hard seeing your father?" she blurted out, as if she had been weighing the question in her mind for some time. "At the coroner's office?"

He hesitated before answering. "A bit, I guess. Not as hard as I would have thought. It was like looking at a stranger."

"When I heard that he had a son who was coming out for his body, I couldn't stop thinking about what it would be like for you to see him that way—after so many years."

"That's something you thought about?"

She nodded. "No son should be reunited with his father that way." She leaned forward and placed her hand over his.

Sean read compassion in her eyes. In the warmth of her touch he felt sincerity. He didn't believe that he had earned either, but he also didn't feel inclined to remove his hand.

"Well, ho-ly shit!" a sharp male voice suddenly called out from the other end of the dining room. All heads turned in its direction.

By the bar stood a disheveled man in his late thirties, wearing faded jeans and a weathered leather vest over a dirty white T-shirt that stretched at his gut. A black bandana with a beer logo covered his head, and he tugged at the zipper in front of his crotch as if he had just stepped away from a bathroom urinal. He wobbled on uneasy footing, staring daggers at Sean and Maria with wide, blinking eyes. His wind-beaten face was flushed underneath his thick, blond mustache. He was clearly drunk. Behind the bar, Al looked nervous.

"It seems that destiny's a'pon me!" the man said with a creepy grin. He had the thick southern accent Sean recognized from the movies—the one he'd envisioned everyone in the region having until he'd touched down that morning. The man raised his arms out like wings and stumbled backward a few steps.

"Oh God," said Maria, removing her hand from Sean's and covering the side of her face.

"You know that guy?" he asked.

"Yes," she admitted with a sigh, shame in her eyes. She looked away from Sean and lowered her head toward her plate. "He's some guy who's been hassling me at work."

He squinted. "You work with him?"

"Not exactly."

The man staggered his way over to their table, still grinning. Al hustled out from behind the bar and cautiously walked up behind him. When the restaurant owner placed his hand on the man's shoulder and whispered something to him, the man shook free of his grip.

Maria was mortified, her face flustered and her nervous eyes peering up at Sean as if she were a timid child. "I'm sorry, Sean," she whispered.

"There y'are, Destiny. That *is* ya!" said the man, teetering to a stop at the edge of their table. He stood around six feet tall and probably weighed a good two hundred pounds. He glared at Maria with a strong stench of alcohol on his breath.

"Lis'n, pal," said Al in a shaky voice and similar accent. "We don't need no trouble'n here t'night. Why don't ya just head on home now?"

"I ain't your pal, Fat Albert," said the man, his teeth disappearing just long enough to utter the response. He kept his focus glued to Maria.

The man crossed his hairy, tattooed arms in front of his chest. His shoulders were crooked. All eyes in the restaurant were watching the scene play out. Even one of the cooks had poked his head out from behind the open kitchen door and was staring at them through a pair of thick spectacles.

"Ya told me you didn't have a boyfriend," the man said, taking a moment to lick his lips and divert his eyes to Sean. "Ya tryin' to make me jealous?"

Sean glared back.

"I *don't* have a boyfriend, Grady!" snarled Maria, removing her hand from her face. She took a breath and clenched her jaw before turning to the man. "He's a friend, and it's none of your business who I spend my time with. We're not at Sunshine's right now. I'm off work. So go away."

"Oh my!" said the man named Grady, taking a step back, his mouth dangling open. He nudged Sean's shoulder with the back of his wrist, and added, "Destiny's gotta sharp tongue on her tonight! I wish she was this feisty workin' the pole. I'd stick more'n singles down that pretty lit'l white thong a'hers." He followed his remark with a loud cackle and an animated slap of his thigh.

Maria buried her face in her hand.

It was now clear to Sean what Maria's night job was.

"You don't want to touch me," Sean told Grady. "What you want to do is turn around and leave."

Grady's eyebrows formed sharp arches and his lips pouted in sarcasm. "Oh? That right, big fella?"

"That's right."

"It's okay, Sean," Maria whispered.

Sean couldn't tell if it was spunk or stupidity that he read in Grady's glazed-over eyes, but the man didn't appear ready to back down. Grady put his hands on his hips, and when he spread open his vest a bit, Sean noticed a sheathed knife strapped to his belt. It looked like a five-inch blade.

Sean chuckled. "Did you buy that thing at a toy store, Cupcake?" He took a sip from his glass of water and set it back down.

The man's face tightened.

"Come on, Sean. Let's just go," pled Maria, her eyes begging him not to escalate the matter.

"I think your idea is *half* good, sweet tits," slurred Grady. "Ya should stay right here with me, and Sean should—"

Sean lunged from his chair and sent a wicked left jab right into Grady's throat like a battering ram. The move was so sudden and savage that every tense onlooker jumped from their chairs in unison. Sean sat back down as Grady doubled over, his desperate eyes bulging as if they were being squeezed out of his skull with a vice. His mouth was shaped in an O, but all that came out was a sick wheezing noise that made Al back away in shock. Grady stumbled backward unsteadily until he collapsed in a heap. He fell to his side with his hands wrapped around his throat, legs kicking and eyes filling with tears.

"What'n the hell ya do to him?" Al asked, his eyes nearly as wide as those of the man on the floor.

"I punched him in the throat," answered Sean matter-of-factly, unsure of what more of an explanation Al needed.

"Oh God," Maria gasped. "This isn't good. This isn't good." Her hands were plastered to her face.

"Oh, he'll be fine," Sean said, swatting down her worries. "He's a big boy. He just needs a moment."

Her eyes were dead serious. "We've got to go, okay? Right now."

"You're not finished with your dinner."

"Fuck my dinner!" she snapped, digging through her purse and laying a fistful of fives and singles on the table. She looked terrified.

He didn't understand her reaction. The way he saw it, he had done her a favor.

She quickly stood up, tossing her purse strap over her shoulder and making a beeline for the door. She darted past Grady, not giving him another look.

Confused, Sean climbed to his feet. Attention of the horrified diners was divided evenly between him and Grady, who was now drooling all over the floor.

Sean placed his hand on Al's shoulder. "Al, the scallops were great," he said with a smile and a pat on the shoulder. It had been a long time since Sean had leveled someone who was truly asking for it. It felt good.

"Thanks," he heard Al mechanically reply, shaking his head.

The screen door slammed behind Sean as he made his way outside after Maria. She was already down the stairs and halfway across the parking lot before he spotted her again. Raindrops peppered his head as he skipped every other stair step and jogged across the sand and shells until he caught up with her. She was near the front of her truck when she spun around to confront him.

"Jesus, Sean!" she growled, squinting from the rain. "Why did you hit him?"

"Because he was asking me to," he answered.

She dug through her purse, shaking her head and jostling its contents until she found her keys. "Sean, I know you meant well, but that asshole drops *a lot* of money at our place. My boss is going to be pissed when he hears about this."

"I can go back in there and make sure he doesn't open his mouth up about this to anyone," he offered.

"No!" she snapped, forcing herself to breath before continuing. "Listen . . . I think it's best if I just play it off like you're some guy I met tonight for the first time."

"I *am* some guy you met tonight for the first time."

She sighed. "You know what I mean . . . I'll just say that I don't know anything about you. My boss . . . He's already in a pissy mood because he's understaffed, and he doesn't like us being seen out and about with men. It ruins the image."

"The image?"

"You know, that we're accessible and into the guys who come in, ogle us, and give us money. I know it must sound stupid to you, but it makes sense from a business standpoint, and I can't afford to lose this job."

He opened his mouth, but she cut him off.

"No more questions, okay?" she said, her shoulders lowered. "You're just some guy who helped me change a flat or something."

He just stared. He couldn't think of a thing to say.

She raised her hand to the side of his damp, rough face. Her touch was gentle. "I'm sorry about your father, and I'm sorry about what happened tonight. But I'm not sorry we met. I'll pray for justice for your father, and that you'll someday be able to forgive him for what he did."

With that, she opened her truck door, slid inside, and closed the door. She cranked the engine hard, waved to Sean as she turned the wheel, and sped off—out of the parking lot and into the night.

Chapter 9

Maria weighed heavily on Sean's mind as he drove back to the motel. He would have never guessed her to be a stripper. He had been hired to watch over girls like her a couple of times at a casino up in Lakeland—a thriving gambling town about seven miles north of Winston. He hadn't liked taking those kinds of jobs but couldn't afford to turn them down in the post 9/11 economy. As unfortunate of a statement on society as it was, booze and table dancers were recession-proof commodities.

The profession was a heart-breaking one: young, usually not-so-bright women—often with drug problems rarely discouraged by their employers—grinding against creepy men's stiff crotches for fives and tens if the girls were lucky. Half of the money didn't even go to them; it ended up in the boss's pocket one way or another. Each girl was someone's daughter. Some were even mothers. Sean had felt dirty being a part of it, even if he was protecting them from ugly, pathetic drunks who couldn't stay in their seats, not unlike the one he'd just knocked to the floor at the Wicked Scallop.

Maria didn't fit the mold. She seemed smarter than that—more together. Then again, he barely knew her.

Sean rubbed the palm of his hand along his wet hair as the wiper blades swished their way back and forth across his windshield. The sky was dropping buckets of water and he found himself having to drive half the speed limit to make out the names on street signs before he sailed right past them. When he spotted a towering bright blue emblem with a large, red number "6" on it, he flipped on his blinker and pulled into the narrow parking lot of a two-story building.

A little over a dozen doors, light teal in color, lined each floor. As Sean pulled in, a man with silver hair and a sagging duffle bag left the room next to his. The man closed the door behind him and lifted the wide collar of his trench coat over the side of his face to protect himself from the beating rain. He looked like a vampire, scurrying down the sidewalk in front of the building before he disappeared in the darkness.

Sean parked and switched off the headlamps. He arched his back to dig into his front pocket for his room's large keychain. He pulled it out, and checked its number: 118.

His gaze shot forward through the windshield; 118 was the room that the man in the trench coat had just left. He gasped and leapt out of his car. He ran to the door through the rain, and reached for the knob. The frame had been splintered. The door swung open with the mere swat of his hand, and when he flipped on the overhead light, he saw that his father's trunk was sitting in the middle of the room with its lid hanging open.

"Son of a bitch!"

He shut the door as best he could and took off at a full sprint in the direction the man had gone, wishing he'd gotten a better look. He noticed that his own body was largely sheltered from the rain by the walkway above, so the only reason the man had covered his face was to conceal his identity from the car he'd seen approaching—Sean's.

A silver Mercedes-Benz E-320 sped out from the side of the motel, whizzing right past Sean and tossing water onto him before clipping a cement parking curb. Someone was making a hasty escape. The Mercedes peeled out onto the side road, in the opposite direction from which Sean had come. He tried to get a look at its license plate when the car crossed under a streetlamp, but there was just an empty frame.

Sean raced back to his rental car and squeezed inside. He cranked the engine, backed up with a loud screech, and then tore out of the parking lot in pursuit. He ignored the impassioned honks of a red Geo he cut off and pressed the gas pedal nearly to the floor as his windshield wipers stabbed at the rain.

The roar of the engine mirrored Sean's anger, his teeth clenched and nostrils flared. Something had been taken from him. He didn't know what it was, but he aimed to get it back and teach the burglar what happens to someone who steals from Sean Coleman.

He rounded a corner and searched for the Mercedes's taillights as best he could remember their shape. He switched to the shoulder of the road, flying past a slow-moving pickup truck and Volkswagen bug. He hydroplaned for a tense moment before regaining some traction and pulling out ahead of them. There were no vehicles ahead. The man couldn't have gotten so far ahead that he was now out of sight; the weather wouldn't have allowed for it.

Sean glanced down each side street that he passed, grumbling obscenities and tightening his grip on the steering wheel with each empty view. The Mercedes had vanished like a ghost.

He entered a residential area where the streets were narrower, tucked in between middleclass homes with yards that hosted large, flush trees that swayed in the downpour. When he spotted a dirt alley that divided two blocks, he slowed to get a good look down it.

About forty feet in, parked beside a chain link fence and just outside the beam of a nearby streetlamp, was a silver car. It was shaped like the Mercedes. Sean might have missed it had it not been for the flash of lightning. The car's headlights were off, but the dome light was on. He wondered if the man hadn't counted on being pursued and was now taking a closer look at whatever he'd taken from Sean's room.

He bit his lip and turned off his headlights, twisting the wheel and sliding into the alley behind the car, trying not to be noticed.

That hope quickly disappeared when frantic movement erupted from inside the car. The vehicle's brake lights switched on for a brief moment, and he knew the driver was shifting into gear. He flipped his beams on, making certain he was targeting the right automobile. Mercedes-Benz E-320. No license plate.

No plate, no brake.

Sean floored the gas and let out a roar, launching his car into the back of the Mercedes like a wrecking ball. He saw the driver's head snap backward a fraction of a second before Sean's view was replaced with a blasting wall of pain.

The airbag smashed against him, filling the cab with white textile. He slammed on his brakes, reeling from the bag's punch. A rank odor and powdery substance filled the air. He coughed and wiped film from his face, cursing himself for forgetting that he was driving a much newer car than the one he owned back in Winston. He swatted his forearms down across the large, deflating bag until he could see through the top half of his windshield.

The Mercedes was twisted at an angle along the edge of the alley. Its bumper was disfigured and appeared to have knocked over a row of steel trashcans.

Sean reached for his door handle but suddenly heard the rev of the Mercedes's engine. The car was backing up to straighten itself within the alley. Its taillights lit up Sean's face. Sean beat down what was left of the airbag, yanking it to his lap as the Mercedes launched forward. Its driver was clearly shaken up, crashing into more obstacles that littered the alley as he fought to get away.

Sean took off after him, steadying the wheel and breathing through the sides of his mouth. He heard something metallic dragging under the floorboard of his car, and he wondered if part of his bumper had been jarred loose. Whatever it was soon broke its hold and slid out from under the car with a series of clunks and clangs. For a brief moment, he remembered that he had purchased the least amount of insurance possible.

A fountain of water and mud shot through the air behind the Mercedes. Most of it splattered across Sean's windshield where his wipers were already battling the rain. Sean's head wove and tilted as he fought for a clear view.

Sparks flew out from under the Mercedes when it left the alley and bounced across a curb gutter. Now back on pavement, the driver doubled his speed. Sean did the same. Warm blood dribbled into his mouth, and he wiped his face with the back of his hand. The airbag had given him a bloody nose.

The Mercedes left the side street and tore onto a wider perpendicular road. It might have been a highway, but Sean couldn't make out the words on the road sign that flew by. The traffic on this road was thin, letting the Mercedes slide past a handful of slow-moving cars on the shoulder. Sean followed, nearly scraping a guardrail as they crossed a bridge.

The reality of how dangerously fast both of them were driving wasn't lost on him. The smart play would have been to let the thief go, report the crime to the police, and give them a description of the car. But Sean knew that the situation he was dealing with wasn't just some random burglary. People who drove Mercedes-Benzes didn't break into cheap motel rooms looking for something to hawk. The man had come for a specific reason: his father's trunk. Whatever was inside, it meant something to that person, and the man somehow knew it was in Sean's motel room. There was a chance, in Sean's mind, that the individual he was chasing was somehow tied to his father's death. Letting him get away wasn't an option.

After passing some more vehicles on the shoulder, he noticed steam beginning to pour out from under the hood of his car. The Escort's alignment felt off, and there were rattles that hadn't been there before, but ahead he saw nothing but the Mercedes and open road. He wasn't going to stop.

A web of lightning danced in the distance. The Mercedes picked up speed, as Sean suspected it would. The two crossed onto a long, narrow bridge, no trees on either side—a body of water larger than a river was likely below. With no cars coming in the opposite direction, Sean swerved into the oncoming lane. The gushing rain and flapping wiper blades fueled his aggression. He stood on the gas, gritted his teeth, and pulled alongside the Mercedes. With nowhere to go, he knew he had the man.

Pulling even with the Mercedes, he looked to the right and saw the driver's side window sliding down. Another flash of lightning lit up the night, and Sean saw a hand clutching what looked to be a pistol pointed directly at him. He gasped, slamming on the brakes, and immediately felt the rear of his car spinout at a sharp angle.

Losing control as the Mercedes bulleted forward, Sean twisted his steering wheel in the same direction he believed he was being pulled in, hoping to equalize his momentum. He collided with the guardrail on his left, a piercing scream of steel pounding his skull. Still sliding forward as sparks flew, he jerked the wheel to his right, crossing back into the right lane and almost taking a breath before he found himself skidding off the road. The bridge had come to an end, and a large tree with a thick trunk was approaching quickly. Even with the brake pedal pressed to the floor, he knew he wouldn't stop in time.

He yanked the wheel hard to the right and the back of his car swung around to catch up with the front just in time to miss a dead-on collision. The car slid across large mounds of earth and rock before striking a wide pool of water, bringing him to an abrupt halt.

He had sailed grill-first into the shallow depths of a marsh and was now surrounded by long, thick grass that pushed up against his windows like the large brushes at a carwash. The engine gurgled and fizzed as water engulfed the front of his car, ending in a sputtering stall.

Sean snarled and beat the steering wheel with his fists, then ripped at the handle beside him and kicked the door open. It fell off at the hinges. "Fuck!"

When he slid out of the car, the water came up to his crotch. The stink of steam and antifreeze taunted him as he trounced his way through grass and mud along the marsh floor that pulled at his boots like molasses. The rain seemed to have grown even stronger as he crawled up the bank toward the road.

A couple of cars facing the other way had pulled off to the side of the highway, their high-beams illuminating the night. Concerned motorists jogged over to him. Sean angrily waved and shouted them off, searching for the Mercedes. He spotted it about a hundred yards down the road, stopped and seemingly waiting. The second Sean took a step toward it, however, he heard peeling rubber and could only watch as the car took off down the road.

Through heavy breath, burning eyes, and a racing pulse, he dropped to his knees in defeat, letting the rain pummel his body.

The Mercedes disappeared into the squall.

Chapter 10

"Yo' don't rush off into some harebrained high-speed chase wif someone who stole fum yo', Mr. Coleman," said the chubby police officer. He was in his sixties and had a long Southern drawl that put even Grady's back at the Wicked Scallop to shame. "Yo' pick up thet dang phone an' yo' call th' po-lice."

Sean eyeballed the back of the officer's rippled bald head through a steel grill from his seat at the back of the moving police cruiser. He couldn't make out much of what the man had just said, other than the term "high-speed chase," which was pretty clear.

"Who said I was speeding?" Sean asked, wincing at the strong stench of mildew in his wet clothes.

"Pfftt!" the officer blurted out, shaking his head. "Oh po-lease. Yo' turned thet rental of yours into a dang submarine, yo' were drivin' so fast. It's a-gonna take ha'f an hour fo' thet tow-truck t'git thet thin' back on dry lan'. An' yer tellin' me yo' chased thet burglar wifout speedin'?"

"That's right, McDaggin," replied Sean, his hand clenching his forehead to nurse a headache he'd had since the accident. "I wasn't speeding." He didn't want to admit to breaking the law, unaware of how much hot water it would get him into with the local authorities.

"Madigan," the officer said with some aggravation. "Mah name's Madigan. Officer Patrick Madigan. An' ah already told yo' thet twice!"

Though it was dark inside the cab, Sean could feel the officer's bloodhound eyes glaring at him through his rearview mirror.

"Either way, it sounds like the name of a damn leprechaun," Sean muttered.

"Whut?"

"Never mind."

The rain had stopped. The only remnants of the storm were beads of water that sporadically glided down the sides of the car windows and the sound of tires treading along wet roads. Sean continued to rub his head.

Madigan cleared his throat, which Sean had learned over the past twenty minutes meant he was about to change the subject. "Boy, yo' sh'd of let th' pare'emedics take a better look atcha. Yo' might haf given yo'seff a corncusshun."

"A what?"

"A corncusshun. Yo' know. A shock t'th' brain."

"I'm fine. I didn't hit my head, and I ain't your *boy*, McDaggin."

The officer shook his head, his body tensing up. "Don't yo' be givin' me enny lip back thar. Thar ain't a law tellin' me ah have t'give yo' a ride back t'yer motel room, dawgone it."

"What?"

"A ride! Back t'yer motel room! Ah don't have t'give yo' one."

"Yes you do, because your boss Quammen told you to. I heard him on the radio. So don't pretend you're doing me some favor. Doing me a favor would be finding out who the guy with the Mercedes is. And how about figuring out who killed my father, while you're at it? You guys do get paid for what you do, don't you?"

Madigan clenched his steering wheel and repositioned his large body in his seat, fighting the urge to respond. Sean could tell he was fuming. After a minute, the officer finally spoke. "We does our job, Mr. Coleman. In th' meantime, yo' sh'd be reckonin' about how you'll be gittin' aroun' fo' th' ress of yourn stay."

"What? What are you talking about?"

Madigan chuckled. "Yo' destroyed a rental, fella. They don't take too kindly t'thet so't a thin' aroun' hyar. They isn't a-gonna give yo' t'other one t'destroy. They'll flag yo'."

When the two pulled into the motel parking lot, another police cruiser was already on the scene. Quammen stepped out of the passenger's side door, clad in a black sweatshirt and gray sweatpants—off-duty threads, though the part at the center of his hair was still sharp. Sean watched him walk over to Madigan's car, waiting for it to stop before yanking open his door.

"What in God's name were you thinking?" Quammen angrily asked Sean.

He climbed outside. "What are you talking about?" he scoffed, pointing to his room's open door. "Some guy broke into my motel room and stole something."

"What did he steal?" Quammen fired back. "Something worth turning my town into a God-damn demolition derby?"

"Oh please. We had a little fender bender."

"Your car's underwater, Sean!" Quammen snarled, throwing his arms up in the air.

From inside the police cruiser, beyond his rolled-down window, Sean noticed Madigan smirk.

"It wasn't my car," said Sean.

"What?" Quammen barked, his chest heaving in and out.

"It was a rental. Lucky Charms McDaggin wrote it down there in his little notepad."

Quammen glared right through Sean. His left eye twitched and a vein revealed itself at the center of his forehead. Madigan shook his head and turned away.

The police chief spun from Sean and took a few steps forward, muttering something and apparently trying to calm himself. It was the kind of reaction Sean was used to receiving from his brother-in-law back in Winston. Apparently, it came with the job. Sean watched Quammen's hefty shoulders raise and lower with each deliberate breath. The lawman finally turned his head to the side and asked in a calmer tone what was stolen.

"I don't know," Sean said. "He had something under his arm in a bag. Something that was in my father's trunk."

"In a bag. So you don't really know that he took *anything* from your room? You just know that he had a bag on him when he came outside?" The statement came out like an accusation rather than a question.

Sean groaned. "The chest on the floor in there is wide open. He broke into it. Of course that's where he got whatever he was carrying."

Quammen turned to face Sean again. "And you didn't get a good look at him?"

"No," Sean said with irritation. "Just silver hair and his car. I gave a description to McDaggin. It's a Mercedes-Benz."

"Madigan."

"What?"

"His name is Madigan. Not McDaggin. And I think you know that."

"Whatever. How hard could a Benz be to track down?"

"Without a license plate? Plenty hard. We don't even know what state it's out of, and we get *a lot* of tourists passing through here."

"Start local."

"I will, and don't tell me how to do my job," said Quammen, showing his teeth. He calmed himself again and added, "Listen. I talked to the motel manager. She'll give you a new room since your door's broke. Take your time tonight, before you move your stuff over. Figure out if he stole anything beyond what you're speculating he took from the trunk. If you know something is missing, call my office in the morning. In the meantime, we'll look into the Mercedes."

"You're not going to dust for prints?"

"Fingerprints?"

"No, toe prints," Sean shot back with a sneer.

Quammen sighed, lowered his head, and rubbed the palm of his hand across his forehead. "Sean, this isn't *CSI*. We don't dust for prints when a motel room gets broken into. Do you have any idea how many people come in and out of a place like this every week? And again, we don't even know if we're dealing with a burglary."

Sean didn't appreciate the condescension. "You're damned right this isn't *CSI*. On *CSI*, they actually solve crimes."

Quammen glared at him, then stepped in close to him. Sean didn't back down, inflating his chest.

The police chief repeated slowly and carefully, "If you figure out that something's missing, call my office in the morning." With that, he walked back to his car and climbed inside. He held Sean's gaze until an officer Sean hadn't seen before exited the motel room and joined him in the cab.

The two pulled out of the parking lot with Madigan following closely behind in his cruiser. Just as Madigan was about to pull onto the street, the officer's left arm floated out of his open window. It rose at a ninety-degree angle, extending a middle finger aimed at Sean.

Sean returned the gesture and added a crotch grab.

Sean hadn't told anyone about the pistol that had been pointed at him by the driver of the Mercedes—primarily because he wasn't convinced what he had seen was actually a gun. It really could have been any object at that speed. Additionally, Sean still resented—despite it being policy—the fact that information regarding his father's death was being kept from him by the police. If they weren't going to be upfront with him, he felt no need to return the favor.

He stepped into his room and sat at the edge of his bed. He sank down deep, the box spring creaking from his weight. Only then did he remember that his clothes from the waist down were still wet. He nearly stood back up and changed, but decided it wasn't worth the effort. He was tired, and he was going to move rooms anyway.

As if he'd sensed it peeking at him out of the corner of his eye, his attention turned to the wooden chest. It still lay open on the thin, well-worn motel carpet. He studied its craftsmanship for a moment, noticing details he hadn't earlier. Its planked wood, beneath a film of filth and grime from long periods of storage, looked to be maple. Scratched brass accents were mounted to the corners, and the thick leather straps at its sides were frayed. Other imperfections in the chest's composition suggested it was handmade, not store bought. He wondered if it was the work of his father.

He took a deep breath and leaned off the bed to land on his knees. His ankle emitted a harmless pop as he dragged himself over to the chest. Inside, amongst the musty odor of age, was a myriad of items: common tools, miscellaneous clothes, some books, wooden cigar boxes, and a jumbled heap of *Playboy* magazines. Nothing seemed of particular importance. He leaned forward and shoved aside clumps of attire. He removed heavier items like hammers and wrenches until he found an overturned toolbox that he pulled out as well. At the bottom of the chest, he discovered a pair of thirty-pound dumbbells along with some round weight plates that accounted for another sixty pounds. His father must have gone through a health kick at some point.

He opened the cigar boxes one at a time, hoping for photographs, letters, or paperwork of any kind. All he found were curious odds and ends like shot glasses, key chains, and even a few rabbit's feet. His father had always had a fondness for collectibles. Unfortunately, the items provided no useful information beyond the names of some bars and restaurants from different cities. He supposed that at some point he could pin up a map of the country and plot out the destinations his father might have enjoyed a sandwich and drinks at, but what would be the point? He had expected to find some documentation—something he could piece together into a timeline. There was none. Not even handwritten notes.

He was perplexed by this. Claudia had said she'd found enough information inside the chest to tie Jack Slate back to a family that didn't bear his name, but none of it was there. He pulled himself to his feet, as he dug into the back pocket of his damp pants. His eyes grew when he felt cardstock. He tugged it out.

The ink on the business card Dusty had given him had bled from being immersed in water, but the handwriting was still legible. With Dusty living at home, Sean assumed the number led to Claudia's trailer. His theory proved correct when she answered the phone when he dialed.

She sounded groggy, having possibly been awoken by the ring. By the third introduction, she understood who she was talking to. Sean pressed her on the paperwork, and she insisted she had returned it to the chest. She described a thick, legal-sized envelope with the pencil sketch of a mountain range across it. She also spoke of a small family photo album with a red marble pattern on its jacket. Neither were there, but he didn't doubt her claim. He remembered the album from his childhood. It had sat on the base of an end table at his parents' house for years before disappearing around the time his father had left. Like the commemorative plates back at Claudia's trailer, Sean had believed it had been thrown out.

Everything else Claudia described seemed to still be there, which meant that the man who'd broken into Sean's motel room had only left with information, not valuables.

The question was *why?*

Chapter 11

I t didn't take long that morning for Sean to figure out that Officer Madigan had been right about the local car rental agencies blacklisting his name. Every rep he spoke to over the phone cited the previous night's police report, which implicated Sean as being negligent for the destruction of the Escort. Word of the incident had traveled quickly, which made sense considering that the service counters of every car rental outfit in Myrtle Beach operated along the same airport wall. The next closest agencies were a couple of hours away, and Sean guessed he wouldn't have any better luck with them.

He plopped down on the unmade bed in his new motel room. It was a carbon copy of his old room, other than a different flower print hanging above the bed. Before long, he found himself glaring out the window. He felt defeated and humiliated, as if he were a child being grounded by a parent. Gazing out beyond the parking lot, he watched a pair of wide-open Jeeps idling side by side at the red light of an intersection. Both automobiles were overflowing with tan, smiling teenagers wearing sunglasses. Once the light turned green, one of the Jeeps peeled out and sped in front of the other. The kids in the trailing vehicle shared a good laugh. They were living the kind of life Sean could have had in his youth had his father's absence not forced him to grow up too fast.

"Assholes," he muttered, resentful that the teenagers had the means to get around town.

He thought for a moment about trying a cab, but he knew it

would cost a fortune with the multiple stops he wanted to make. He was already dreading the bill for the damage to the rental car. It would add up to thousands of dollars, even if the insurance covered a portion of it. Sean had only a few hundred to his name, sitting in a local bank back in Winston.

He chased his financial predicament to the back of his mind and thought about walking over to the front desk and seeing if they could give him a public bus schedule. That's when Maria's name popped into his head.

It was a Saturday, so she may not have been working her day job. And though she'd made it clear that her nighttime boss didn't want her seen around town with men, Sean was convinced that she had cared enough about his father that she would be willing to help him if he asked.

He couldn't find a Maria Ortíz in the phone directory, so he pulled Claudia's number back out and began punching it into his phone.

———————

A colorful menagerie of latex creatures spanned the entire length of the car's dashboard. Some of the animals were shoved into tight corners where the windshield met vinyl. Others were secured with wads of clear tape. A couple, which looked like unicorns wrapped together in a sexual position, dangled from the rearview mirror like an ornament. Though repulsed by the display, Sean had a hard time peeling his eyes off it.

He was sure the *Looney Zoo-looney*, as the collection was crudely labeled with a piece of masking tape and a black marker, hadn't been inside the Datsun the night before. They must have been the loose animals he'd seen inside his father's old trailer. Why they had been migrated to the vehicle was a question Sean didn't want to ask.

When a deep exhale of breath let out beside him, he spun to look at the driver and said, "Don't do that shit while we're driving, okay?"

Dusty's eyes bulged exaggeratedly at Sean's words, as if he were imitating an old-time comedian like Jackie Gleason. His hair even now looked like Gleason's, from the actor's *Honeymooners* days, slicked down with a sharp part on the side.

Hugging the steering wheel with his bare thighs below denim shorts, Dusty released the half-filled balloon from his hands. It sailed through the cab of the car, slapping off the passenger window and a dangling monkey before landing on Sean's lap. Sean clenched a fist and bit his lip.

Dusty laughed uproariously at the stunt, bouncing around in his chair and looking like a jack-in-the-box in his tight pink polo shirt. When he reached for Sean's lap to retrieve the balloon, Sean shoved his arm away.

"Don't touch me," he warned, scolding Dusty further with his eyes. "Just drive." He brushed the balloon off his lap onto the floor.

Dusty's face morphed into a mime-style pout, and Sean had to fight back the urge to punch it. Never in his life had he encountered anyone like Dusty. Sean couldn't tell if there was something mentally wrong with him, or if the kid was truly performing some continual, eccentric monologue, as his mother had suggested. If it was the latter, that meant that Dusty was purposely refusing to step out of character and act like a normal person, and it was more than enough to piss Sean off.

"Just get us there without all the bullshit, all right?" Sean said forcefully, pointing through the dirty windshield.

Dusty held his hand to his forehead and saluted.

Sean shook his head in irritation.

He had been hoping to avoid Dusty altogether, and was relieved an hour earlier when it was Claudia who'd picked up the receiver after he punched in the number on the "balloon enthusiast's" business card. She gave him Maria's cell number, but when Sean dialed it, it had repeatedly gone to voicemail. When Sean begrudgingly called Claudia back and explained his predicament, she offered up Dusty's transportation services as payment for the "one free event" Sean had earned for having a balloon popped in his ear the day before. The agreement was absurd, and Sean nearly rejected the proposal, but he realized he was left with no better options if he was going to dig into the mystery surrounding his father.

Still, he nearly reconsidered his decision once Dusty began whistling the opening theme from *2001: A Space Odyssey*.

How did my father live with this idiot? he thought before flipping on the car radio and drowning out the anthem with an oldies station. Dusty eventually halted his performance, instead swaying to the melody of an Elvis Presley ballad coming from the radio.

The cool air that poured out of the dashboard vents slowly began to calm Sean's nerves, and before long, even the rustle of balloon animals wasn't quite as irritating. At least he was finally getting somewhere, instead of being stuck back at the motel.

When the swirling rhythm of a Ray Charles tune called "You Don't Know Me" climbed up from the speakers, Sean thought of an old girlfriend. He smiled at the memory of her telling him how she'd fallen in love with that very song after watching Bill Murray and Andie MacDowell dance to it on a gazebo in the movie *Groundhog Day*. She once even tried to get Sean to emulate the scene with her, but he, being Sean, would have none of it. He wished now that he had at least put forth the effort.

Sean gazed out of his window at the small souvenir and hammock shops that passed by. A lot of people out and about—mostly old folks and families dressed in bright colors, enjoying the weather and laidback atmosphere. When he noticed a seabird glide by with a small fish in its clenches, he knew they were close to the ocean.

Dusty had become so quiet that Sean glanced over to make sure he was paying attention to the street signs. That's when he noticed that Dusty's chins had tightened and his eyes were beginning to well up. Sean hadn't a clue what had brought on the display of sudden despair. *The song? My shortness with him? Maybe it's just another performance*. Whatever the catalyst, Sean didn't feel his curiosity was worth the price of initiating an awkward conversation. When the song ended, Dusty turned off the radio and used the back of his arm to brush away a tear.

Tense silence accompanied the two as the car turned onto Beach Bridge Road. It was a narrow, well-kept street. On the right, there was nothing but forest and a lone dirt path from the street that disappeared into it. On the left, tall concrete walls, staggered trees, and signs that read "Private Beach" warned commoners to stay away from the row of extravagant homes beyond them. Each high-arching residence they passed presented a long, stately driveway of near-white gravel and steel security gates blocking access to them. Shiny, expensive cars and stone fountains occupied the drives.

After a dozen homes or so, Sean spotted 625, the number Claudia had written down for him the day before, on one of the gates.

"Pull over here," ordered Sean.

Dusty nodded somberly, then sniffed.

When the car slowed to rest on the thin shoulder, Sean opened his door and told Dusty to wait for him. Dusty nodded and turned off the ignition. There was still a hint of sadness in his face, but he had for the most part pulled himself together.

When Sean stepped out of the car, he heard Dusty mutter, "Hold on." Dusty reached to his side and popped open the glove compartment.

Sean stewed impatiently as Dusty waded through papers and candy wrappers. He finally pulled out a hand-sized, paper hole-puncher. He raised it in the air and presented the palm of his other hand to Sean. He then glared at Sean, suggesting that Sean should understand whatever he was inferring.

"What?" Sean asked, his gaze blank.

"The card," Dusty replied in a surprisingly adult tone.

"What card?"

"The card I gave you. My business card."

Sean's mouth hung open. "Are you kidding me?"

"Listen, I'm trying to run a professional business here," stated Dusty, who had momentarily dropped the persona and was suddenly presenting himself as a seasoned capitalist.

Sean scoffed, shook his head, and jammed his hand into his pocket. He pulled out the business card and shoved it into Dusty's hand. Dusty punched a hole directly through the card's center, right across his hand-written note from the day before. He then handed it back to Sean.

"This is stupid," Sean muttered. He ripped the card into confetti and tossed it back at Dusty. Dusty winced as the pieces brushed his face.

"You're going to wait right here, right?" said Sean.

Dusty nodded. "Yes, at the hourly rate, which I'm fine breaking down into minutes because I need to be out of here in half an hour."

Sean's eyes widened. His glower burned a hole right through the performer.

"Hey, I'm not a chauffeur," explained Dusty. "I've got an afternoon gig I need to get ready for. You're cutting into my time, and time is money."

Sean snarled and lunged inside the car, quickly kneeling on the passenger seat and grabbing Dusty by the shirt collar.

"Oh God!" Dusty wailed in panic, trying to cover his face with his arms.

"Listen up, you tubby little shit," Sean hissed through clenched teeth. "I'm not paying you a dime. You gave me a ride out here. You're giving me one back. Got it?"

"Okay, okay! Geez!"

Sean's grip had pulled up the bottom of Dusty's shirt, exposing hairy, overlapping flab that jiggled with each movement.

"You'd better still be here when I come back, or I'll—" A stray gust of wind whipped through the open door and smacked one of the balloon unicorns from the rearview mirror into his face. "Dammit!"

He released Dusty and yanked the unicorns from the mirror. With the face of a madman, he stretched them apart until a double-pop ended their romance.

"No!" Dusty bellowed like a parent who'd just watched their child fall off a cliff.

"Enough!" Sean shouted. He shook his head and backed out of the car. "It's a sick thing, Dusty! You and these balloons! It's not normal!"

"I said I was going to stay here!" Dusty shouted back. "You didn't have to—"

Sean yanked the keys out of the ignition and shoved them into the pocket of his pants, silencing Dusty's protest. Sean then stepped out and slammed the car door shut. He walked in front of the car, checked for traffic, and crossed the road.

Controlling his breathing, he stepped past clusters of leafy vines that crawled up the face of the residence's sandstone-colored brick wall. When he reached the front gate, he gazed through it at a large, brick home with arched eaves above every door and window. The home rested between tall trees with thick trunks and full branches that provided ample shade from the sun. A pair of concrete pathways hugged its north and south walls. Parked in the driveway, beside a lush flowerbed, was a red Maserati convertible.

Sean spotted a callbox mounted to the gate and pressed a button at its center. After fifteen seconds or so, an upbeat female voice streamed through its speaker.

"Hello! How can I help you?"

"Hey, listen, uh . . ." Sean tried again. "My name is Sean. My father worked for you. He cleaned your pool. I just wanted to ask you—"

"Jack? You're Jack's son. Oh, I'm *so* sorry. Wait just a second. I'll be right down."

A brief buzzing sound emitted from the side of the gate. It then began opening inward on an automated track.

Sean's eyebrows arched upward. "Well, that was easy."

Before entering the grounds, he stole a glance back at Dusty. The kid was climbing out of his car. He walked back to the trunk, his hand tugging down on his shorts to relieve some tightness. Sean wasn't sure what the kid was doing, but he was confident the car wasn't going anywhere.

Sean made his way across the driveway, his gaze shifting across the property as he did. To his left, a white wooden swing swayed in the breeze, dangling in the shade from ropes under a large tree limb. To his right, a statue of a woman without arms oversaw a small fountain that might have served as a koi pond. A short, well-trimmed lawn, along with a couple of pine trees, occupied the space between the driveway and the building.

It was an impressive spread by any standard and the crashing of waves and cries of seagulls confirmed that it sat just off the beach—the beach where Sean's father had stolen the surfboard the night he was killed.

The broad door at the front of the house suddenly flew open, and a short, well-groomed woman with a colorful blouse, turquoise necklace, and khaki pants emerged. She was probably in her early sixties, and wore sympathetic eyes and a hesitant grin. She shuffled her way across a short walkway toward Sean.

"Jack did such good work for us," she blurted out, as if she felt that complimenting a father's work ethic was the kind of gesture his son would appreciate while mourning his death. She slowed down her pace as she neared him, seemingly weighing whether to extend a hug or a handshake. She elected for the handshake once her eyes finished scrutinizing him. "I'm Linda. Linda Kent." Her perfume was strong and musky, nearly drawing a wince from Sean as he gripped her frail fingers. "I was so sorry to hear what happened to him," she said.

"Thanks. He was killed not far from here, you know," said Sean. He released her hand and slid his eyes over to what little he could see of the inside of the house through the open front door.

"I know," she said with lowered shoulders and some empathy in her voice. "I watched the police cars and ambulance from our back patio that morning. All of the flashing lights and activity, over by the bridge. I could tell they were pulling a body up from the water. I didn't find out until a couple of days later, on the news, that it was Jack. It's all so tragic."

He nodded. "Did you see or hear anything that previous night, out by the beach? Gunshots or anything?"

"No," she replied with an odd chuckle. "My husband and I turn in pretty early. We both have sleep apnea and are plugged into CPAP machines by nine each night. A car could crash into the side of our house and we probably wouldn't notice it."

"When was the last time you saw Jack? How often did he clean the pool?"

Her eyes blinked and then narrowed at the continued inquiry, but she answered, "Oh, he'd stop in once a week, on Wednesdays. That's when I saw him last—the Wednesday before . . . you know." She grimaced. "He spent no longer than an hour on the pool. Usually closer to thirty minutes. He would just come, do his thing, and leave."

"He'd have no reason to be here on a Sunday night then?" he asked.

"No, none that I can think of," she answered. Her eyes drifted off to her side in contemplation for a moment before returning to his. She bit down on her lip.

"What?"

"Well, he *did* keep some of his pool equipment and chemicals here, in our shed out back, just so he wouldn't have to drag them up from his van every time. I can't imagine him needing to stop by to get them, though, especially at night. He had the key code to get through the gate, so I suppose it's possible."

He nodded and crossed his arms in front of his chest. "Did the police talk to you at all?"

"They did that evening, the day they discovered the body. They asked if there were signs of a break-in at our home. An officer even searched the grounds a bit. He didn't find anything of interest, and nothing was stolen from us. I didn't know at the time, of course, that it was Jack's death they were investigating."

"The police didn't know he cleaned your pool then?"

Linda pursed her lips. "No, I suppose not."

"And you didn't call and tell them that later?"

She inclined her head and shrugged her shoulders. "I saw no reason to. Should I have?"

"No, I suppose not," he said, emulating her aloofness.

She nodded. Her eyes peered up at him as if she was expecting another question. He wasn't quite ready to ask one, instead letting his gaze float along the perimeter of the property.

"Well, Sean," she began. "I'll go ahead and write the check out to you if that's okay. And if you want to circle around the house to the shed and grab his things, that would be great."

"What check?" Sean asked.

"For your father's work. We owed him from last week. I assumed that's why you were here."

"Yeah." He nodded, seizing the opportunity to further peruse the grounds. "Don't make it out to me, though. Make it out to Claudia Bouche." He sought no restitution from his father, even in death.

She smiled, confirmed the spelling of the name, and hustled inside after directing him to the concrete pathway on the side of the house. "I'll meet you out back!" her voice echoed through the open door.

Sean walked along the pathway, ducking under some low-hanging branches and stepping through small puddles left by a morning sprinkler. He passed by a couple of large windows framed with ivy. Between colorful drapes, he spotted the lush furniture inside. Nothing about Linda's demeanor struck him as deceptive, and he had no reason to believe she wasn't telling him the truth. Regardless, the close proximity of her home to where his father had been found kept his eye keen.

He jogged up a short set of stairs and soon found himself standing on a concrete patio overlooking a private tennis court that took up most of the backyard. Beyond it, over the top of a brick wall that largely concealed the beach, was the ocean. White crests from incoming waves toppled over one another, as the laughter of unseen children in the distance greeted their arrival. Further out, a sailboat glided along with grace, away from a low-lying bridge that connected the mainland to the island. He knew it had to be Pritchard Bridge, where his father's body had been found.

He gazed at the bridge and its concrete pillars for a moment, before turning his attention back to the patio. At its opposite end, flanked by a handful of collapsed deck chairs, a covered hot tub, and some inflated water toys, was the pool. Shaped like a kidney bean, it struck Sean as being somewhat small for the size of the property. Still, simply *owning* a pool was impressive in his book.

Linda's spread stood a bit higher than the neighboring residences, giving him a decent view of their yards. The one to the north was exploding with overgrowth; other than roofing, a vacant flagpole, and the tops of trees and hedges, there wasn't much to see. The view to the south was a different story.

It was a broad, stately-looking home with slate walls, white trim, and tall lattice windows that overlooked the ocean horizon. A row of four large, white pillars that resembled Greek columns rode along the far-stretching wooden porch at the home's back entrance. About six feet below the porch was a cement patio with a pool and hot tub that were both larger than Linda's.

When a bright shimmer of light suddenly flickered across Sean's eyes, he turned his head to the far end of the neighbor's patio. There, beside the pool was a young woman in a skimpy white bikini, reclining in a chair and sipping on a beverage from a tall, thin glass. Sun caught the glass a second time. Its flicker forced Sean to narrow his eyes. Once he readjusted, he noticed how attractive the young woman was. She had a very fit body, with bronze, moist skin that shone under the sun with the same glare as her dark sunglasses. An exotic mane of wavy blonde hair, wet likely from a recent swim, spiraled down to her shoulders. She was oblivious to Sean's presence, which let him stare at her all the longer.

"She's beautiful, isn't she?" a young voice spoke out from behind Sean, prompting him to spin around in surprise.

Standing behind him, wearing a teal bathing suit, flip-flops, and a bright smile, was a little girl. She was probably no older than nine, with short, dark hair, and freckles sprinkled across her cheeks.

He glanced up at the house, searching for an adult, but found only an open sliding door from where the girl had likely come.

"I'm Nicola," said the girl. "What's your name?"

"You know, you shouldn't be talking to strangers," he said with a hint of a scowl. He switched his attention to the neighbor's sprawling, masterfully-landscaped courtyard that led out to the beach. The foliage that surrounded statues, small gardens, and a thin pathway was dense, but very well kept.

"You're not a stranger. You're my grandma's friend. I saw you talking to her out front, from upstairs."

"Well, we're not actually . . ." he began before deciding that it was a waste of time to explain the relationship to a child. "My name is Sean."

"Hi, Sean. What are you doing back here? Are you our new pool guy?"

"No," he said, the girl's question drawing his focus back to his purpose for being there. He asked Nicola about her grandmother's shed. She pointed down a short hill to a small shelter tucked away behind some thick foliage.

"She's an amazing swimmer," said the girl just as he began making his way down the hill.

He paused for a moment. "Who?"

She pointed at the woman by the pool next door and said, "The Goddess! That's what Grandpa calls her. He doesn't know her real name. Every morning, she walks down to the beach and swims across the ocean—right through the waves—to a big boat. Then she eats breakfast out on its deck! It's like in a movie. Grandpa watches her. Sometimes with binoculars."

"I bet," he muttered. "I need to grab some stuff from the shed. Tell your grandma I'll be back up in a minute, okay?"

"Okay!" she shouted louder than she needed to.

Sean trounced his way down the steps carved out of rock, and then across a gravel pathway to the shed. It was a small, wooden building that couldn't have had more than eight feet of depth to it. Pinned beneath the wide-stretching branches of two out-of-control live oaks, it stood just inches from a tall stone wall that marked the edge of the property where "the Goddess" was enjoying the sun.

Sean twisted the rusted, metal latch at the shed's face, and when he swung open the door, its dry hinges wailed. There wasn't much inside the dark and musty shanty: a work bench, some yard tools, and the pool equipment he was told belonged to his father. He sifted through the odds and ends, which included a retractable net, a coiled hose, some oversized buckets, a long-handled bristled brush, and a half-empty gallon container labeled Algaecide. He wasn't sure what he was expecting to find, but whatever it was, it wasn't there. He stacked the buckets and consolidated as much as he could inside the top one. He then dragged everything outside. He had no interest in the items, but it would have felt wrong returning Linda's kindness with the burden of leaving her to deal with his father's belongings.

When he glanced back at the house, he saw Linda standing next to her granddaughter. The two were talking. Both wore smiles. It struck him at that moment that Jack had never known about his own granddaughter who lived halfway across the country. Whether or not he would have cared was a question Sean found himself pondering, though the answer made no difference in his mind.

Linda had the check in her hand. She waved it in the air when she saw him looking up at her. He smirked, shook his head, and tossed the long handles of the pool net and broom over his shoulder. He was reaching for the buckets when something little Nicola had said began to take shape in his mind. The thought stuck with him all the way back up the steps.

"How early does the Goddess go swimming?" Sean asked Nicola, just as Linda was about to say something.

"*Really* early," the girl answered. "Just after the sun comes up."

"The who now?" asked Linda, confused.

"The hottie next door," Sean answered bluntly. "The one your husband watches. Would my dad have known her?"

"Oh," Linda said, her eyes wide and her hand brushing her face in embarrassment. "I don't think so. I never saw them exchange words. Why?"

"Who's your dad?" Nicola interrupted.

"This is Jack's son," Linda quickly explained to her.

Nicola's eyes widened and her hands went to her face. "I'm so sorry, Sean," she said with sadness. "I'm so sorry your daddy died."

"It's fine," he said dismissively, turning his attention back to Linda. "No one else over there would know him either?"

"Just Bobby," said Nicola.

He tilted his head back to the girl. "Who's Bobby?"

"The man who cleans the Goddess's pool," Nicola said. "He and Jack were friends. They sometimes talked over the wall, anyway."

"*Someone* has a crush on Bobby," said Linda with a playful grin, angling her head toward her granddaughter.

Nicola blushed.

"Hey, you have good taste," Linda added. "Bobby's a good-looking young man."

"Grandma!"

Sean leered back over the wall at the Goddess, who had turned onto her stomach. "Why don't you give me a few more minutes, okay, Linda?"

"Oh," Linda said uncomfortably as she watched him set the buckets and other equipment down on the patio. "Okay . . ."

Sean made his way back down the steps. When he reached the oak tree to the right side of the shed, he latched onto one of its low branches and pulled himself up along the trunk. He could only imagine the expression most certainly stretched across Linda's face as his weight bent limbs and sent spooked birds fluttering off into the air.

"What are you doing, Sean?" Nicola's voice echoed in the distance.

Sean negotiated his way out onto a thick branch that hugged the stone wall, cursing at the leaves that smacked him in the face. Several fairly fresh stubs from broken off twigs suggested that someone had recently gone through the same motion of scaling their way across the branch. Probably Nicola's dirty old grandfather.

Sean ventured out as far as he could go before wood groaned beneath him. He leaned forward and clasped his arms over the top of the wall. From there, he had a good view of the Goddess's tight glutes.

"Hey!" he hollered at her.

Her head spun to the side. When he shouted out again, she twisted into a sitting position. Her eyes scanned the trees along the wall.

Sean waved awkwardly at her as he struggled to keep his balance, and her attention zeroed in on him. She raised her hand to her sunglasses but seemed to consciously stop herself from removing them.

"Hey! I need to talk to you for a minute!" he shouted with his hand cupping his mouth.

She stared, stone-faced, at him.

"Can you come here for a second? I need to talk to you about something!"

She quickly stood up. Appearing nervous, she waved him off with her hands, glancing behind her at windows at the rear of the house, as if she was afraid that someone inside would hear Sean's voice.

"Listen!" he continued. "Were you swimming in the ocean on Monday morning?"

She shook her head, seemingly not in reply to the question, but rather to the premise that she was even going to entertain it. She turned around and made a beeline for the back door of the residence.

He called for her to wait, but she ignored him, jogging up a short flight of stairs and past some large, decorative pots that were filled with flowers of many colors. Within seconds, she had made her way across the wooden porch, through some French doors, and inside the house.

"Dammit," Sean grumbled.

Through the tall lattice windows that rode the back wall, he could still partially see the Goddess. She was now engaged in what looked to be an animated conversation with an individual he couldn't distinguish through the glare of the window. Her arms waved defiantly as she spoke, like a television lawyer laying out a dramatic closing argument to a jury.

A moment later, someone brushed past her on their way toward the French doors. It was a tall, dark figure who Sean made out to be a black man once he emerged from the home. The man had a shiny bald head and wore a dark gray, well-tailored suit with a bright white shirt underneath. The shirt was unbuttoned down to his sternum where a couple of gold chains hugged his chest.

Sean watched the man let his eyes adjust to the sunlight before he lifted his gaze to the sight of Sean draped over the top of the wall.

The man's nostrils widened with annoyance. "We got a problem here, man?" he called with a raised hand. He had an accent that resembled Chief Quammen's but with more of an inner-city snap to it.

"No problem," replied Sean. "Just a conversation."

The man power walked down the stairs to the patio, the soles of his polished black shoes clapping the cement. He entered the yard, crossing between some short hedges and skirting a flower garden.

Sean glanced up at the house. The Goddess was still inside, watching the scene play out.

The man didn't slow his pace until he was just a few yards from the wall, focusing on Sean the entire time. He stopped and placed his hands on his hips. His eyes were unusual for an African American— turquoise-blue. They were not only distinct in color but in their piercing magnetism. Sean felt as if he were gazing at the face of a tribal statue with gemstones in its orifices.

The strong scent of Aqua Velva aftershave grabbed Sean's nose. He recognized it from a gift set his sister had given him last Christmas. The man must have been wearing a ton of it, too, because Sean was up-breeze from him.

"Man, why you gotta be up on that wall hasslin' the woman?" asked the man. Sunlight flickered off a gold stud in his ear. "I know how she looks, but—"

"I wasn't hassling her, *man*," interrupted Sean. "I was talking to her."

"Whut ya need to talk to her about?"

"About whether she saw anything out by the beach on Monday morning."

The man's face tightened. "They pulled some man's body out uh that water on Monday mornin'. Is that whut ya askin' about?"

"More or less."

"Yeah, we saw it, man. The whole damn neighborhood saw it."

"How about before that? Earlier in the morning. The people who live here told me your wife goes swimming in the ocean every day, out to some boat."

The man snickered, a twisted grin forming along his lips. "She ain't my wife, man. No way, no how."

"I don't care if she's your dentist," said Sean. "All I care about is whether or not she saw anything while she was out there."

"She didn't see nothin', man," he said in a resentful tone. "She'd have told me if she had."

Sean glared at him. The man glared back. Tense seconds marched along before the man finally scoffed and turned his back to Sean. He began walking back toward the patio, his gold necklaces clinking against each other.

"What about Bobby?" Sean shouted. "Did Bobby see anything?"

The man froze. With tense shoulders, he slowly twisted his head toward Sean. "Whut did ya say?"

"Bobby. The guy who cleans your pool. Was he here on Monday?"

The man walked back over to Sean with questioning eyes. "Bobby doesn't work for us no more."

"Why?"

"It's none uh yo' damn business," the man said with a sneer.

The topic of Bobby had clearly struck a nerve, though Sean didn't know why. "What's your name?"

The man shook his head and winced in what Sean initially believed was a rejection of his request. Then a certain calmness and confidence settled along the lines of the man's face. His eyes homed in on Sean's again, and within seconds his demeanor oozed something that resembled pride.

"Blake," the man said, chin raised in a taunt or perhaps a show of superiority. "Titus Blake."

Sean nodded, his eyes steady. "I'm Sean. Sean Coleman."

Neither man spoke for a bit as they sized each other up.

"So Titus," Sean finally said, breaking the stalemate. "You know where I can find Bobby?"

Blake said nothing. He seemed so intent in his assessment of

Sean that Sean began to believe that the man hadn't even heard the question. Sean opened his mouth to ask again.

"No," Blake said, cutting him off. He then turned his back to Sean for the second time, and walked back up the patio toward the porch.

A piercing scream suddenly erupted from somewhere behind Sean, causing Blake to spin around. Blake's hand slid into the jacket of his suit, as if reflexively reaching for a gun.

Sean's pulse shot through the roof. He turned his head, but could see little through the thick leaves of the oak behind him—just some movement. When a second scream wailed out—this one more horrifying than the first—Sean was sure it belonged to little Nicola.

Chapter 12

S ean's jaw tensed as he leapt to the wall, hooking his arms along its top edge and letting the rest of his body swing to it. He dangled for a moment before falling to the uneven ground below. He stumbled but managed to keep upright. He hurried through shrubs and limbs and then charged up the stairs to the house.

"Stay back!" he heard Linda warn someone.

"Grandma!" Nicola shouted.

Air was spewing from Sean's mouth by the time he reached the last step. He gasped at the outrageous sight of a stocky man bedecked in a curly neon green wig wearing a loud, colorful clown outfit. Thick white makeup covered most of his face. The clown had his hands out in front of him with spread fingers, pleading with Linda and Nicola for calmness.

Linda stood stoutly in front of her granddaughter, shielding the girl's small body with her own. "Leave right now, or I'll call the police!" Nicola clung to her hip.

"Oh God," Sean muttered, suddenly realizing the clown was speaking with Dusty's voice. "What in the holy hell?" he yelled with tight fists and a puffed-up chest. He stepped in front of Linda, facing down the clown with fire in his eyes.

"I told you I had a gig to get to!" Dusty cried. The curls of his wig bounced as he spoke. "You were in here so long I was starting to think you weren't coming back!" His voice was higher pitched than before.

"So you come here in this moronic get-up and scare the hell out of a little girl?"

"The gate was open!" he pleaded. "The birthday party starts in *ten minutes*, and no one was answering the doorbell! I can't afford for my reputation to take a hit in this town—not on the birthday circuit!"

"The *birthday circuit?* What the . . . ?" Sean was beside himself. He momentarily shifted his focus across the top of the south wall at the neighbor's house. There he saw Titus Blake standing on the porch, absorbing the spectacle with a blank glare, his hands now at his side. He held Sean's gaze for another few seconds before shaking his head and walking inside.

"I apologize for this idiot," said Sean, facing Linda. He watched Nicola cautiously poke her face out from behind her grandmother's hip. "I'll get him back in his clown car, and we'll be out of your hair."

Linda nodded, her agitated eyes now revealing a hint of relief. She held out the check she had written. "Don't forget your father's things."

Sean nodded, taking the check and sliding it into this pocket. "Help me with this stuff, Bozo," he said to Dusty, motioning toward his father's pool equipment still sitting on the ground.

Dusty rolled his eyes and collected the hose, brush, and the chemical container. His over-sized yellow shoes seemed to get in his way as he consolidated the items in his arms. Sean swung the net over his shoulder and tucked the buckets under his opposite arm.

"Are there other clowns in your clown car, mister?" Nicola asked of Dusty, suddenly brave enough to step out from behind her grandmother.

Dusty cocked his head back and let out a loud, obnoxious laugh. "Not today, my lovely," he said in theatrical fashion. He was back in character mode and now spoke in a Mary Poppins accent. He leaned forward to meet Nicola's wide-eyed gaze. "But I do have lots of balloon friends who keep me company. By any chance, do *you* have a birthday coming—"

The conversation abruptly ended from Sean sliding the circular frame of the pool net over Dusty's head and giving it a stiff yank.

"Gah!" Dusty gasped as the frame hooked under his chin. He stumbled backwards, his large shoes shuffling for balance while he strained to keep the items in his arms from falling. He was out of character again. "Take it off! The netting—the mesh! Dammit! It will jack up my wig! I'm serious!"

"You said you were late!" Sean mocked with some satisfaction. "No time to hand out business cards. Let's go."

Nicola giggled at the display, while Linda remained stone-faced, unsure of what to make of it. Sean finally released Dusty, who grumbled some more about his wig before collecting himself and briskly following Sean toward the side of the house.

The two bickered all the way back to the car. Sweat was starting to eat through Dusty's makeup as he rolled down one of the back windows. He let the heads of the oversized broom and net dangle out of it. He and Sean then shoved the rest of the equipment onto the backseat.

"Okay," Sean said, wiping sweat from his own brow. "I'll drop you off at the party. What time do you want me to pick you up?"

"The hell you will!" snapped Dusty, placing his hands on his hips. He was one angry clown. "No, no, no. I'm done with you! Your card was punched! The *event* is over, and no one drives my car but me."

It was the reaction Sean had expected, but he knew that confiscating the keys had earned him some leverage. "You're wasting time, Dusty, and time is money. We don't want that birthday circuit reputation of yours to take a hit. No one likes a tardy clown. Now get in the car and I'll get you where you need to go."

Dusty glared at him as the seconds ticked by. "Son of a . . . !" he finally shouted, tightening his fists and stomping his large shoes on the ground.

"Don't give me that pouty Shirley Temple bullshit," Sean taunted, prying the keys from his pocket. "Time's a tickin'. Get in the car."

Dusty groaned and treaded around to the passenger's side of the car. Sean smirked and climbed into the driver's seat, taking a moment to adjust the seat lever for more leg room. Balloon animals fluttered from both men's presence as Sean revved the engine. He popped the transmission into drive and the car lunged forward. He drove down to the next driveway before turning around, which gave him a chance to look through the neighboring gate to see what kind of wheels Titus Blake owned. A dark Cadillac sat in front of a cement fountain in the shape of a large, upright fish with water pouring from its mouth. The car had Jersey plates.

"No Mercedes," Sean muttered.

Chapter 13

Martin Schofield frantically rushed to the stern of the boat, his trembling legs giving out before he could reach the handrail. When he crashed to the deck, the binoculars tethered around his neck bounced off of the wood and struck him in the jaw. He gasped and crawled forward with clenched fists, belching out the first heave from his stomach. Bile dripped from his lips.

He reached the edge of the boat, where he grabbed a metal cleat and pulled his head over the ocean. Vomit erupted from his mouth, immediately gaining the attention of a passing seagull that swooped into the cloudy, clumpy water for a taste.

Once Schofield had emptied his stomach, he pulled himself to his knees and wiped his mouth with the back of his arm. The sound of his own heartbeat echoed through the inside of his skull as he kept low and lumbered his way past a couple of deck chairs, a short row of cinder blocks, and the breakfast table he'd cleared off earlier that morning. He trotted up a short group of stairs, rolled open a tinted-glass sliding door, and collapsed into a cushioned chair at the captain's helm. He lowered his quivering hand below the dashboard of dials and monitors, and grabbed the handheld microphone of a mounted CB radio.

Out of breath, he held the microphone to his mouth and pressed its button. "Mr. Blake. Mr. Blake. The guy . . . the guy you said to keep an eye out for. I see him!"

When he received no answer, he slammed his fist on the wheel in frustration. His focus slid up to a rearview mirror that hung from above. There he found his own bloodshot eyes, tired and stinging from nights of restless sleep, glaring right through his soul. He didn't recognize those eyes. They looked as though they belonged to a stranger. He looked away when he could no longer bear their guilt. His fingers went up under his chaotic red hair where they clawed his scalp with the malice he knew he so richly deserved.

An angry voice finally sounded out from the radio speaker. "Not on the open air, dammit!"

"Shit!" Schofield whimpered, dropping the microphone and letting it dangle by its curled cord as he reached to his side for a duffle bag. He dragged the bag onto his lap, unzipped it, and rifled through its contents until he was holding a cell phone in his palm. It was already vibrating.

He pushed a button and half a second later was assaulted with an angry tirade from the man he knew as Titus Blake.

"Whut did I say? Not on the open air, ya stupid son of a bitch! Cell phones are bad enough, but on a public channel, man? Stupid as shit! We don't need some repeat uh the other night. It's daytime. People are awake! They'll hear ya."

"I'm sorry," Schofield moaned. "I'm sorry, Mr. Blake. I'm just not . . . I'm just not . . ."

"Ya just not cut out for this shit?" Blake finished, his statement left dangling with silent implications that terrified Schofield.

"No! I didn't say that. I didn't say that. I just . . . The man you said to look out for. The big guy. He's checking out the yacht!"

The phone went silent for a moment. Blake then asked, "Is he at the damn pier? Right now?"

"No. He's on the beach. I'm still anchored. I saw the guy looking directly at me through a pair of binoculars. He's there right now! Scoping out the yacht!"

"Ya can see him on the beach? How close are ya to the shore?"

"I'm just in the regular spot, Mr. Blake. Honest. I was checking out the beach through my binoculars! We made eye contact—Or binocular contact. Whatever you want to call it. He's gotta know something!"

A few seconds went by before Blake spoke again. "Is he with some asshole dressed like some clown?"

"A what?" Schofield asked with a cocked head.

"Is he with anyone?"

"Just a minute," said Schofield before snatching a hold of the binoculars still dangling from his neck. He raced to the boat's side window and trained the lenses through the tinted glass toward the beach, taking a second to push his red bangs out of his eyes. "Oh shit!" he gasped once the scene came into focus.

"Is there something in particular you're looking for?" asked an overweight Italian-looking man with thick silver eyebrows. He had a crisp, commanding voice with a depth worthy of movie narration. A wide-rim hat and a pair of gold-framed sunglasses shaded his face.

The man sat by himself in a reclining chair made of wood and canvas. He looked in his late seventies or early eighties and was partially hidden by an umbrella that offered his round, wrinkled body some protection from the sun. He held a glass in his hand, half-filled with a blood-red cocktail and ice.

Sean gathered from the man's question that he was anxious to get his borrowed binoculars back.

"Just checking out the view," he answered, holding his gaze through the lenses.

He watched the yacht—mostly white in color with dark windows—anchored a couple hundred yards from the beach. He searched for the conspicuous man with topsy-turvy red hair who'd fled to the other side of the boat, seemingly in response to Sean's surveillance. The redhead was now nowhere to be seen.

"*The Closer*," Sean read off the bow of the yacht.

Having unloaded Dusty in front of a crowd of cheering kids in a front yard flush with food tables and party decorations, Sean had driven back down the coast to the beach. He wanted to take a look at the location where his father was last seen alive—where he had stolen the surfboard.

"What do you know about that boat out there, *The Closer?*" he asked the old man over the shouts of some children who were playing in the nearby water under the watchful eye of their parents.

"Ah," the man chuckled, leaning back in his chair with a grin now spread on his face. "You're asking about the Goddess, aren't you? You have to get up pretty early in the morning to catch that show, my friend." He had a hint of an upper east-coast accent.

Sean lowered the binoculars from his face and handed them back to the man, whose curly white chest hair poured out of his burgundy, unbuttoned Polo shirt. The man wore long, khaki shorts, and a pair of expensive-looking leather sandals lay upside down in the sand just a foot or two away.

"Does *everyone* call her that?" Sean asked.

"Call her what?"

"I met with the Kents earlier," answered Sean, tossing his thumb toward the back of the family's property. "They call her the Goddess, too."

The man's grin widened. "Yes. I suppose one of us dirty old men probably coined that phrase. Some of us get together for a poker game once a week. I'd be lying if I said she never came up in conversation." He punctuated his remark with a salacious laugh that quickly disintegrated into a coughing fit.

"Has the topic of that dead body they pulled out of that water on Monday come up?" asked Sean, ignoring the man's hacking. "With you and your poker buddies?"

The man turned his reddened head and spit out some phlegm before meeting Sean's gaze again. "Yes it has, as a matter of fact," he wheezed with damp eyes. "He was the Kents' pool cleaner. Someone killed him. The police were asking around about break-ins, but there weren't any to my knowledge."

"Yeah," Sean said. "That's what I'm hearing, too. Did any of you hear anything like shouts or gunshots that night?"

"No, we did not."

"Do you know of anyone around here who drives a Mercedes-Benz E-320?"

"No, I don't."

For some reason, the man showed no curiosity in why he was being interrogated, which was fine with Sean, who was in no mood to explain it. He folded his arms in front of his chest and glanced at the yacht again before his gaze drifted along the ocean horizon to the bridge that his father had been found under. Seabirds sat on its railing, searching the water for a late lunch. A few cars rode along its deck, heading toward the island.

Sean felt lost, and that his coming there had been a big waste of time. He had scoured the private beach, ignoring the inquisitive stares of the handful of residents there enjoying the sun. They likely wondered whose guest he was—this large, fully clothed man kicking at rocks, examining footprints, and combing through long grass. The only peculiarity of note was the squirrelly, red-haired fellow on the yacht, who may very well have been reacting to a jerking fishing pole at the back of the boat.

A diluted but familiar scent piggybacking on a light breeze suddenly caught Sean's nose, and he twisted his head away from the ocean to seek its source. What he found were the cold, blue eyes of Titus Blake glaring back at him. Blake was standing behind the mesh of a chain-linked fence a couple dozen yards away. He was no longer wearing his jacket. A tight vest now overlaid his white shirt underneath his folded arms.

"Ah, the sentry," said the old man, his head turned the same direction as Sean's. He sipped some of his cocktail through a thin straw.

"The sentry? Why do you call him that?"

"His job is to watch things. Watch the Goddess. Watch the property. Just look at those magnificent eyes. He's like a hawk." The words came out as admiration.

Sean turned his gaze back to the old man. "Who does he work for?"

"For the man who owns that spread, of course. That big house. The yacht. The Goddess's husband. He's some big shot from up north."

"Do you know his name?"

"Anthony Albano," said the man with a curious but unmistakable sense of pride. He then raised his hand in the air and snapped his fingers.

Sean's eyes narrowed in confusion.

Back at the fence, Blake began untying his shoes. Within seconds, he had removed them along with his socks and was making his way over to a gate. He fiddled with the latch for a moment, and then swung the gate open. With bare feet, rolled-up pant legs, and an icy disposition, he walked along the beach toward Sean.

Sean switched his attention back and forth between Blake and the old man, who was now gazing back out at the ocean horizon with a confident smile, as if he hadn't a care in the world.

Blake was making a beeline directly for Sean.

Sean tightened his body and clenched his fists, preparing for a confrontation. To his surprise, however, Blake walked right past him. Only the shift of his crystal eyes acknowledged Sean's presence. Blake approached the old man, leaned forward, and yanked the umbrella out of the sand with a grunt. He then collapsed it and set it down on the ground. As if going through a routine practice, Blake next circled around in front of the man and held out his hand. The man took it, and Blake carefully assisted him to his feet.

"You're Anthony Albano," said Sean.

"Yes I am," said the man, trying to slide his foot into one of his sandals as Blake held his arm. "But you may call me Tony if you like. And what can I call you?"

"Coleman," interjected Blake, his eyes lifting to meet Sean's. "Sean Coleman."

Albano nodded. "Ah, you and Mr. Blake have already met. How splendid."

"We have," said Sean. "But your butler wasn't being very helpful."

Blake's eyes burned through Sean's. He looked like he wanted to say or do something, but Albano commanded his silence with a subtle shake of his head.

Sean continued. "I wanted to ask your wife the same questions I asked you, about early Monday morning. Maybe I could even talk to the guy out there on your boat—the one who looks like Carrot Top."

Albano chuckled. "None of us saw anything, Mr. Coleman. The police asked us the same question, and we gave them the answer I just gave you. Now, in case you weren't aware, this is a private beach. Unless you're someone's guest, you don't belong here."

Blake folded up the beach chair and tucked it under his arm. He draped the umbrella over his shoulder. Albano was standing without assistance, but he looked frail. The ice in his cocktail tapped against the inside of his glass, the result of a now-noticeable hand tremor.

"Come on," Albano finally muttered to Blake after staring down Sean for a moment. "We have some packing to do." He walked slowly and carefully, each step deliberate. Blake stayed close behind, ready to latch onto him and keep him from falling if needed.

"Going on a trip?" Sean asked.

"It's the end of the summer, Mr. Coleman," answered Albano. "It's time to head on home."

The two brushed past Sean and, without turning back, made their way toward the gate.

"You don't want to know why I'm asking these questions?" Sean shouted at them. "Why I want to know what happened Monday night?"

Nearly to the gate, Albano stopped and carefully turned around. His face oozed smugness. "You're asking because the dead man was your father."

Blake grinned.

Chapter 14

A *lbano must have talked to the Kents after I'd left*, Sean told himself. It was a simple explanation for how the old man had known of his relationship to the deceased.

Still, the arrogance with which he'd spoken the words seemed to suggest that there was something more to it—as if the knowledge had been presented as a message of omniscience. It didn't sit well with Sean, and on his way back up the coast, he spent his idle time at red lights angrily stripping balloon animals from the dashboard and windshield and tossing them onto the backseat.

Sean realized from his roadmap that the county coroner's office wasn't that far out of the way from the house where he'd dropped off Dusty, so he decided to make another stop.

When Sean passed the small funeral home where he had signed papers the day before, he thought of his father. He wondered if the body had already been taken over there and put away in some cold, metal drawer until it would be time to shoot him up with chemicals and pack him away for the long trip home.

In Winston, Jack would be put on display for the family and the few old buzzards left in town who still remembered him and then buried under the earth of his abandoned past. Sean pondered whether or not he'd ever drop by to visit the gravesite after the funeral.

Only one car sat in front of the coroner's office, a reminder that it was Saturday and that Warner was a government employee. He was probably on-call, and the car, which was a late 1980s Mustang with a bad paint job, likely belonged to a janitor. Sean turned into the parking lot and was about to flip a U-turn when he noticed movement at the side of the building. Someone with a heavy trash bag hoisted over his shoulder was making his way toward a large dumpster. Sean edged in closer and recognized the person to be Warner's nephew, Jordan. He was dressed in a tank-top and long shorts. Some broken-down cardboard boxes were pinned under his opposite arm. He was facing away from Sean and was grooving his thin shoulders to whatever tune was spilling from his ear buds.

Sean watched him for a moment, shaking his head at the boy's tightly wound helmet of hair that bounced like a spring with each movement.

Sean parked the car, climbed out, and approached the kid from behind. Just as Jordan dropped his bag in the dumpster with a hollow thud, Sean made his presence known with a stiff slap on the boy's shoulder. Jordan's body jerked in surprise and spun around to meet Sean. When he realized who'd tagged him, his eyes widened and he nervously yanked the ear buds from their holes.

"Whoa," Jordan said with a crackle in his voice and his hands raised defensively in front of him. "I'm sorry about what happened yesterday. I was just fucking around with my uncle. I didn't mean any disrespect, okay?"

"Don't worry about it, Curly," Sean said dismissively. "I've got a question for you. How closely do you work with your uncle?"

Jordan's head tilted to the side. His eyes shrunk into a squint. "Uh. What do you mean?"

"What I mean is, do you help him with his work? Do you assist him when he examines the bodies that are brought in here? Does he talk to you about their causes of death?"

The boy frowned in confusion. "Uh. This is . . . kind of a weird conversation, man," he said. "I should probably call my uncle." His skittish eyes turned toward the side door of the building, as if he was looking for someone to rescue him from the situation.

"Yes or no, Jordan? It's a simple question."

"Well, yeah, I guess so."

"Good." Sean jammed his hand into his back pocket and pulled out his wallet. He slid out some crisp twenties and let them dangle at eye-level.

Jordan's eyes widened. They shifted back and forth between Sean and the cash. His lips curled into a half smirk.

"Do you know what kind of gun my father was shot with?" Sean asked, his tone serious.

Jordan pushed aside some reluctance and nodded, still leering at the cash. "I only know of the one because my uncle wouldn't shut up about it."

"The one what?"

"The one bullet. The guy—your dad—he was shot with two different guns. The bullet in the shoulder was the one that had Uncle Malcolm creaming his pants."

Sean's eyes lowered to the pavement as he processed what the intern had said. Two guns likely meant two different people had shot his father. "Why?"

"Why what?"

"Why was your uncle creaming his pants?"

Jordan glanced to the side door again, this time seeming to make sure no one was eavesdropping on their conversation. He leaned closer to Sean. "It was something called a Geco," he whispered. "Metal-piercing. Very rare."

"A Geco? Like the lizard?"

"Yeah, like in the commercial. I think that's how you say it, anyway. It's a nine millimeter."

Being that his late uncle was a firearms aficionado, Sean knew a fair bit about guns. Yet he'd never heard of the Geco brand and half believed Jordan wasn't saying it correctly. Either that or the bullet was truly as rare as the intern believed. "Do you know if that brand meant anything to Quammen? Have any leads come from it?"

"I have no idea, man," answered Jordan. "I just know that it's rare. I'm sure Quammen knows that, too."

Sean had no reason to doubt the boy and asked him other questions about the autopsy. It was apparent, however, that Jordan was very limited in his responsibilities and wasn't privy to any other specifics.

"All right," Sean said, confident the well was dry. He shoved the twenties back inside his wallet. The billfold quickly disappeared into his pocket.

"Whoa, whoa, whoa," protested Jordan. "Where's my money?"

"What money?"

"The fucking money you just flashed in my face, man! Are you serious? The money for the info!"

"I'm not sure what you're talking about, kid. I didn't promise you shit."

Jordan's face turned red with anger, but his eyes went timid when Sean homed in with a wicked glare. The boy took a step backward.

"I'd say we're now even for the puppet show you put on yesterday. You agree?"

The boy nervously nodded his head, his eyes still averted.

Sean smirked and placed his hand on Jordan's shoulder. He pulled the boy in close like a schoolyard bully about to extract milk money. "And let's keep this conversation between the two of us. Got it?"

Sean was nearly back to his car when he spotted a white Jeep Cherokee enter the parking lot. It slowly pulled up to the front of the coroner's office, the driver assessing Sean's presence. When the glare of the sun left the vehicle's side window, Sean could tell that it was Warner. He parked next to Sean, killed the engine, and stepped out wearing a white T-shirt, Bermuda shorts, and a scowl.

"What are you doing here?" he asked, adjusting his glasses.

"Just doing some sightseeing," replied Sean.

Warner shook his head in irritation, glancing over Sean's shoulder at his nephew. Sean could see the reflection of Jordan shrugging his shoulders in the Jeep's back window.

"What are *you* doing here?" Sean asked Warner. "You look like you're on your way to a barbeque."

"I was called in. We've got a body on its way in—a suicide."

"You get many of those out here?"

"Very few, but it happens," Warner replied, placing his hands on his hips. "About ninety percent of the people that pass away in this county are the elderly—retired folks who either moved here for the weather or are here on vacation. Heart attacks, strokes, you know."

The coroner sounded like a tour guide, presenting death stats rather than geographical history. When Warner's head turned toward the road, Sean followed his gaze.

An ambulance with its lights off had turned off of the street. It bobbled over a gutter and crept its way toward them.

"Have you heard anything new from Quammen on my father?" Sean asked, scratching his jaw.

"Since yesterday? No. And I don't suspect I will. My involvement's over, unless more paperwork comes along. Your father's body has been turned over to the funeral home. All evidence and reports are in the hands of the police."

Sean weighed bringing up the metal-piercing bullet Jordan had described but decided against it. He knew Warner wouldn't give him anything, and he worried the coroner might tip off Quammen that he knew about it. Sean didn't need another lecture about letting the *professionals* handle things.

The ambulance came to a halt just a few feet away from them, its engine purring for another few seconds before it was killed. A couple of young men with dark hair and wearing EMT uniforms stepped out and acknowledged Warner before slipping around to the back of the van. There, they opened the doors and pulled out a gurney. They propped it into place.

"Unless there's anything else I can help you with, Mr. Coleman, I have some work I need to attend to," said Warner.

"Go ahead," said Sean, digging into his pocket for his keys.

Jordan joined his uncle beside the ambulance as Sean slid into the Datsun. He rolled down his window and stuck the key in the ignition. That's when he heard a name uttered by one of the paramedics that sent his heart collapsing into his stomach.

He heaved the door back open and lunged to his feet, eyes bulging and heart racing. The pavement below him suddenly felt slanted and in motion, forcing him to latch his arms around the side mirror of the ambulance after taking only a few steps. He gasped and staggered forward, pulling himself along the side of the van until he reached its rear. There, the only face that wasn't blurred through the prism of his tunnel vision was Warner's. The coroner's eyes were wrought with puzzlement and concern over Sean's manic state.

"Sean?" Warner asked, leaning forward and placing his hand on Sean's shoulder.

Sean slapped his arm away and shoved one of the EMTs so hard he knocked the man to the ground. At the opened back of the ambulance, there was a filled body bag. It lay on a stretcher in the bed. When Sean grabbed for its zipper, multiple voices from different directions pled with him to stop. Hands were prying at his shoulders and arms, and Sean snarled as he fought savagely against them. His fingers gripped the zipper strap and yanked the bag open as the name he'd heard muttered only seconds earlier echoed up from the depths of his soul.

Maria Ortíz.

Inside was the delicate, lifeless face of a young woman. Her skin was pale but pure. On her nose was a silver stud in the shape of a small butterfly.

Chapter 15

S ean had barely budged for the past couple of hours, plastered to the seat of a decaying cement bench at the middle of a small courtyard in front of the coroner's office. The sun had long set. The traffic on the street had thinned out. The light from a glazed window at the edge of the building was all that let him see the cracked sidewalk that led up to the entrance.

The news, as told him by Quammen, was devastating. Shortly after Dusty had left Claudia's trailer that morning to pick up Sean, the mother had been notified that her only daughter had taken her own life. It had happened sometime overnight. A neighbor who was to have coffee with Maria early that morning had found her apartment door unlocked, and entered to discover her unresponsive on her bed with a bottle of prescription sleeping pills spread out along her nightstand.

Claudia hadn't been able to get a hold of Dusty. She didn't know where he had taken Sean, nor did she know the address where Dusty was working. Once Quammen had arrived at the coroner's office, Sean rode shotgun with him over to the birthday party, providing directions. Along the way, he had told Quammen of the troublemaker at the Wicked Scallop and how Maria was afraid that being seen with a man would get her into trouble at work. Quammen seemed to discount its relevance, noting that he had been told by Claudia that Maria had a long history of depression and that it wasn't the first time she had tried to kill herself. The news nearly floored Sean.

Dusty had been waiting under a tree to be picked up when the men arrived. Though the party had long been over, he was still decked out in full clown attire and makeup, twisting a pink balloon into what looked like a rabbit for the birthday boy's little sister. A wide smile had adorned Dusty's face. It matched that of the young girl, who was ecstatic about the gift he had presented to her. The sight proved a haunting contrast with the loud wails that came just a minute later, once Quammen had carefully broken the news to Dusty.

The tears hadn't been from some character as part of a performance; they'd come from an inconsolable sibling—one whose heart had just been broken.

Once back at the coroner's, Sean had placed a call to the Winston Police Department back in Colorado. Lumbergh wasn't in the office, but Sean left a message with the receptionist for the police chief to look into the significance of Geco nine millimeter bullets. If they were half as rare as Warner's nephew believed, such information might prove important in Sean's father's death. At that particular moment, however, his father wasn't occupying his mind. Maria was.

From his bench slab, Sean watched shadows dancing along the bright window of Warner's office. After some more shuffling around inside, things finally went dark. A minute later, Warner emerged from the front door. He locked it and made his way toward the parking lot. When Sean stood up, the unexpected movement in the night startled the coroner.

"Who's there?" he shouted.

Sean announced himself and watched Warner's shoulder's relax.

"Jesus. What are you still doing out here?"

"Was it a suicide?" Sean asked, not wasting another breath. "Did she really kill herself?"

Warner sighed. "I told you that hours ago."

"I know what you said. And I'm asking you, now that you've examined her, if you still believe that."

"Listen," said Warner. "I'm not supposed to discuss this stuff with anyone who's not immediate family."

"Oh, cut the shit, Warner!" Sean cried. "It's a simple question. I was with this girl just hours before she died. She wasn't depressed. She wasn't suicidal. But she *was* afraid—afraid of the person she worked for. If there's any chance that she was murdered . . ."

Sean suddenly felt himself choking on his own breath. He turned away, bent forward, and placed his hands on his knees to compose himself. He couldn't remember the last time he had let his emotions get the better of him that way, especially in front of another person. It left the taste of humiliation in his mouth.

"Sean," said Warner, his tone sympathetic. He rested a hand on Sean's shoulder. "You've been though a lot. Two people you know have died in a very short period of time, and—"

"I didn't know either of them," Sean said somberly, twisting his body to disconnect from Warner. "Not really. And this isn't about my father. It's about a girl with her whole life ahead of her dying in a way that doesn't make any sense." He turned to face Warner again. "Now was it suicide or not?"

He could hear Warner's uneasy breathing in the dark, and though he couldn't make out the details of his face, he imagined it was contorted in conflict.

"The toxicology report is going to take a while," he said at last. "But I don't see any other likely causes at this time. There are no signs of physical trauma. No known health conditions. No signs of illegal drug use. Her body just stopped working. That's consistent with an overdose of sleeping pills."

Sean couldn't decide if Warner's words were what he wanted to hear or not. Either way, they didn't bring him any sense of relief or closure. In his gut, he believed that there was more to what had happened to Maria than pent-up depression. When she had left him in the restaurant parking lot the night before, she had done so with a message of hope. She had treated him with compassion, and it didn't make sense to him that she could muster up that kind of persona at a time when she felt so helpless that the only answer left was to end her life.

"Where's your car?" Warner asked, pulling Sean from his haze.

"Quammen's officer drove it back to the Bouches'."

"Need a ride, then?"

"Yeah, I'll take one. Thanks."

"Where are you staying?"

"I don't want you to take me back to my motel."

"Where then?"

"Ever hear of a place called Sunshine's?"

Chapter 16

Warner must have thought Sean was some kind of freak, asking to be dropped off at a shady strip club south of Murrell's Inlet in the wake of a young woman's death. Sean could see it in the coroner's eyes once the reversed image of the club's neon-pink letters reading "Southern Hospitality" slid from his glasses.

Sitting behind the wheel of the idling Jeep in the parking lot, the coroner shook his head. "You just want me to drop you off here for the night? At a . . . at a titty bar?" The question came out of his mouth like it was the first time Warner had ever uttered the word "titty."

"Yeah," replied Sean. "I'm going to drown my sorrows in bare breasts and thongs. Want to join me?" The words were intended to scare off Warner.

It had become clear on the ride over that the coroner wasn't aware that Maria had worked at the establishment. It was information he had no reason to be privy to. Sean saw no point in getting him involved.

"No. No thanks," said Warner, swallowing. "I'm going to go home to my family. And listen . . . you're welcome to come with me if you like. My wife's going to warm up some dinner. We could turn on some *Quincy M.E.*" He gave a weak smile.

Warner was a good man—of that, Sean was sure. He might have even taken him up on his offer had his conscience not convinced him that he owed it to Maria to figure out how she'd spent her final hours. "Textbook suicide" or not, there had to be more to the story. Even if the pursuit of the truth led him nowhere, it was a journey he had to take.

"Thanks for the ride, Warner," he said, opening his door and climbing out.

The half-full parking lot was littered with cigarette butts and beer bottles. A Mötley Crüe song filled the night air, streaming out of an open door at the front of the poorly lit building.

"How are you going to get back to your motel?" Warner asked, leaning across the passenger seat.

"I'll figure out something. Don't worry about me." Sean closed his door and nodded his head in gratitude.

Warner nodded back with pursed lips before sinking back into his seat. He slowly navigated his way out of the parking lot, his headlights cutting through the muggy night.

When Sean turned back to the building, he saw a lanky black man with a bit of an afro, a leather vest, and a cigarette dangling out of his mouth. He was sitting just outside the door on a wooden stool. He climbed to his feet when Sean approached him.

"I need to see your ID, man," he said matter-of-factly.

"Do I look underage to you?"

The man snickered. "Nah, man, but we got to do it. The city sends in narcs from time to time. Ya know, to make sure we're law-abidin' folks. They'd love nothing better than to pull our license and shut this place on down."

"What a shame that would be for the community," Sean quipped. He dug into his pants for his wallet and presented his driver's license.

The man looked it over. "Colorado, huh? You on vacation?"

"Something like that."

"You do a lot of skiin' out there in Colorado?"

"No."

"Fishin'?"

"Yes."

"All right, man. All right. I get it. You'd rather be lookin' at naked women than small-talkin' with the brother. Am I right?"

Sean ignored the man's question. He wasn't in the mood for

chitchat. He took his license back, slid it into his wallet, and walked inside. He entered a room where neon spotlights pierced through thick clouds of rank cigarette smoke. The red and purple beams swung in rhythm with the eighties metal music that blared from loud speakers pointed outward from a small circular stage. At the center of the stage was a thin pole that stretched to the ceiling. An oily-haired girl hung from it wearing knee-high boots and not much else. She was upside down, her legs scissoring the pole in obvious innuendo.

There were fewer than twenty patrons inside. All men. Most of them sat by themselves at small round tables just off the stage. Their glazed-over eyes were trained on the stripper like a cheetah stalking a baby antelope. A few others occupied some stools at a bar along the wall where a middle-aged woman with thick makeup and large hair like Claudia's served drinks. Sean watched her flash a friendly wink at the obese deejay in the corner—a bald man, probably in his thirties, sporting a thick, bleached-blond goatee and a red velour jogging suit. He stood behind a waist-high wooden enclosure and didn't notice the woman's gesture as he shuffled frantically through CD cases.

Mötley Crüe was soon replaced with Warrant, and when the girl on stage stepped off to mingle and fake-flirt with customers, a new girl came out from behind a pair of curtains near the stage to take her place. This one was blonde and was starting off with a white silk robe.

Sean made his way over to the bartender and asked for a diet pop. The order drew an odd look from a large bearded man sitting at the bar with his back to the stage. He wore a gray T-shirt with the sleeves rolled up to his tattooed shoulders. When Sean returned his glare, the man shifted his focus back to the glass of hard liquor in his grease-stained hands.

It was the first time in over a year Sean had stepped foot inside of a bar. He used to maintain an almost permanent residence in one back in Winston called O'Rafferty's. Back then, when he wasn't losing his shirt in games of pool, he was downing boilermakers until two in the morning from a stool beside the wall. Those memories—as fuzzy as they were—crept back in this mind as he watched the man with the beard clench his glass as if it were a lifeline.

Sean had never gone through a recovery program for his alcoholism. He went cold-turkey after his uncle's death—a method that several people had told him would never work. But it had worked for over a year, despite the urges. The fact that he could now stand mere feet from a wall of liquor bottles and, while mourning Maria's death, order a pop, lent him assurances that he had conquered that beast.

While the bartender was scooping ice, Sean struggled to recall Maria's stage name, which he'd heard from the troublemaker at the Wicked Scallop the previous night. It came to him just as the bartender slid a large glass with a thin straw in front of him.

"Is Destiny working tonight?" Sean asked, feigning ignorance.

The bartender's eyes widened. She swallowed and scanned the room before leaning in close to him.

"I'm sorry to have to tell you this, darlin'," she began in a charming Southern accent. "Destiny . . . she died last night. Poor thing passed away."

"What? How?"

Sadness flooded the woman's eyes, and it was clear that Maria had been on her thoughts. "The rumor is that she . . . Well, they think she killed herself."

He let his mouth hang open and did his best to act surprised by the news. Out of the corner of his eye, he noticed a thin man at the end of the bar with a black baseball cap pulled tightly over his head quickly stand up and make his way for the bathroom. Sean paid him little mind.

"That's awful," he said, pulling up a stool and taking a seat at the bar.

"It sure is, darlin'. It took us all by surprise."

"Were you two friends?" he asked.

"Well, I'd like to think so," answered the woman, scrunching her nose. "But we were really more of acquaintances, I suppose. We talked and all, but we didn't spend any time with each other outside of work."

"Do you know if she was dealing with anything? If anything had been bothering her?"

The woman took a step back. Her face turned suspicious. "Now, who are you again, darlin'? And how did you know her? I don't believe I've ever seen you in here before."

He answered with the first thing that came to his mind. "I'm her mechanic."

"Her mechanic?"

"Yeah. I . . . I work on her truck from time to time."

"Oh. Okay."

He berated himself in silence for the weak explanation but kept himself talking so as not to prompt any more questions about his identity. "You know, I asked her out once and she said it wouldn't be a good idea. Something about her boss not wanting her seen out and about with men."

"Oh yeah," said the woman, wiping her hands with a towel and rolling her eyes. "That's Rockline's thing."

"Rockline?"

"He's the owner." She looked pointedly at the bald deejay. "Everything's about keeping the dream alive."

"What dream?" asked Sean.

The woman chuckled. "The dream that these sorry sons of bitches who come in here have of leaving with a new girlfriend."

The man at the bar with the beard lifted his head and flashed a toothless smile at the woman.

"Present company excluded," said the woman with a smile. She slapped the man's broad shoulder with her towel. "Bob here's a real gentleman. He just comes in for the conversation. Isn't that right, Bob?"

Bob snickered. Sean narrowed his eyes, nearly into a scowl.

"Oh, don't worry there, darlin'," the woman said to Sean. "That's not the kind of business we run. No one goes home with anyone. We make certain of that. It's just part of the game, like that cartoon coyote that chases the roadrunner. He never gets the bird in the end."

Sean took his beverage, removing the straw and leaving it on the bar. He swigged some of the drink straight from the glass and felt the carbonated burn flow down his throat to his empty stomach.

The girl on stage was already down to her lingerie and garter straps, swinging around on the pole in her heels like a slow-moving propeller. The one on the floor was sitting on one of the patron's laps, running her finger along his jaw line while grinning from ear to ear. Her hand slid down to his crotch when he waved some bills in front of her. Sean found himself visualizing Maria's face on the girl, and the image turned his stomach.

His eyes drifted to the deejay again, who was looking him over. Rockline arched his eyebrows and flashed a creepy smile, welcoming who he believed was a new customer to his harem. Sean's face remained deadpan. He took another drink and then set his glass down on the bar. He then slowly began making his way over to the corner of the room. Rockline's eyes had dropped back down to his sound equipment. He didn't notice Sean's approach.

The rock anthem's volume surged as Sean passed between some speakers, the vocals wailing at the height of the bridge. He stepped down to the wooden floor and began negotiating his way around chairs, tables, and the shady clientele too focused on the stage to notice his existence. When the oily-haired girl approached him with swaying hips, a devilish smile, and a verbal proposition he couldn't hear above the music, he waved her off.

Sean scoped out the entire room for any bouncers besides the man he'd met out front. There were none. The only person who had eyes for him was the man with the black baseball cap, who had left the bar when Sean had ordered his drink. The man was now standing behind a cloud of cigarette smoke in front of the hallway that led to the bathrooms. The angle of his neck and the rim of his hat mostly covered his face, but Sean was convinced he had the stranger's full attention. When Sean held his stare for a moment, the man nervously turned his head toward the bathrooms, as if pretending to wait his turn. Maybe he wasn't pretending, but Sean cared little either way.

Sean's eyes slid back to the deejay who was almost within reach. He was pulsing his shoulders and mouthing the lyrics. When he turned his head to Sean, Sean opened his mouth to speak. The introduction was immediately disrupted, however, by a loud shriek that blasted out from somewhere on the other side of the stage.

All heads spun in the direction of the clamor, where a short, stocky man with dark, frazzled hair and a tie-dye shirt stood. When a fluctuating purple spotlight randomly pinned itself to the man's face for a second or two, his eyes revealed an almost demonic intensity. His right arm slowly rose into the air, exposing a wooden baseball bat grasped tightly in his hand. The top of it glistened from a dark red liquid that looked like blood. Patrons at nearby tables launched to their feet, backpedaling and stumbling through chairs to put some distance between themselves and the madman.

It was Dusty, sans makeup and clown hair.

"Shit," Sean muttered.

"You killed her!" snarled Dusty, his face pure rage as he focused on Rockline. He wrapped both hands around the bat's handle and swung it through the air in a downward motion as if he were splitting a log with an axe. When the bat met the top of a small, round table, shattered glass and alcohol sprayed through the air. The strippers fled to the back of the room, one of them tripping and falling on the way.

The blood on the bat had to have belonged to the bouncer at the door, otherwise the man would have been inside by now, checking on the sound of the chaos. *What the hell did Dusty do to him?*

Dusty suddenly made a beeline for the deejay, his teeth clenched like they were ready to split his jaw in two. CD cases flew from Rockline's hands as he scrambled to climb out from behind his small enclosure, his girth handicapping the effort. With wide, frantic eyes, he screamed for someone to call the police. After two failed attempts, he managed to swing open a gate at the side of the booth. Before he could step outside of it, Sean launched forward and kicked it shut.

"Stay there!" Sean shouted, pointing a stern finger at him.

Dusty was nearly on top of them by the time Sean turned back around. Sean grabbed Dusty's raised bat and swung his shoulders to the side, sending Dusty down to the floor on his back. Dusty landed hard but wouldn't release the bat until Sean forcibly yanked it from him.

"Stay down!" Sean warned him, raising the bat.

The song had ended, and patrons began coalescing in confusion. Some slowly moved in for a closer look, buzzing with curiosity.

"It's his fault, Sean!" yelled Dusty with some crackle in his voice. "He did this!"

"Tell me what you mean!" demanded Sean. His eyes shot back and forth between Dusty and Rockline.

"This place. It . . . it stole her innocence." The words felt scripted yet unpracticed, as if Dusty was so overcome with emotion that he had instinctively borrowed the line from a movie.

When Sean heard the rattle of the gate behind him, he turned and yelled, "I said stay there, asshole! And sit down!"

Rockline timidly removed his hands from the latch. "There isn't a chair in here."

"I don't give a shit. Sit your ass down!"

The deejay nervously nodded his head. He swallowed before awkwardly lowering his body down to the floor until only the top of his sweaty head was visible above the enclosure. He looked like a three-year-old in a timeout.

The bartender was on a telephone behind the bar, presumably talking with a 9-1-1 dispatcher. Sean eyeballed her for a moment before turning his attention back to Dusty.

"Dusty," Sean said, controlling his breathing. "What did you do to the man outside?"

Dusty's chest heaved in and out. His gaze swam around the room. "He . . . he wasn't going to let me in!"

"What did you do to him?"

Dusty said nothing.

Sean lifted his head to the crowd of men hovering behind him. "Someone go check on the guy at the front door."

Bob, the bearded man at the bar nodded and hobbled his way over to the entrance.

When the loud, opening riff of Poison's "Unskinny Bop" abruptly belted out from the speakers—presumably the last song Rockline had cued before the ruckus had begun, Sean winced and shouted at the deejay to turn it off. Rockline's meaty hand shook as it slid up to a control board in the mixing booth and the music cut off.

"And turn off the neon!"

The hand flipped a switch beside the board, and then another on the wall. The colorful beams were replaced with standard but dim overhead illumination.

"Dusty," Sean said in a more measured tone, his chest heaving in and out, "what was Maria mixed up in here?"

Dusty's lower lip shook. He let the back of his head press flat to the floor and gazed up at the ceiling as if he had suddenly given up on life. "It's a strip joint," he muttered, his eyes filling up with hopelessness. "Guys. Hanging all over her. Treating her with no respect. Asking her for favors."

"She was afraid," Sean said. "Afraid of upsetting the fat-ass sitting on the floor in there. Why?"

Dusty shook his head, his eyes still lost. "I don't know. I don't know."

Sean sighed and turned his head to the deejay. "You in the sound booth! Get up!"

Rockline's hands clasped the edge of the enclosure and he carefully pulled himself upright. He was breathing heavily and his eyes danced with fear. "All she did here was her job, man. H-H-Honest!" he said with a stutter. He had eavesdropped on Sean's exchange with Dusty. "I run a clean joint. She just stripped."

"Bullshit!" Sean roared. "She didn't go home and kill herself last night just to get out of doing lap dances. She was scared. Scared of disobeying *your* rules!"

"Rules?" Rockline stammered. "The only rules I have is that the girls stay clean and don't be seen alone with guys in town. What's the big fucking deal?"

When a door swung open over by the bathrooms and a light lit up the hallway, Sean looked past the man with the black hat who still stood there. His attention focused on the new figure that emerged. It was a taller man dressed in denim and leather, who wore a black bandana around his head. Gazing down at his own crotch and oblivious to the scene on the floor, the man tugged at the zipper on his jeans. After some trouble, he raised it to full-mast. When he lifted his head, his shoulders tensed at the unexpected silence in the room. Sean then made out a blond mustache hanging below a familiar pair of glassy eyes. It was Grady, the belligerent drunk Sean had made short work of at the Wicked Scallop.

Grady met Sean's eyes, processed the situation for a moment, and then reached for his belt, unsheathing the knife he had flashed the night before. The man with the black hat backed away from him in fear, as did a couple of other patrons who were standing close by.

"Stay here and don't do anything else stupid," Sean said to Dusty, who was still lying flat on his back. Sean then tightened his grip on the bat and started walking toward Grady. He carried himself boldly but with enough restraint in his pace that Grady wouldn't feel as though he were under assault—not yet, anyway. "I want to talk to you," Sean said loudly.

"If ya want some, ya come and get some," Grady said, voice hoarse from taking a fist to the throat the night before.

Sean stopped just out of arm's length. The tension was thick among the onlookers. "Who did you tell about that beating I gave you last night? Did you say something to the fat-ass deejay behind me?"

"What are ya talking about, asshole?" said Grady, his eyes shifting around the room. He lowered his body into a defensive posture. He seemed inebriated again, but not quite as witless as the previous night.

Sean slowed his words when he spoke again. "Did you tell the fat-ass that you saw Maria with me?"

"I don't know any fuckin' Maria."

"Destiny! Did you tell him I was with Destiny?"

When Grady glanced at Rockline, Sean positioned his body in between the two, not wanting the deejay to gesture him an answer.

"You told him, didn't you?" Sean growled. "And now she's dead."

Grady's face twisted in puzzlement.

"Guys!" a panicked voice sounded out from the entrance of the building. It belonged to Bob. He was out of breath and leaning against the wall, one hand on his side. Splotches of blood stained the front of his shirt. "He's all fucked up," he said. "He just stumbled out to his car. He's headed back in here with a gun! Said he's gonna shoot someone!"

The room went totally silent.

Sean's attention spun to Dusty, who was now sitting up on the floor with wide eyes. Rockline mirrored Dusty's expression. The deejay gasped and shoved open his gate. When he exited the booth, he lost his footing and toppled to the floor.

Patrons exchanged anxious looks before their heads began to twist in multiple directions, presumably searching for hiding spots.

A couple of men took off down the bathroom hallway, while another scrambled behind the bar, nearly tackling the bartender. A blond-haired man with a mullet slid underneath some conjoined tables, while others lumbered around in disarray. One of the strippers screamed hysterically. Panic had overtaken the establishment.

"Sean!" Dusty suddenly yelled in warning.

Sean looked toward Grady, who was lunging forward with his knife. Sean side-stepped his assailant, feeling the blade whisk past his shoulder. Sean snarled and swung his bat into the swell of Grady's back as he flew by. Grady fell to the floor, his knife sliding along the polished wood until a fleeing customer inadvertently kicked it in another direction. As Grady was pulling himself to his hands and knees, Sean sent an NFL-worthy punt squarely into his solar plexus, toppling him to his back.

Sean swung his attention to the front door just as the bouncer slogged through it, his face drenched with blood and his hair matted on one side. One of the man's eyes was swollen shut, but the other one bobbled wildly, searching for his target. He held a pistol out in front of him.

"Wait!" Rockline wailed hysterically, waving his arms from the floor. "Put the gun away! We'll sort this all out!"

"Fuck you, fat man!" shouted the bouncer, spit spraying out of his mouth. "If someone's gonna treat me like a nigger, I'm gonna *show* them a nigger!" His finger was on the trigger, and he looked more than willing to pull it.

"Shit," Sean whispered, holding still. He was very much within the bouncer's line of sight, but he knew he wasn't who the man was scoping for—Dusty was. Nonetheless, when the bouncer's eyes shifted to Sean, they stayed on him.

"That bat in your hand!" the bouncer yelled. "Where's the asshole who came in here with it?"

Sean could hear Dusty shuffling around on the floor somewhere behind him. "He ran out the back," Sean answered firmly.

"What the hell you talkin' about, man?" the bouncer fired back. "If someone goes out the back, the fire alarm goes off!"

As if on cue, the fire alarm suddenly blasted on. Its pulsating, high-pitched shriek signaled that someone had indeed just fled out the back door. It just wasn't Dusty.

The bouncer's eyes widened and he took off toward the back of the room, his gun clenched tightly in his hand. He only made it a few steps, however, before Sean caught movement out of the corner of his eye. Dusty had lunged to his feet and was now rushing toward the sound booth.

"Stupid!" Sean grunted. His attention flipped back to the bouncer, who had stopped and was raising his gun at Dusty. "Hey!" he shouted to draw back the bouncer's attention.

Sean planted one foot forward and, with both hands, hurled his bat at the man. It cartwheeled through the air and connected just as the gun went off. The discharge sounded like a cheap firework, muffled by the piercing alarm still screaming like a banshee. The bouncer stumbled backwards, colliding with the customer wearing the black baseball cap who was fleeing toward the front door. The cap flew from the customer's head upon impact, exposing red hair. Sean immediately recognized it as belonging to the man on Anthony Albano's yacht he'd seen through binoculars.

The redhead spun toward Sean, his eyes wide and his mouth open, and then took off for the entrance again. Sean would have pursued him, but the bouncer was still armed, and Dusty was still in danger. Sean scanned the room and found Dusty climbing over the sound booth wall, reaching inside it. The overhead lights went dark, quickly replaced with the swiveling, neon spotlights.

The play was idiotic. Though the darkness and flashing lights added to the confusion, Dusty had exposed himself to his would-be assailant—a man who would have otherwise left the building. To Sean, the plan made little sense, which seemed to be the case with all things Dusty.

Still, with the alarm continuing to sound and neon beams adding an anarchic sense of motion to the room, no clear shot was going to be fired. Sean prayed the bouncer wouldn't begin taking blind ones. He kept low as a precaution.

He made his way in the direction of the sound booth, his knees bouncing off chairs and tables. When he felt someone's shoulder strike his shin, he latched onto their shirt and dropped to a knee.

"Don't shoot! Jesus! It's me! Don't shoot!" the man cried.

Sean rubbed his hand on the man's head, confirming that it was Rockline. He quickly shoved the deejay out of his way.

"Dusty!" Sean yelled, his voice mostly lost in the sound of the alarm. He heard no answer.

When he reached the sound booth, there was enough of a glow from the control panel to see that Dusty wasn't there. Sean hoped he had found his way outside, along with the other fleeing bodies that could be made out in flashes of neon, streaming toward the entrance.

Sean turned to follow suit. That's when the purple, bloodied face of the bouncer flared up right beside him. Sean sent a right cross directly into the man's nose before lunging forward and grabbing the man's right arm with both hands. A shot fired and its blast lit up the room for a split second. Sean slid his hands down to the man's wrist and then found his gun. The man maintained a death-grip on the weapon until Sean cocked his neck and sent the side of his head into the man's face. He delivered a second headbutt before stripping the gun from between his fingers.

Sean held the weapon tightly and pistol-whipped the man across the head, sending him to the floor. The bouncer went down hard. Sean shoved the gun—a revolver—under the back waistline of his own pants for safe keeping. He then pinned the man on his back with a knee pressing into his sternum. He grabbed on to the collar of the disoriented bouncer.

"This is over! Got it?" Sean yelled, leaning over him.

The man groaned and squirmed, but Sean had good leverage on him. He wasn't going anywhere.

"The customer," Sean continued, "the redhead who was in here wearing a black baseball cap. You had to have checked his ID. What's his name?"

"F-fuck you, man," the man growled, barely audible over the alarm.

Still holding the man to the floor with his right knee, Sean cocked his left fist and rammed it hard into the prone side of the man's ribs. The bouncer gasped in pain.

"Who is he?" Sean shouted. "And speak up!"

"Fuck if I know," the bouncer said, fighting for breath. "Never . . . saw him before. He . . . he slipped me fifty bucks. Fifty bucks to let him in without an ID. Figured . . . figured he was under-age. Ya with the city or something, man?"

"Yeah, asshole." Sean leaned in with a sneer. "I'm from fucking *21 Jump Street*. Now if I let you up, are you going to calm the fuck down?"

"Don't ya do me no favors, white boy!" he shouted. "If ya let me up, I'm gonna kick your ass!"

"That's what I thought," Sean muttered. He lifted the man's torso just high enough off the floor to land a devastating uppercut under the man's chin. The man's body jolted and then went limp. Sean gently eased him back to the floor.

Sean climbed to his feet, ears ringing from the continuing alarm. He stumbled into furniture and over broken glass until he'd made his way to the entrance of the building. There, illuminated by an outside light on the wall, was Grady, dazed and crawling toward the fresh night air. He'd barely broken the plane of the building when Sean delivered a hard foot to his rear. It sent him barreling forward, off the cement step, and flat to his stomach in a patch of dirt.

In the parking lot, men were fleeing to their automobiles. Engines cranked, headlamps lit up, and tires sped across gravel. A few lingerers remained, including the bartender, but Sean didn't spot Dusty among them. His car wasn't there.

When the fire alarm came to an abrupt halt, the silence only lasted a few moments before it was replaced with police sirens whining in the distance. Sean didn't plan on sticking around to greet the officers, but he had unfinished business. The moment Rockline emerged from the building, Sean grabbed him by his blonde goatee and shoved him into Grady, who was just beginning to climb to his feet. The men crashed to the ground in a heap of intermingled limbs. Sean hovered over them like a drill sergeant.

"No more bullshit!" He grabbed the pistol from his pants, identifying it as a .38 Special with a five-round capacity. He pointed it at Grady. "What did you tell Fat Santa here about what happened at the seafood joint last night?"

"Nothing, man! I didn't say shit!" Grady shouted in a raspy voice, his hands out in front of him. "Why would I want anyone to know I was taken down with one punch?"

"I swear to God," Rockline pleaded, drawing the aim of Sean's gun. "I don't know what either of you are talking about! I didn't harm Maria. She came in last night, did her set, and left. I don't know why she killed herself. She seemed fine to me. She liked working here! She was making good money—better than usual, because one of the other girls left!"

Sean didn't know what to believe. He turned his attention back to Grady as the police sirens grew louder. "You didn't tell *anyone* about last night?"

"No, man. Just the cop."

Sean's eyes widened. "What cop?"

"The one who showed up at the Scallop after ya left! Someone at the restaurant called the police because of the fight. The manager gave him your description. Your first name, too, because everyone had heard it. All I told him was that I knew Destiny worked here—at Sunshine's."

Sean's eyes narrowed. "What was his name?"

"Who?"

"The cop, goddammit!"

Grady eyes squeezed shut as he struggled to remember. The sirens were close, and red and blue lights began to flicker behind a row of nearby trees.

"Quammen!" Grady finally blurted out. "His name was Quammen!"

Chapter 17

He lay under the cover of darkness in the midst of a wild tangle of grass and overgrown shrubs that had swallowed up the open area of land just south of the strip bar. His eyes were glued to the spectacle playing out before him near the entrance of the building. The large individual, whom he'd first met through a pair of binoculars from the yacht, had tossed a couple of grown men to the ground like rag dolls and now had a gun trained on them. He couldn't make out what the brute was angrily demanding of them, but he was sure it had to be about the girl—the stripper.

Up until that night, Martin Schofield had never stepped foot inside Sunshine's. He'd only driven Albano and Blake there a couple of times and hung out in the car while they inspected the package. No one would have recognized the twenty-four-year-old—who looked more like a teenager—from behind the tinted windows. That's why Blake's demand that morning had made no sense.

Blake was adamant that Schofield stay clear of the strip club, his tone threatening and absolute. At any other time, Schofield would have followed his orders, just like he had reluctantly done that fateful night. But with the growing standoffishness he'd been sensing from them all, he'd begun to suspect it wasn't his safety or best interests that concerned Blake. He'd increasingly felt as though he had a target painted on his back, and the others were just waiting for the paint to dry before pulling the trigger.

At least Albano needed him for the yacht. He was the only one of his men who knew how to sail it and that made him indispensable for the time being. He had his late father to thank for that, having raised him in the tourist industry down in Jacksonville, Florida. As a teenager, Schofield used to tag along on outings at least three days a week, teaching wealthy travelers from across the country how to deep-sea fish. The wannabe anglers all seemed to like him and enjoyed teasing him for how quickly the sun would turn his skin the color of his hair.

That damn hair of his. He should have just buzzed it off. Its bright shade of red and floppy appearance was so distinctive that it had given him away the moment his hat had been knocked from his head. The stranger, who hadn't recognized him previously, had identified him instantly; Schofield could tell by the look in the man's eyes. He was sure that revelation would seal his fate. It would take only the big man showing up again at the house and saying something to Albano, and then all bets would be off. Schofield would end up as dead as the others—as dead as that stripper.

That's what Blake hadn't wanted him to discover at the bar—that the stripper was done breathing. She was the only outsider who could have tied it all together, not through some brilliant Sherlock Holmes detective work, but simply because of where she happened to work. She was the unfortunate victim of some very bad luck, just as Schofield had been when a bout of insomnia led him to taking the yacht out earlier than usual that morning. When all the shit came down, as he now termed it, he had been the only one in a position to put an end to it. And put an end to it he did.

Blake was right. He wasn't cut out for this line of work—a gruesome, nightmarish profession he'd never asked for but had nonetheless found himself trapped in. He thought he had struck gold a year earlier when Albano had hired him. It wasn't every day, after all, that a well-connected real estate mogul from Mendham, New Jersey, offered a good-paying job to a deck hand on a chartered boat. Schofield was just supposed to be a "transportation guy"—a pilot for the yacht Albano was about to purchase and a personal driver to get him around town. He hadn't known the extent of Albano's empire, nor the way the man conducted business. Real estate wasn't his only game. There was also gambling, drugs, prostitution, and every other sin that they spawned. By accepting the position, Schofield had effectively sold his soul to the devil.

The others recognized his discontent. His squeamishness. Of that he was sure. It oozed off their dry faces whenever he'd ask delicate questions or expressed any form of doubt. Pulling the trigger that night may have been what Albano wanted from him, but it also made him a loose end—just like the stripper.

Schofield noticed the big man's face in the lot suddenly turn sober in reaction to something one of the men on the ground had said. With the approaching police sirens blaring through the humid night air, Schofield could no longer hear their voices. It was certain that whatever had been said was of vital importance to the man.

The police would be there at any second, and Schofield knew he couldn't afford to be seen. As red-and-blue flashing lights trickled through the thick greenery, he edged his way backwards on elbows and knees through damp earth and grass. When the big man's head swung in his direction, Schofield stopped. He held perfectly still, refusing to breathe even after a buzzing insect landed on the middle of his nose. The big man appeared to be looking right at him. Had he been seen?

The man's head turned toward the approaching police cars, and Schofield finally released the air from his lungs. He watched the man slide the pistol under the back of his shirt and take off on foot for the woody area spread out behind the bar. Within seconds he disappeared into the night.

Schofield waited until he was sure he was totally hidden behind ample-sized trees and wild bushes before climbing to his feet. His chest throbbed as he contemplated his situation. Listening to the distant sounds of car doors slamming and animated voices, his mind was a labyrinth of desperate ideas and implausible scenarios.

Whatever hope he'd had of things blowing over and life returning to what it had been prior to the night he'd put a bullet through a man's skull was eviscerated.

They'd killed the stripper. Whether it would be tomorrow or the next day, he would be next.

Schofield walked about a mile through darkened marsh and the sounds of unseen critters scurrying among the brush before he reached the gas station he'd been dropped off at earlier in the night. The trek had been much easier at dusk, when he could still see where he was going. Now his shoes squished and smelled of mildew. Sticking to the side of the building where the glare from the lights in the shelter over the pumps found little resonance, Schofield dug into his pockets for change. He fed it into a payphone and dialed the number of the cab company he'd used to get there.

He stuck to the shadows until the cab arrived, wincing for a moment when the driver tooted her arrival. Once inside the car, he muttered out his destination to the large, jovial woman behind the wheel. She repositioned herself in her seat, brushed her dreadlocks to the side of her dark face, and drove out of the parking lot. Schofield kept his head pointed at the floorboard, addressing the woman's attempts at small talk with simple yeses and nos. Without his cap, he was more easily identifiable, so he did his best to avoid eye contact through the rearview mirror.

The Cadillac was back at the house. Schofield wouldn't be able to get to it without punching in the front gate code, which would alert Albano inside. It was best to forget about the car anyway. His plan was to fall off the planet to escape the clutches of a man who wanted him dead; it was best not to do it in a car registered to his pursuer.

Schofield's belongings were aboard the yacht, whose hull he'd been staying in the past several nights. It was tied up at a pier along a secured dock a couple of miles south of the house. He'd have no problem gaining entry, grabbing his things, and staying in a motel overnight until he could catch a bus down to Charleston in the early morning. There, he'd empty his bank account through multiple ATMs, and then figure out a destination and means of travel. That was the extent of his plan for the time being. Whenever he attempted to think beyond that, his exhausted mind petered out.

When the cab pulled up to the dock, Schofield paid the driver and instructed that she wait. She grinned when she was handed an extra $20 for her trouble. She pulled out a well-worn paperback book from her glove compartment, flipped on the dome light, and got comfortable. Schofield exited the cab and walked up to a chain-link gate at the edge of the fence that surrounded the marina. He punched the four-digit entry code into the keypad. His hand a bit shaky, he managed to unlock the gate on his second try.

Thick wooden planks creaked under his feet as he made his way past a number of smaller, older boats that bumped up against their supports from the light breeze that drifted in from the ocean. The half-moon that beamed through an opening in the clouds above offered hope of a fresh start, and for a moment, Schofield began to feel as though he had already broken free of his master's chains.

He mused about what kind of life he could now lead. The man he had killed had stayed off the grid for thirty years, or so he'd been told by the others. What was stopping Schofield from doing the same? He had no family left. Few ties to his past. He could move to the West Coast and hook up with some seafaring outfit that wouldn't put any more effort into scrutinizing his background than they did with the illegal immigrants from Mexico they hired.

How hard would Albano try to find him? Would he eventually realize that, when the police never showed up at his door, the man who'd killed Jack Slate had no more reason to spill his guts to the authorities than the guy he had done the job for? It made sense in Schofield's mind.

"Time heals all wounds," he whispered, leaping from the pier to the stern of the yacht.

He pulled a set of keys from his pocket and unlocked the sliding glass door at the rear of the cabin. He stepped inside the pitch black compartment and slid the door shut. His heart stopped when he detected a strong scent of aftershave.

The beam of a flashlight suddenly switched on, lighting up his face and forcing him to wince. He gasped.

"Marty" came Blake's eerily confident voice from behind the glare. "Whut a'ya doin' out so late? I thought ya liked to turn in early."

Though Schofield couldn't see Blake's hand, nor much of the rest of his body, he was certain he was holding a gun.

Chapter 18

Quammen had known about the altercation at the Wicked Scallop the night before, yet he hadn't mentioned it—not after the high-speed chase, and not after Maria's body had been discovered, and that bothered Sean. *Why? Was he cutting me a break, or had he kept it under wraps for another reason?* The questions continued to torment him as he walked along the quiet, darkened shoulder of a lonesome two-lane road.

Sean had found his way onto the road after leaving the forest behind Sunshine's. Some signs had pointed him in the direction of the highway, though it had yet to present itself. A couple of cars had made their way down the drive since then, their headlights carving through the mist. Each time, Sean left the road until they passed, fearful they'd have police markings on their doors. He planned on now keeping a low profile until he was sure who was on his side and who wasn't.

Despite Maria's fear of getting in trouble with her boss at work, Sean no longer believed it had something to do with her death. Pride had compelled Grady to keep his mouth shut, and Rockline seemed as clueless to the incident as he did to life in general.

If not for what Sean had learned about Quammen, he might have been ready to accept once and for all the coroner's conclusion that Maria had taken her own life. But the police chief's secrecy had to mean something. Until Sean could iron out a logical explanation, he was no longer willing to regard Quammen as an ally—even an unhelpful one.

The presence of the redhead from Albano's yacht was a separate curiosity—one that nagged at Sean as he scratched an itch at the base of his skull. The man couldn't have followed him and Warner to Sunshine's. He had already been inside, sitting at the bar, when Sean entered. It was certainly possible that the man was just another patron who'd wanted to watch naked women on a Saturday night, but the fact that he'd paid off the bouncer to avoid presenting an ID suggested otherwise. So did the cap that he had pulled way down over his head. Like Quammen, he had something to hide.

Sean's mind churned like a computer's hard drive as he gazed at a streetlamp in the distance. Before long, he could make out a section of the highway it illuminated. A car quickly flew by and another passed in the opposite direction. In the briefest of moments—for a reason Sean couldn't explain—his exhausted mind imagined the two cars colliding with each other and exploding into flames. As if his consciousness had suddenly been freed of its bonds, he found himself allowing for the possibility that the deaths of his father and Maria might somehow—in some way—be connected.

The notion unsettled Sean's stomach and he drew a deep breath from his lungs. He stopped walking as his mind sought for clarity.

What if his father's death hadn't come from him having simply stolen from the wrong person? What if it was part of a bigger scenario—one that included Maria? Between where Jack Slate's body was found and the redhead turning up at Sunshine's, there was a common thread that led back to Anthony Albano.

Maybe Quammen was well aware of that thread, even before Maria's death. Maybe he had been tight-lipped about her because he feared Sean pulling on that thread and unraveling his father's murder investigation. There was a much worse possibility, one that brought a chill to Sean's spine: Quammen being part of the fabric himself.

Sean had assumed back at the beach that Albano had learned that he was Jack Slate's son from the neighbors next door. But what if Albano had been told it by Quammen—one of the few other people who knew? The notion seemed farfetched, but Sean couldn't bring himself to discount it.

Once he reached the highway, he thought about raising his thumb to try and hitch a ride back to his motel. In the dead of the night, however, he'd more likely get the attention of a cop than an average citizen willing to offer a guy looking like him a lift. It wasn't worth the risk.

To the north, there was a bright yellow, lit-up sign. It stood tall and proud, just off the road. When Sean squinted, he made out large red numbers below it. It was a gas station, and it looked open. He made his way toward it, keeping far to the side of the highway so as not to be noticed from the road. There were plenty of trees and shrubs to disappear behind if needed.

When he was within a hundred yards from the gas station, he watched a yellow taxicab pull up to the front of the building. It came to a stop underneath the lit structure that sheltered the pump area.

"Holy shit," Sean uttered in astonishment. He couldn't remember ever having been the beneficiary of such good luck.

His pace evolved into a swift jog, and he moved closer to the road so that he was less likely to trip over something in the dark. As he drew nearer to the gas station, the details of the cab began to sharpen. There was someone at the helm, but no passenger. The triangular-shaped sign mounted to its roof was lit up, which meant the driver was available. This brought the corners of Sean's mouth into a curl as air rushed in and out of his lungs.

Just then, a figure emerged from the shadows at the side of the building. It was a man, dressed in dark colors. He jogged over to the cab, and when his body fell under the bright light of the shelter, Sean spotted a head of disheveled red hair.

"Son of a bitch!" he grunted, eyes widening.

It was the man who'd run out of Sunshine's—the man from the yacht. He hadn't left the strip bar in a car. He'd done so on foot.

Sean clenched his teeth and accelerated into a full sprint. The redhead disappeared inside the cab, shutting the door behind him.

"Hey!" Sean yelled, frantically waving his arms to get the attention of the driver.

The cab pulled forward, flipped a U-turn in the parking lot, and made its way back to the highway. Sean continued to shout and wave, but knew he was virtually invisible in the dark. He kept running, putting as little space between him and the car as he could before it took off down the highway in the opposite direction.

"4Y54!" he spewed out with a gust of breath. The cab may have gotten away, but its dispatch number hadn't.

His momentum dwindled to a halt. He leaned forward, braced his hands on his knees, taking in wind. He repeated the number aloud over and over, desperate to remember it. He noticed no other cars in the lot as he hurried over to the entrance of the building's small convenience store. He pulled his shirt down, making certain the gun he'd taken from the bar was not exposed.

A ding sounded as he pushed open the pair of doors. Inside, he was welcomed with two short aisles of junk food and a wall fridge stocked with pop and energy drinks. The refrigerator hummed loudly, as if it wasn't working quite right. By the register, about twenty-five rows of lottery tickets dangled sloppily from the ceiling, but no cashier was present.

"Hello?" Sean said as a head popped up from behind the back aisle. It belonged to a brown-skinned man with short, black hair.

"Yes sir!" the man replied enthusiastically in what sounded like a Middle Eastern accent. "How may I help you?"

"4Y54!" Sean said, pointing at the man.

The man's eyebrows bent inward. "Excuse me, sir? For wife?"

"4Y54," Sean said again, shaking his head and walking over to the register counter. "I need a pen. Do you have a pen?"

"Yes sir!" The clerk said, quickly making his way down the aisle and intercepting Sean in front of the counter. He retrieved a ballpoint pen from the front pocket of his colorful uniform shirt.

Sean took it and wrote the cab's number in large lettering along his forearm. The clerk seemed amused by the display, a wide grin stretched across his face.

"The man that just left here in a cab," Sean said. "Do you know him?"

"The man who left?"

"Yes. Just now," Sean said, his voice now rising. "In a taxicab. Do you know who he is?"

"I'm sorry, sir. I did not see this man. This was in the parking lot just now?" The clerk's grin didn't falter.

"Yes," Sean answered in frustration, considering only then that the redhead may have never actually entered the store. "Forget it. How many cab companies are there in this town?"

"Taxicab companies?"

"Yes!" Sean groaned.

"Just one," he said, holding up a long index finger. "Brookside."

"And they use yellow-colored cabs, right?"

"Yes sir. Do you need a cab?"

Sean glared at him for a moment. "Yes. I *do* need a cab. Can I use your phone?"

The clerk nodded and made his way around to the backside of the register counter. He pulled a phone from the wall and plopped it down on the counter in front of Sean.

"I have the number here," said the clerk, his eyes straining as they examined a messy collage of Post-It notes, business cards, and fliers on the wall behind him. "Just a moment . . . Yes!"

The clerk punched in the number, and a minute later, Sean was talking to a dispatcher and requesting cab number "4Y54." When asked why he needed that particular cab, Sean struggled for a moment before stating, awkwardly, that he was fond of the driver. He was told that the cab was currently working a fare, and that a different driver could pick him up sooner. Sean declined, saying he would wait.

"Mind if I make another call?" Sean asked after hanging up the receiver.

"Is it a local call?" the clerk asked.

Sean glared at him. "Yes."

"Okay then," said the clerk. He picked up the receiver and held his fingers to the buttons. "What's the number?"

 Sean looked straight ahead. "Uh . . . One. Three zero three—"

"That's not a local number," the man interrupted, shaking his head. His smile was as wide as ever, which Sean found disconcerting under the circumstances. "There is a public payphone outside, sir. You can make long distance calls from it."

"Fine," Sean said, grumbling. "Can you make change?"

"Yes."

Sean reached into his back pocket for his wallet.

"If you buy something."

Sean squared his jaw, glaring right through the man. He was half tempted to pull out his gun and wave it in the man's face, just to see if he could wipe the smile from his face. Instead, he bit his lip, pointed to a lottery ticket, and laid out some bills. Before heading back through the doors, he rubbed the gray off of his ticket with a penny from the coin cup next to the register. He won nothing.

After a couple of flubbed tries on the payphone outside, Sean finally heard ringing. Upon the third ring, there was a click and then the loud, familiar wails of his niece exploding through the receiver.

"D?" Sean asked, holding the phone back a couple of inches from his face.

"Hello?" he heard his brother-in-law say. His voice was muffled but the stress in his tone was unmistakable. "Is anyone there?"

"Gary. This is Sean. Is everything all right?"

"What? Who's this?"

Sean closed his eyes and shook his head. "Sean!" he shouted

with such volume that the clerk inside probably heard him. "Your brother-in-law." He swatted at a bug buzzing near his face.

"All right, I'm hearing you better now," said Lumbergh.

"What the hell's happening?"

"Ah. Ashley keeps waking up. I'm letting Diana sleep. What do you need?"

"Listen. There's some weird stuff going on out here. How much do you know about this Quammen guy?"

Lumbergh sighed. "He's a chief of police, Sean. He's the guy in charge. I hope you're not giving him any shit."

"Don't worry about that. What do you know about him?"

"As much as either of us needs to know, which isn't a whole hell of a lot. He's a public servant. A man doing his job." Lumbergh hesitated before continuing, raising his voice to carry over Ashley's crying. "What the hell's happening, Sean? You're just supposed to be picking up Jack's body."

"Just . . ." Sean began. "Just look into him for me, okay? See if there's any dirt on the guy. Any controversies or—"

"Why? Are you trying to blackmail him or something?"

"Gary, Jesus. Just shut up, okay? I'm out here for the family, and I'm not asking you to do a whole hell of a lot. Just look into him. Also, some guy named Anthony Albano. He's some rich asshole who owns a home out here. I think he's from somewhere up the coast."

Ashley suddenly let out a piercing cry so loud that Sean nearly dropped the receiver. He then heard Diana's voice. She was angry and began trading barbs with her husband. The details of the argument were mostly muted. Lumbergh was probably holding the phone to his chest. A few seconds later, Ashley's voice tapered off.

"Gary?" Sean asked.

When Lumbergh answered, his tone was sober and direct. "Quammen and Albano. I'll look into them. We finished?"

"Geco bullets. Did you find out what they are?"

"Oh God. Why, Sean?"

"What do you mean, why? Didn't you get my message?"

"I got the message and I researched the bullets. Why do you need Geco bullets?"

"I don't need them. I just want to know what they are. Who uses them? Is it a state secret or something?"

The line went silent. Sean could picture Lumbergh pulling at his hair while deliberating whether or not to answer his question. He finally did.

"It's a very rare German ammunition. Metal piercing."

"German? Is it only made in Germany?"

"Made there, but sold exclusively through two distributors in the United States. They're expensive as hell, and they serve no practical purpose—"

"Where are the two distributors?"

"Why does it matter? It's a stupid purchase, Sean."

"They're not for me, dammit! They're the bullets my father was shot with. Now where are the distributors?"

When Lumbergh spoke after a lengthy pause, his voice was calmer. "California and New Jersey."

"New Jersey," said Sean, narrowing his eyes and nodding his head. The Cadillac parked in front of Anthony Albano's house had a Jersey license plate.

Chapter 19

"Some big shot from up north," Sean grumbled in the dark beside the gas station, recalling the phrase Albano had used to describe himself back on the beach.

Albano was from the same state where the bullet that had shot Sean's father had been purchased. Though it was far from proof that he was behind Jack's death, Sean was convinced that pursuing the "big shot" was the right course of action. He'd start with the redhead, who wasn't as well-protected as his boss.

Before hanging up the phone, Sean had told Lumbergh not to bother trying to reach him at his motel. He planned on moving to a different one—one outside of Quammen's jurisdiction and outside of everyone else's radar.

Within ten minutes, the cab had returned. It crept around the side of the gas pumps until Sean made himself visible. He verified that it was the right one, reading "4Y54" from above its roof. The cab pulled up to Sean, stopping just a few inches from him.

Through the rolled-down driver's side window appeared the dark, round face of a woman who looked in her early forties. A broad smile formed below the dreadlocks that sprouted from her scalp like a well-watered potted plant. She assessed Sean, her eyes moving up and down his frame.

"Mmm-mmm-mmm," she said in a deep, sassy voice. Her head moved in circles like a slow-moving record player. "So y'all the tall drink of water that requested me?"

Sean nodded, taken back.

"Well, get in, baby. I'll getcha where ya need to go." Her smile shifted into more of a pucker, flaunting a coat of bright red lipstick. Her long, thick eyelashes fluttered.

He snorted and shook his head as he pulled open the back door of the cab and slid along the worn vinyl seat. To keep from having to bury his knees in his chest because of the tight quarters, he sat at an angle. The scent of incense was in the air.

The woman twisted her large body around to meet Sean's eyes again. She folded her arms in front of her across the top of the backrest. "Now, I know we've never met before, sugar. I'd remember y'all." She held his gaze for a couple of uneasy seconds before continuing. "So how is it that I, specifically, can help?"

It wasn't clear whether the query was purely business or part innuendo, but Sean decided it was best just to cut to the chase. "You're right. We've never met. I need you to take me to wherever it was you took your last fare."

Her face stiffened. She leaned back. "Wait a minute. Are ya following that quiet, red-haired man?"

He hesitated before responding. "Yes, I am."

"'Cause this is exactly where I picked *him* up, too."

"I know. I saw."

She squared her chin and shook her head in protest. "No, no, no. Huh-uh," she said. "I'm not supposed to do that, not unless a cop is askin'. A passenger's destination is their own business. Y'all a cop?"

"Yes," he said immediately.

She tilted her head to the side, her eyes thin with disbelief. Sean could nearly hear a BS detector sounding off in her brain.

He sighed. "Okay, I'm not a cop, but this is part of a police investigation." He took a deep breath before continuing. "Listen. My father was murdered—just a few days ago—and the guy you picked up is somehow involved with it. I'm sure of it."

Her face loosened. Before he could continue, she cut him off. "Well, then, sugar . . . why don't y'all just call the cops?"

He clenched his jaw, half regretting he'd been so candid. "Because I don't trust them."

"Oh, I don't blame ya there, sugar," she replied. "These boys put themselves on a power trip 'round here."

He knew all about that. "What's your name?"

She seemed to think it over before answering. "Lakeisha."

"Lakeisha, I know you don't have any reason to help me, but I need to talk to that man. It's very important."

Her eyes softened and her head lowered. She looked up at him as if she was peering through a gateway into his soul. When she finally spoke, her voice was soft and tender. "My daddy's dead, too."

He frowned, not sure what direction the conversation was headed.

"I'm gonna help y'all. Awright?" She spun forward and popped the transmission into drive, accelerating so fast as she turned the steering wheel that Sean's face nearly collided with the window at his side.

Within a second or two they were flying down the highway with Sean's large back plastered to his seat. Lakeisha twisted a radio knob, and suddenly the loud guitar wailings of a Lenny Kravitz song were bouncing around the interior.

"I knew it!" she shouted over the music. "I knew there was something wrong with that ginger biscuit. He wouldn't look me in the eye, you know. Just kept his head low. Acted like he was mindin' his business and all, but I knew. I knew he was hidin' something."

He grabbed the back of her seat and battled against the force of gravity to pull himself forward. "Where was it you took him? Was it a big house on Beach Bridge Road?" He hoped the answer was no. He wanted the redhead outside of his boss's fortress.

"No, no, no, sugar. I took him to a private marina down south. He's gotta have a boat tied up there somewhere. He also has a friend with him."

His eyebrows bristled. "Bald black dude?"

"No. A black and blue dude!" she quipped.

"What do you mean?"

"The guy's all beat up. Some white boy who looks like he went a couple rounds with Lennox Lewis."

Sean thought back to the coroner's office and the bruises shaped like a row of teeth across his father's knuckles. He pulled the revolver from the back of his pants and asked Lakeisha to flip on the dome light. She did, and when he checked the gun's barrel, he discovered only three live rounds; two had been fired off by the bouncer at the strip bar.

"What are you doin' back there?" asked Lakeisha, craning her head over her shoulder.

He ignored the question, slyly sliding the gun back in his pants. "Listen," he said, his voice loud to overcome the music. "When we get there, I don't want you sticking around, okay?"

"Oh, I don't mind waiting, sugar," she shouted back, her eyes connecting with his in the rearview mirror. "I won't even charge you for it."

"I'm not worried about that," he said. "I'm worried about you. I don't know what's going to go down, and it's best if innocent bystanders don't get mixed up in things."

She let out a loud laugh. "Sugar, I ain't that innocent, I'll tell y'all that right now."

He smirked. "You know what I mean. Just drop me off at the closest street. I don't want them to see us coming. Then just take off, all right?"

"I'll tell ya what," she said. "I'll do as y'all say, but I'm gonna give y'all my cell number. This is my personal line. If you need me to come back, just give me a call." She scribbled down a number on a sheet of paper and handed it back to him.

"Will do, Lakeisha. Thank you."

"And if y'all want to give me call for any other reason, y'all do that too, awright, sugar?" Her long eyelashes batted in the mirror.

Sean shook his head, a soft grin twisting across his face. "I will."

He sank back in his seat, and his mind began working on a plan for when they reached the marina. He'd have to wait until he saw the layout before deciding on a point of entry, but it was how he would confront the two men that clung to the forefront of his mind.

"Do you know which boat he's on?" asked Lakeisha.

"Yeah. *The Closer.*"

Chapter 20

"I-I-I was just going out for a walk," Schofield sputtered nervously, his eyes squinting from the flashlight's sharp glare.

"A walk?" said Blake, his voice chilling from the darkness of the yacht's hull.

"Yes. Yes, sir."

"That was one hell of a long walk."

Schofield took a step backward. Immediately, the door he'd just come through slid open. He swung around and saw the figure of another man enter the room.

"He came here in a cab, Mr. Blake," said the man. It was Eddie, Blake's favorite stooge. "I tipped the driver and sent her on her way. Told her old Marty here had changed his mind."

Schofield visibly cringed.

"Did he leave anything in the cab?" asked Blake.

"No. I asked," answered Eddie.

Blake's light slid up to Eddie's face for a moment, revealing two black eyes and a taped nose—souvenirs from the pummeling Jack Slate had given him on the beach that night. It was no wonder Albano had kept the thug in hiding ever since. His appearance would have surely struck anyone investigating what had happened as suspicious.

His escape route blocked, Schofield turned back to Blake.

"Listen. I . . . I can explain," pled Schofield.

"Whut's to explain, my man?" Blake asked. "I tell ya t'keep ya head low, and ya take some little joy ride in t'town, doing God knows whut. Maybe ya gonna tell me that ya just wanted to know whut it felt like t'be driven around by someone else for a change."

"I didn't talk to the police, Mr. Blake. I swear." Schofield's pulse was racing, anxiety crippling his body and making it hard to breathe.

Blake chuckled. "Oh, I know ya didn't talk to the cops."

How could Blake know that? Schofield thought briefly. But he had more pressing matters to consider.

His mind shifted to his duffle bag. It was somewhere on the boat, but he couldn't remember where he'd left it. His gun was inside. Whether it was on the captain's chair or hanging on a knob in the coat closet, it might as well have been a mile away.

He began to feel faint. He took a step back, but Eddie shoved him forward with what felt like the muzzle of a gun against his back.

"Where were ya headed?" asked Blake. "Where was that cab driver gonna take ya?"

Schofield struggled to come up with an answer that wouldn't make matters worse. "Come on, man," he whimpered, his eyes still squinting from the flashlight. "I did what I was asked to do, didn't I? Slate didn't get away that night."

"Oh, that's true," Blake replied almost amicably. "And I'm sure Mr. Albano was real appreciative of that, just like he was with your help with that clean up the next night. Other than losin' track of Slate's dead ass on the surfboard, ya did good."

Eddie chuckled from behind Schofield. The gesture brought a smile to Blake's face.

"I mean," Blake continued, "the cinder blocks. Figurin' out the tides and the no-wake zones, or whatever they're called. I think Eddie even picked up some sailin' pointers from ya. All in all, we're pretty damned satisfied. And we feel awfully confident that the bodies of that bitch and Captain Hot Tub are never goin' t'be found."

"Then what?" asked Schofield, shaking his head. "Why are you two here?"

Blake said nothing, seemingly relishing the display of Schofield's shaking body and moist eyes.

Schofield spoke again. "Are you gonna shoot me? Right here, right now?" His voice quivered. "Who's gonna drive the yacht?"

"Marty, Marty, Marty." The words left Blake's mouth in a patronizing manner. "No one's gonna shoot ya. Mr. Albano doesn't want a mess in his yacht. But we do appreciate ya pickin' up more cinder blocks than ya needed ta. It helps us out. And I think Eddie's now got the hang of the yacht."

Schofield suddenly felt something slip past his hair. Before he could blink, he felt a violent jerk and then immense pressure around his throat. His eyes bulged as he was pulled backwards into the chest of the man behind him. His hands went for his neck, his fingers trying to wedge themselves under whatever was cutting into his throat. With no luck, he tried to swing his elbow into the ribcage of his attacker. Instead, Eddie dropped down to his back, taking Schofield with him.

Blake laughed. It was a deep, maniacal laugh—one that carried all the way up from the pit of his stomach. He kept the flashlight trained on Schofield's face as if not wanting to miss one second of the man's life being stripped from his body.

Eddie gripped Schofield's waist with his knees and hauled back even further. Schofield's arms and legs flailed wildly. His foot struck the leg of a barstool, tipping it over. A sick wheezing sound whistled from between his lips as his face turned the color of his hair. Blake's hideous laughing grew louder and louder until it was all that Schofield could hear or feel, occupying the last of his dwindling senses.

Chapter 21

Sean watched Lakeisha's taillights shrink into the dark until her cab hung a right and completely disappeared from view. Only then did he jog across the street—gun in his hand—to a chain-link fence beside the open entrance of the marina parking lot. Pushing his way through shrubs and stumbling across a large puddle of water he didn't see, he entered the gravel lot. Staying low, he took cover behind a white commercial van.

He dropped to a knee and peered around the fender of the vehicle. There were only two other cars in the lot, meaning that few if any of the docked boats had people living on them. While the lot itself was barely lit, two intense lamps hung directly above a closed gate at the center of a secondary chain-link fence that separated the cars from the boats. Beyond the fence and in the light of the moon, he could make out the silhouettes of three or four masts pointed to the sky. They towered above the fence line.

Beside the gate was a security booth large enough to host a single guard, but it was empty and unlit. Sean looked for video cameras mounted on either the booth or fence. He saw none, but that didn't mean there weren't any. What was visible was a large keypad at the center of the gate, which was most certainly locked.

Sean gazed along the fence, searching for a dark area to climb over. His best shot seemed to be a spot to the left where the lot met with packed dirt. There, the ground was angled downward along with the fence. He stood up and slid to the back of the van. His heart jumped when he spotted another car parked just yards behind the van. It was a dark Cadillac.

Sean wrapped himself back behind the van, straightened his arms before him, and pointed his pistol directly at the Cadillac's windshield. He searched for movement and listened for sound. Neither came. It looked as though no one was inside, but he kept his gun aimed on the windshield as he walked steadily toward the car. His eyes quickly lowered to the front bumper. New Jersey plates. It was the same car that had been parked outside of Albano's house. Now it was tucked neatly out of sight from anyone entering or leaving the parking lot. He glanced through the windows, finding no one. He then placed has hand on the vehicle's hood. The engine didn't feel warm. The car had probably been there for at least an hour.

As he jogged over to the darkened area of the fence, his gaze flickered to the gate. Once he reached the railing, he was well shadowed. He listened for a moment, hearing only water from the ocean slapping gently against wood and the jostling and creaking of hulls. When Sean grabbed a handful of steel and placed the tip of his foot through a diamond in the netting, the mesh at the bottom of the fence caved inwards. The dirt at the bottom of the fence had eroded away from high tides and weather. Sean realized that he could more discretely pull himself under the fence rather than over.

The cobweb of metal scraped his face as he pulled himself under it, but he made it to the other side easy enough. "Shit security," he grumbled.

Sticking his gun back in his pants, he trudged through wet dirt and washed-in debris along the uneven shoreline. He then climbed up the lower half of a thick pillar and slid under the railing onto a wooden platform.

A sudden, loud screech and a heavy thrashing noise made Sean freeze in place and sent his heart galloping. He'd awoken a large seabird, whose wings flapped noisily to carry it into the night. He stayed still until he was convinced the noise hadn't alerted anyone.

Tied to several horn cleats beside him was a large, weather-beaten sailboat. It was white with a bare mast that looked, from his vantage point, as though it reached high into the heavens. He grabbed his gun and pulled himself along the planks with his elbows for a few yards. He then cautiously climbed to his feet and made his way down the bumpy platform to the center of the marina—a wide wooden pier with a couple dozen slots of secured boats on each side.

The surrounding sea crafts were of varying shapes and sizes. Their bows all pointed inward. At every third or so access point was a lit colonial-style street lamp, built to pay homage to another era.

Sean knew that he was exposed as he moved steadily down the walkway. The vulnerability made him uncomfortable, but there was little he could do to minimize the risk, other than keep a sharp eye open and a finger on the trigger.

Boards creaked below his boots as he edged himself forward. Every nautical instrument around him bumped and rattled from the water's current. He had to discipline himself not to fixate on each sound; instead he listened for voices. He had just about reached the end of the pier when he heard one. It came with a light breeze, just as the pier's last lamp cast clarity on a large bow reading *The Closer*.

The stately yacht was even larger than it had looked from the beach, the length of its thick hull taking up nearly the full stretch of pier that ran perpendicular to the main walkway. On the side of the boat were good-sized, horizontal windows that spread across the extent of the bridge. They were high up off the water and blocked with curtains, making any attempt to peek through the glass futile.

A light from inside the hull projected shifting shadows across the curtains. At first, Sean believed the glow came from a television screen, but when a circular beam fell directly against the window for a moment, he deemed the source to be a flashlight.

He hunched low, worried at first that he might have been detected. When the voice returned, followed by a second, he decided he hadn't been. He couldn't make out what was being said, but the conversation was definitely between two men. One spoke with confidence. The other one sounded nervous, even panicked.

Suddenly, there was a loud thud from inside the yacht. It was quickly followed by the sounds of a violent scuffling and objects crashing against other objects. When boisterous laughter erupted from behind the walls, Sean decided that the clamor inside would keep him from being heard boarding the boat.

He maneuvered to the stern and hopped onto its wooden deck. With his gun pointed forward, he negotiated his way around a couple of deck chairs and a stacked pair of cinder blocks to a short staircase that led to a sliding glass door. He kept to its side, resting his shoulder against its rail before angling his head to glance inside.

Other than the bright glare of a flashlight angled toward the floor by an unseen figure, the room was completely dark. The man holding the flashlight was the one laughing. His laughter was intensifying.

Sean thought for a moment that those inside were engaged in some kind of game, possibly alcohol-induced. It was only when he made out the silhouettes of two people savagely struggling on the floor did he realize the situation was deadly serious.

The beam of the flashlight suddenly left the men on the floor and jolted straight up to Sean's leering face. The laughter stopped. Sean gasped and swung out of view. Two loud pops fired off from inside the hull, shattering the glass door beside him. Large shards crashed to the deck as smaller shrapnel sprayed Sean's face.

A man's voice belted out a panicked instruction, but Sean's racing adrenaline wouldn't let him decipher it. His instinct told him to return fire, but his conscience pleaded for the unknown person who had been under assault. He didn't understand the situation he'd walked in on, but he knew someone was in trouble aboard Albano's boat. That person might be an ally. Sean wasn't going to fire back until he needed to.

There was frantic movement from inside. The flashlight had gone dark, and furniture was being knocked around as aggressive whispers were exchanged. There was a sick, gasping noise from someone who sounded like they couldn't breathe.

"I've got a gun, assholes!" Sean shouted. "You try and rush me, and I'll make you eat it!" The line had come from a cop show he had watched a while back. He couldn't remember the series or actor, but he'd always liked it.

"Bullshit!" a man from inside yelled out after a couple of seconds. "People with guns don't slap their jaws about havin' one! They fuckin' use 'em!" The man sounded like Titus Blake, but Sean couldn't be sure.

"Then come out, tough guy!" Sean yelled back. "Let's see those big balls of yours slide right on down these steps. I'll shoot them off for you!"

There was more shuffling inside, more whispering. Unfamiliar with the design of the boat, Sean couldn't be sure that he was covering the only access point in or out. At any moment, one of the occupants could pop out from the side or roof of the boat and lay in a shot.

The safe play would have been to abandon whoever had been attacked inside—to fire off a couple of rounds in the air and then bolt down the pier all the way to the parking lot. But that wasn't who he was. That wasn't the man his uncle had taught him to be.

A loud, disoriented voice suddenly sounded out from behind Sean, off in the distance. "What the hell's going on out here?" It sounded like a woman—an older woman from somewhere inside the marina, on another boat.

"Stay inside and call the police!" Sean yelled, twisting his head and cupping his hand to his mouth.

"What?" she yelled back.

"Dammit. Call the police!" Even with his suspicions about Quammen, getting the police on the scene was the safest gamble.

When loud footsteps stormed toward the demolished cabin door, Sean took a brisk step back. He straightened his arms, set his jaw, and prepared to fire.

"Don't shoot!" wailed a raspy, desperate voice. A male figure in dark clothing crashed through what was left of the door. One of his hands was wrapped around his throat, while the other floundered frantically through glass and splintered wood.

Sean held his fire, but the men inside didn't. Blasts rang out, lighting up the interior of the boat. The man's body buckled. He cried out in pain, falling from the stairs and crashing down to the deck on his stomach.

Sean snarled and swung his arm inside the doorway, squeezing off a shot. He would have fired another, but he knew he only had two bullets left. He swung back out of the entry, hoping the proof that he had a gun would give them pause.

"What's going on?" the woman in the distance screeched like a hawk.

Sean guessed the she was drunk, dumb, or half-deaf to not grasp how dangerous the situation was.

The downed man on the deck was spasming in pain, a bullet or two almost certainly lodged somewhere in his back. Though he was lying lower than the cabin area, he was a sitting duck for a clean shot from inside.

Sean had only two shots left, with at least two assailants inside. He had to be smart with his ammunition. He also knew the injured man was in bad shape and prone to a kill shot. Sean bit his lip and curved his arm inside the hull, firing off another round. He then lunged low and latched his free hand onto the collar of the writhing man's shirt. Clenching it in his fist, he dragged the man across the deck on his side. More shots popped off from inside the cabin.

Something shattered across Sean's shoulder just as he crossed back out of the line of fire. Burning pain stretched across his flesh.

He didn't feel as though he'd been shot, but perhaps cut by a chunk of wall blown off by a bullet. Whatever the damage, it could wait.

Without warning, a broad, blinding beam of light suddenly lit up the back deck of the yacht. Its intensity burned across the side of Sean's face. He and the wounded man were totally exposed under its glare. In that moment, Sean got a quick, clear look at the head of the man he was trying to save. He had red hair that sprouted out from his scalp like thick strings from a mop. It was the man he'd come to the boat to find. Blood shined along the back of the redhead's shirt. It was spreading out quickly and pooling across the deck.

Sean turned his head toward the bright light, showing his teeth as he squinted. It was coming from the top deck of a boat docked not far down the main pier. There was someone manning it and waving their hand around. Sean could make out little more than the person's silhouette.

"What's going on? What the hell's happening down there?" It was the same loud female voice as before. She was the one directing the spotlight.

"Turn that fucking light off! You're gonna get us killed!" Sean roared. "Call the police! Now!"

A shot fired out from what felt like the side of the yacht.

The woman's head jolted to the side at a sick angle, dark spray filling the air in front of the light as she tumbled backward on unbalanced footing. She collapsed out of sight.

"Jesus Christ!" Sean gasped. He popped his head around the side of the yacht just long enough to see a hand with a pistol disappearing back inside a small window along its hull. The men weren't planning on leaving any witnesses.

Sean didn't know if there was anyone else within earshot hearing the commotion. He didn't remember seeing any nearby homes or open businesses when the cab driver had dropped him off. All he knew was that he had one bullet left in his gun and it wasn't going to take the men inside much longer to figure out that there was a reason he was using his firearm sparingly.

The redhead rolled onto his back, a wheezing noise filtering through his bloodied mouth. "I'm sorry," he whispered, looking up at Sean with a quivering lip and glazed over eyes. "They made me do it. They made me shoot him." The words came out like a deathbed confession.

"My dad?" said Sean, glaring back at him.

When Sean heard a noise inside, he turned his attention back to the cabin. Through his peripheral vision, he noticed the redhead nodding in reply.

"Why? Why did it happen?"

"He . . ." the man struggled to speak. His eyes shifted back and forth from a pair of cinder blocks to a coiled chain that sat on the deck beside him. "He saw them kill her. Kill her . . . and the pool guy."

"What do you mean?" Sean said. "My dad *was* the pool guy."

"No. Other one . . ."

A confused frown stretched Sean's face. At first he thought the man had lost too much blood and didn't know what he was saying. That's when he remembered the name Bobby. The little neighbor girl, Nicola, had mentioned that he was Albano's pool boy. She had said he was a friend of Sean's father. Blake said that Bobby had been fired, but what if he hadn't been? What if he'd been killed?

"You said *her*. What woman are you talking about?" asked Sean, knowing the injured man had to have been referring to someone other than Maria.

"The . . . the Goddess," he moaned. His face twisted in pain as the words left his mouth.

"Shit," Sean said, shaking his head.

The man had to be delusional. His words made no sense. Sean had seen Albano's trophy wife alive and well just yesterday—days after his father had been killed. Though the redhead wasn't of coherent mind, the real story of what had happened was locked away somewhere inside his skull. Sean couldn't just take off and leave him for dead. He needed to get the man to safety, get him some treatment, and hear his full account.

There was a crash from inside the cabin. It was close. The men were getting braver. The scent of Aqua Velva caught Sean's nose.

If Sean tried to make his way down the pier the same way he'd come, Blake and whoever else was inside would likely pick him off from the side of the yacht, like they had the woman on the other boat. Her spotlight still lit up the scene, leaving them with little visual cover. The other end of the walkway spread out past the stern of the yacht led only to water.

Sean took a breath and made a decision. "You're fucking with the wrong guy, assholes!" he shouted in the most intimidating voice he could muster. "You *want* some pain? I'm gonna *give* you some pain!"

When Sean heard the men shuffling for cover inside, he spun and stretched his gun out toward the spotlight on the other boat. Closing one eye to aim, he pulled the trigger. The recoil rushed through his hand. Glass shattered and sparks flew above the deck of the other boat. The spotlight went dark. Sean shoved his gun in his pants and latched both hands around the front of the redhead's shirt. With a loud grunt, he yanked the man up to his feet and then over his shoulder.

Blind return-fire whizzed by them as Sean climbed out of the boat and slogged his way to the left, away from the main walkway. The positioning of the yacht would give him some cover, but only for a few seconds. He could hear the men inside shouting at each other as they grappled to get a bearing on where their adversaries had fled. The redhead whimpered in pain as his fractured body bounced on Sean's shoulder with each lunge forward.

When Sean heard something drop along the planks behind him, he feared at first that it was the close footsteps of a pursuer. A hand-sweep determined that it was his pistol. It had fallen from his pants, but it didn't matter. He kept moving, knowing an empty gun would do him no good.

He saw the outline of the platform, but just barely. When he could see the dim reflection of moonlight along the water just a few feet in front of him, he hoisted the redhead down in front of his chest, as if he were holding him like a sleeping baby. Sean dropped to his butt and baseball-slid off the edge of the pier into the water.

There was a splash, but it wasn't loud enough to grab the distressed gunmen's attention. Sean felt the burn of saltwater along his shoulder. His boots quickly filled up with water weight and he slid them off with his feet, letting them sink. Twisting his body so that he could float on his back, he wrapped his arms around the redhead, who was now motionless. He pinned the man's back against his chest with one arm, while extending his other to scull them away from the pier. Sean kicked his feet under water. As he did, he felt shallow breath against his neck from the man's mouth.

Just outside the yacht back on the pier, the flashlight was back on. Its beam swung quickly back and forth from the other boats in the marina to the open sea on the starboard side of the yacht. The men hadn't figured out where Sean had left the dock.

When the beam spread out in Sean's direction for a moment, he stopped swimming, letting the water calm around him until the light had passed. Once he'd negotiated a couple of slimed-up buoy ropes and put about 300 feet between him and the marina, he began angling himself toward the shore where he spotted the contour of a couple of darkened shacks.

In the distance, a boat engine fired up. It was soon followed by a hideous scraping sound that echoed off the water like fingers on a chalkboard through a loudspeaker. A lethargic chuckle filtered out from between the redhead's lips, the first sign of life he'd exhibited from the moment they'd left the pier.

"Dumb fucks," he mumbled drunkenly, as if he were lost in a dream. "Don't . . . know how to drive . . . the yacht."

"Stay with me," said Sean, leaning back. His legs were tired from kicking, but he kept them pumping as best he could. "We'll get you to a hospital . . . get you talking to the police."

"No," he whispered, his head shifting ever so slightly. "Don't trust . . . police."

"Why?" Sean asked aggressively. "Is Quammen in bed with Albano?"

The redhead didn't answer.

"Come on, man." Sean jiggled the redhead's body to try to wake him up. "Why shouldn't I trust the police?"

Only silence.

Chapter 22

S itting in sopping wet clothes on a dark, breezy beach next to the dead body of a man whose name he didn't know, Sean's limbs shivered uncontrollably. With his arms crossed in front of his chest and his legs drawn up against them, he stared at the man lying across from him on the shore.

The man had murdered his father. He had robbed Sean of answers to questions that had tormented him for thirty years. Sean wanted to hate him, but he couldn't bring himself to. The guilty truth was that Sean had *wanted* his father dead.

He'd mused over the notion from time to time throughout the years, typically in moments of weakness and despair. It wasn't until he'd learned of his father's death that the sentiment had been validated—no longer confined to a morbid daydream. While his brother-in-law's words washed over him that day beside the reservoir, he'd formulated in his mind a hypothetical scenario: his father still alive—his life and whereabouts still unbeknownst to the family he'd abandoned—or his father remaining dead and his death providing that family with the closure they'd never had.

He had silently decided on closure. Though the choice had already been made for him, it didn't keep him from feeling less guilty now as he peered down at the dead redhead, whose face lay sunken in wet sand. Sean felt like a cohort—an equal partner in shame. The redhead hadn't taken from Sean a lost relationship he had hoped to one day rebuild. What he'd stolen was the knowledge of why his father had left. The truth. To Sean, it still felt like the larger casualty.

Still, it wasn't the redhead who was ultimately to blame. He was just a tool—an instrument. The man responsible was Albano. Sean was sure of that. His men had killed the redhead to try and sever their connection to Jack's murder. Tying up loose ends also had to be the explanation for Sean's motel room being broken into. The thief had to be one of Albano's men. Something in Jack's trunk must have linked back to Albano—a paper trail, perhaps.

It was clear that Albano had to pay for his actions. If there was any truth to the cryptic babbling that had left the redhead's mouth before he'd died, there were other acts of murder beyond Sean's father. They just hadn't been uncovered yet.

The yacht had now been gone for some time. The loud screeching noise that had echoed across the water had come from the portside of the boat dragging its way along the pier. It was sloppy captaining by an inexperienced driver desperate to flee the marina before police officers showed up and found a dead woman on one boat and another's deck stained with blood.

Sean had watched the boat's navigation lights make their way north along the coast. He didn't know the yacht's destination, but he guessed another pier—a spot to regroup. The men had likely split up, one of them leaving in the Cadillac; it would have made sense. It was possible the driver was even casing the area at that very moment, searching the streets and shoreline for Sean.

The authorities never did arrive at the marina. It was obvious that no one had heard and reported the shots. The dead woman's body, as well as the redhead's, would have to wait until daybreak to be found by sailors or beachcombers. Sean wasn't going to call the police. If he did, he might end up as dead as the others. Any grain of trust that he had left in Quammen had vanished upon hearing the redhead's dying words: *Don't trust the police.*

The name Seedorf entered Sean's head. It belonged to the county detective who was the primary investigator in his father's death. Sean had yet to meet him, as Quammen had been serving as a go-between.

Maybe the detective was worth reaching out to directly. Then again, who was to say that Seedorf wasn't exactly who the redhead had warned him about? The web of mistrust was maddening.

Sean crawled over to the dead man's body, his knees sinking in the sand as he did. He took a breath and dug his fingers into the back pocket of the man's pants. He pulled out a Velcro wallet and pried it open. Inside, he felt cash, credit cards, receipts, and other slips of paper. Behind an overlay was a driver's license. He forced it loose. He had trouble making out the name on it in the dark, but he was sure he saw "New Jersey" written in a large font along the top. He returned the card to its sleeve and shoved the wallet into his own pants. It felt wrong stealing from a dead man, but with information in short supply, he deemed it necessary.

In another of the man's pockets, he found a keychain with half a dozen keys. One felt like it went to a car. One maybe a padlock. The others he wasn't sure about. He slid them into his pocket as well. The gash on his shoulder barely hurt now. There was a tear along his shirt where he had been hit with debris, but he didn't seem to be losing any blood—not any more, anyway.

Still shivering, he gave the body one last glance before trudging up to a grassy area above the beach. In the dark, wearing only socks on his feet with holes at the big toes, the ground was cold and hard to negotiate. Still, he chose to stick to the terrain, walking south along the coastline away from the marina. To his left was the beach. To his right, a couple hundred yards away, was a road, possibly the one Lakeisha had brought him in on, though he wasn't sure. Sticking in between the beach and the road, and keeping an eye on both of them, seemed like his best chance of not being seen by the wrong people.

As he made his way down the coast, the occasional sharp rock or shell was met with a muffled profanity. He spent the rest of his time thinking about the people whose murders his father had supposedly witnessed.

Bobby, Albano's pool boy, made sense. His name had certainly startled Blake the other day when Sean had spoken it from atop the Kent's wall. Mention of the Goddess, on the other hand, seemed to have no substance. Sean had seen her alive and in the flesh, literally as well as figuratively. The Grim Reaper must have garbled the redhead's thoughts.

Thick clouds over the skyline to the east began to glow orange from the impending sun. Sean briefly lost himself in the sight. His grumbling stomach brought him back to his senses.

He ducked down in the grass when he spotted a couple of early-morning joggers along the beach—a young man and woman bouncing in tandem in the direction from which he'd come. They'd be the ones to find the redhead if they went a couple more miles. As Sean knelt, waiting for them to pass, he witnessed a pinprick of unfiltered sunlight pop up from the ocean horizon.

"Come on," Sean whispered, repeating the words he recalled an old girlfriend saying on a road trip to Nevada about a year ago. With her delicate hand caressing his shoulder, she'd been gazing out the rear windshield at the birth of a new day in the Utah desert. "Come on."

When a wider ray spread out along the water, Sean let a corner of his mouth curl. "There you are," he said in conjunction with the memory. He remembered the way she'd looked at him after she'd said those words. Her eyes were aflame with the same kind of beauty and promise he now beheld. It wasn't until that moment that he realized just how much he missed her. Lisa.

Lisa was the love of his life. He had met her in the wake of Uncle Zed's death, while in pursuit of his murderer and the murderer's associates. The men had also been responsible for the death of Lisa's husband. Sean and Lisa's brief romance was perhaps doomed from the beginning, having risen from deep loss and doubt. But she was the light that had guided him out of his darkest days. She had awoken him from a dead sleep, and the few months they'd spent together were the happiest of Sean's life.

But that was then. Seemed so long ago.

About thirty minutes later, after squatting behind some tall weeds as a police car raced by on the nearby road with sirens blaring, Sean spotted in the distance another marina clinging to the seaboard. As he came closer over another thirty minutes, he saw that it was much larger than the one he'd left—public, commercialized, and already filling up with people, cars, and boat trailers. Long wooden shops with arched roofs lined a wide boardwalk that separated a parking lot from the harbor. Out in front of them, food vendors were pitching table umbrellas across from fishermen casting their lines. Vehicle-reverse beepers could be heard, along with the occasional honk. Activity was brewing everywhere.

Sean's clothes were still quite wet, unassisted by southern humidity. He worried that if he walked down to the marina, his appearance would make him stick out like a sore thumb. As he got closer, however, he decided that passersby seemed too preoccupied with their own interests to care about how he looked. Many were carrying ice coolers and food; others were jostling long fishing poles. Attire along the boulevard ranged from work overalls to even a few tank tops and swimsuits.

Sean leaned against a tree trunk and pulled off his damp, grungy socks. He rolled them into balls and shoved them into his pockets. He then used his fingers to fix his hair. Deciding that the tear and the dried blood along the shoulder of his shirt shouldn't stand out too much, he walked down a lush green hill to the boardwalk. There, he slid in behind a large, boisterous family. They were all wearing cowboy hats, enormous belt buckles, and loud boots as they hooved their way along the walkway. He kept his head low, subtly glancing around for police officers. The closest thing he saw were a couple of security guards engaged in a light conversation that had them both chuckling. They seemed oblivious to the action around them.

After passing under an arched sign reading "Forenoon Marinas" that spanned the width of the boardwalk, Sean spotted a payphone. It was at the side of a frozen yogurt stand that had yet to open. He went next door and made change at a pastry shop with the purchase of a jelly doughnut. He gulped down the doughnut in four bites and let out a belch as he approached the phone. An elderly woman in a sun visor scowled at him as they passed.

Sean called Lumbergh's office first. When no one picked up, he remembered the time zone difference. He chose not to leave a message and called his home number instead. Surprisingly, there was no answer there either. Someone should have been home that early in the morning, even if it took them a few minutes to roll out of bed and answer. Instead, both attempts went to voicemail. He left a message on the second call.

"Gary, listen. A lot of serious shit went down last night. I don't want to explain it over the phone, but we need to talk. You're the only one I can trust. If you get a call from Quammen today, don't tell him that you heard from me. I don't think he's right. I'm pretty sure he's in cahoots with the people that—"

Beep.

"Dammit!" Sean snarled, slamming the receiver down on the hook. Their voicemail never allowed enough time for a decent message.

He almost called back but didn't have enough coins left to make another long distance call. He could have returned to the pastry shop for more change but decided it didn't make sense to leave another message. What he needed was to speak to his brother-in-law in real time.

He counted through his silver and found that he had enough for at least a local call. He searched through his pockets and wallet looking for Lakeisha's number but didn't find it. He must have lost it in the shootout or in the ocean, and there was no phonebook at the booth for him to be able to look up the cab company. He couldn't find the business card for *Looney Ballooney* either, recalling seconds later that he had torn it up and tossed it in Dusty's face the day before. Fortunately, after a moment and a deep breath, he remembered the number.

"Looney Ballooney Enterprises!" Dusty's enthusiastic voice sung out after the second ring. "Dustin Bouche, owner and operator speak—"

"Hey! Asshole!" Sean angrily interrupted, Dusty's inexplicable cheeriness striking a nerve. "Where the hell did you go last night?"

"May I ask who this is, please?"

"What? Are you fucking kidding me?" Sean clenched his fist.

"Yes, I sure do," Dusty continued in a gamely tone.

"You sure do what? What are you talking about?" He was beside himself, confused by Dusty's jovial demeanor and incensed by the bizarreness of his responses. The last time he'd seen the kid, he had just caved in a bouncer's head. Now he was behaving like a smartass adolescent. Sean nearly exploded on him when his instincts warned him to take a step back. Wariness settled in. "Dusty, is there someone there with you?"

"Absolutely!"

Sean's stomach dropped. He quickly tempered himself. "Is it the police?"

"Mm-hmm."

"Can they hear me right now?"

"Nope. No worries."

"Okay. Listen. Don't let on that you're talking to me. You've already figured that out. Are they arresting you or anything? For last night?"

"Well, I do work on Sundays in the daytime. Just not on Sunday evenings."

Sean squinted. "I don't know what that means."

"No, I sure won't."

"You won't be arrested?"

"Correct."

"Did they come there looking for me?"

"Oh, absolutely!"

Sean rubbed the palm of his hand along his forehead. "Are they going to leave soon, or are they—"

"Oh, anytime. Anytime."

Sean nodded. "Okay. Good. Dusty, do you know of a place called Forenoon Marinas?"

"Sure, I've been there many times. I even worked a party there once."

"Good. Once they leave, I need you to go there and pick me up—out in the main parking lot. Watch for police cars following you. If you spot any, don't come. Go somewhere else. If you're not here in an hour, I'll figure that's what happened."

"Sounds like a plan!"

"All right," Sean said, taking a deep breath and lowering his head. "One more thing. Do you or your mom own a gun?"

Chapter 23

"**M**artin Schofield. Mendham, New Jersey," Sean read off of the redhead's driver's license. From the birth date, Sean found that he was twenty-four years old. "Just a kid."

Schofield's hair was longer in the photo. His freckles were more noticeable too, though Sean had never really gotten a close look at his face. After gazing at the half-grin in the picture, Sean shook his head and returned the license to the wallet. He thumbed through the other items that were tucked away in sleeves. When he found a slip of paper with a handwritten, four-digit number followed by a pound sign, he removed it and shoved it in the front pocket of his pants. With any luck, it was the gate code to Albano's estate.

Sean had used a little of Schofield's cash to buy himself a cheap baseball cap, a T-shirt, and sunglasses from a kiosk vendor. He figured it was the least the guy could have done for the son of the man he killed. The purchase wasn't a matter of principle, however; if the cops were following Dusty, Sean didn't want to be easily recognized in a crowd.

He also picked up an article of clothing he had long sworn he'd never be caught dead in: flip-flops. His only footwear choices from the boardwalk vendors that were already open were those and something called "water shoes," which looked even goofier. To Sean, men walking around in public with thongs between their toes were a product of an emasculated society, but in a predicament such as his, they were more pragmatic and discreet than bare feet. He chose the manliest color he could find—navy blue—but it didn't keep him from feeling like a fool.

Standing up from his bench under a shaded area at the southeast end of the parking lot, he took another look for Dusty's car. It had been nearly forty-five minutes since he'd placed the phone call, and he'd begun to worry that the young man he had little trust in to begin with wouldn't show. A minute later Dusty arrived.

The Datsun's loud, lime-green paint job distinguished it from the other cars that had just entered the large lot from the street in a slow-moving convoy. Sean watched the vehicle meander up and down a couple of rows, searching for an empty space. No other cars were trailing it, leaving Sean with some confidence that Dusty hadn't been followed. Dusty eventually found a spot and pulled in. He stayed in the car.

Sean watched the parking lot until his nerves subsided. Placing his hands in his pockets and trying to appear casual, he waited for a truck hauling an empty boat trailer to clear its way of an adjacent loading zone before making his way toward the Datsun. He kept his head low, the bill of his cap and his sunglasses covering a good portion of his face. The soles of his flip-flops slapped under his heels, irritating him.

When he was within a couple of rows, he noticed movement inside the car through its back window. Seconds later, a hand emerged from the driver side window clutching the strings of three or four colorful full-size balloons. Sean hesitated for a moment, unsure of what the display meant. The balloons were suddenly released. They floated steadily up into the air. The breeze quickly carried them off to the north, above trees and power lines.

Sean shook his head and proceeded toward the car. He squeezed himself in between it and the side of an SUV parked uncomfortably close. He opened the Datsun's passenger door and navigated inside. His knee knocked a balloon rhinoceros to the floorboard.

Whipping off his sunglasses, he turned to Dusty. "Why did you do that? That thing with the balloons?"

Clad in a tight yellow T-shirt, navy jogging pants, and a dwindling grin, Dusty glared back. "It was a homing beacon," he said. "So you'd spot my car."

It was the explanation Sean had guessed. He had seen the same stunt pulled by an orange robot on the 1980s detective show *Riptide*. "Your car's the color of the Land of Oz! I didn't need help spotting it. All you did was draw attention to us. Is that why it took you so long to get here? You had to go find a helium tank somewhere first?"

Dusty's upper lip receded from his lower. This time, the display didn't appear to be part of an act. Guilt flowed through Sean's gut, censuring him for lashing out at someone who was dealing with the fresh loss of his half-sister.

"A grocery store down the street lets me use their helium tank," Dusty offered with some timidity.

"It's okay," said Sean with a sigh. "Listen, I'm sorry. I'm sorry that your family's going through this. I'm sorry about Maria. I'm sorry that I yelled at you."

"It's all right," mumbled Dusty. "None of it's your fault."

"What happened to you last night? Where did you go?"

"I left," answered Dusty, collecting himself. "That guy at the bar was crazy. He was likely to kill someone."

Sean let a snort escape from his nose. "Oh, you think?" he said, keeping his tone soft. A grin crossed his face. "You hit him in the face with a baseball bat. Who could blame him?"

"I don't care," Dusty said, eyes narrowing as he gazed out the windshield. "I know the guys at Sunshine's had something to do with Maria's death. They're creeps."

Sean cocked his head and exhaled noisily. "Dusty, I don't think they did. I can't say for sure what happened, but that bald asshole in the red jumpsuit doesn't look to have been any part of it."

Dusty's eyes stayed on the windshield. He wiped his mustache with the back of his arm. Sean couldn't tell if his words were sinking in or not.

"She could have just been sadder than I'd thought," Dusty finally conceded. "I wish I understood what she was thinking—what was going through her mind."

Sean nodded. "Me, too." He placed his hand on Dusty's shoulder. "How's your mother doing?"

"Not good," he said, swallowing. His eyes lowered to his lap. "She raised Maria over all those years. I was different. I grew up with my dad, out in Houston. My mom took me in just a couple years ago, after high school, when my father got sick of me living at home. He didn't get my art. Most people don't. He wanted me to move out and work a *real* job." Dusty took in a breath. "He was probably right."

"You and Maria weren't close before that?"

"No," Dusty answered, shaking his head. "We weren't even all that close *here*." His eyes rose to Sean's. "But I loved her. She was nice to me. And most people aren't."

Sean nodded. "You're going to have to be strong for your mother now. She helped you, when you needed it. Now she needs your help."

Dusty nodded, his eyes somber.

"What did the police say to you, back at your trailer?" Sean carefully asked.

"Chief Quammen's trying to find you. He knows you were at Sunshine's last night. I guess he doesn't know I was there, too."

Sean shook his head, finding it highly unlikely that Quammen wouldn't have been able to place Dusty from the descriptions given to him by witnesses.

"I never showed the bouncer my driver's license," Dusty added.

"No, just the side of your bat," said Sean. "Quammen didn't mention anything else? Nothing about anything happening later in the night? Early this morning?"

"No," replied Dusty, his eyes narrowing. "Did something else happen?"

"Yeah, but you're better off not knowing. You've got enough to worry about." Dusty opened his mouth to pry further, but Sean interrupted him. "Did you bring it?"

"Bring what?"

"Really?"

"Oh, the gun. Yes!" He sprang to life, spreading his legs and reaching under his seat. When his hand reemerged, it was holding a silver pistol. "It was Jack's. I didn't know he owned a gun until this morning. Mom was going through more of his stuff late last night, and . . ."

Dusty continued on, but his words faded into a monotonous buzz as Sean's eyes adjusted to the pistol. It was a six-inch-barreled Colt Python with a nickel finish, identical to the one Sean's father had taught him to shoot with just days before he left. Sean still owned the gun, which his father had left behind. It was back at his place in Winston. The one Dusty now held in his hand was a dead-ringer for it, down to the seasoned wood grip.

He leaned over and took the gun from Dusty, silencing the monologue. Sean then rested back into his seat and popped open the weapon's cylinder. "Bullets?" he asked, swearing he could faintly smell chewing tobacco on the firearm.

Dusty reached back under his seat and pulled out a small cardboard box. It was white with subtle lettering on the outside. "This is all we found. There aren't many in it."

Sean glanced it over. "It will be enough."

"Enough for what?"

"Just get me back to Beach Bridge Road."

Chapter 24

When a row of old shops glided by on the right, Sean knew they were only a mile or so away. They were the same buildings he'd noticed a day earlier when Dusty had chauffeured him to the same location. This time, however, the bright colors of their walls felt warped, nightmarish. Sean rubbed his eyes, writing the perception off to sleep deprivation—that and the vengeance burning through his body.

Dusty hadn't said much since they'd left the marina. He listened to the radio and hummed a few tunes but had otherwise suppressed the theatrics entirely. He was acting like a normal person—one who had no idea what his passenger was about to do.

Sean had told himself dozens of times on the way over that he was making a mistake, that he should get a hold of his brother-in-law before doing anything rash. Lumbergh would surely attempt to talk him out of a confrontation with Albano, maybe offer a better solution. He'd urge a calmer head, and it would be good advice. Still, Sean probably wouldn't have taken it. His anger was guiding him forward . . . as was an opportunity.

If the Pawleys Island Police Department was in Albano's pocket, as Sean believed, Albano wouldn't be expecting officers to show up at his doorstep. Instead, he'd be waiting to hear from them with progress on their search for Sean. Albano's men were likely out doing the same or focusing on what to do with the yacht. With any luck, Albano was sitting inside his fortress alone, by the phone, riding out the storm. At least, that was the theory.

Sean brushed his hand along his pants pocket, tracing the bulge of the key ring he'd taken off of Schofield's body. If the four-digit number he'd taken from the wallet got him through the front gate, one of the keys might get him through a door.

The opening piano solo for a brisk-paced oldies song belted out through the Datsun's door speakers. Dusty, who'd been focused on the road, turned emotional. He let out a loud sigh, and within seconds, his shoulders began shaking and his eyes started to water. When Sean heard the discernible vocals of Ray Charles join in with the piano playing, he twisted the volume knob to the left until the song went silent.

"What's with you and Ray Charles?" he bluntly asked, keeping his eyes forward and removing the cap from his head. He tossed it in the backseat. "Bad memory or something?"

Dusty's face was wooden. "I think about him at times. About what life's been like for him."

Sean turned to look at him. "Why?"

"Because he has so much working against him. He went blind when he was a kid, you know."

"Yeah, I know. It's not exactly a secret."

"Can you imagine? No longer being able to enjoy life—not to its fullest, anyway. Not like he used to."

Sean's eyes went back to the road. "I'd say he's done pretty damned well for himself. Household name. Filthy rich. Millions of fans."

"He can never see colors again—bright, beautiful colors," Dusty said, his voice shaking. "Nothing but darkness. Forever. All he has left is entertaining others."

He had known Dusty less than two days. In that time, he hadn't been able to figure out if the kid had something clinically wrong in his head or if he was simply eccentric, as his mother had insisted. The answer still wasn't clear, but after the exchange about Maria back at the marina, Sean now believed he could distinguish between when Dusty was being earnest and when he was putting on a show. Right now, Dusty wasn't performing. And though his conduct wasn't any less strange, Sean no longer felt inclined to ridicule it.

Maybe Dusty believed himself to be, like Charles, someone who was blind to the world around him—a casualty of limits beyond his control. Maybe he'd become an entertainer to try and escape from those bonds—to become someone else and establish his worth through how he was received by others. Maybe he just needed a little hope and some affirmation that he hadn't wasted his life.

"I'll let you in on a little secret, Dusty," he said, sinking back in his seat. "I actually met Ray Charles last year."

"You *what*?" Dusty's eyes were large, suddenly shifting his focus between Sean and the road.

"Yeah. He performed a concert in a town called Lakeland, a few miles north of where I live back in Colorado. It's a gambling town, up in the mountains. I worked security at the auditorium that night. I met him after the show."

Dusty gasped. "Met him? As in shake his hand or—"

"Yeah, and a little more than that. We talked for a bit. You know, shot the breeze. You want to know what really surprised me about him?"

"What?" Dusty answered eagerly.

"I have never met anyone who loves life more than him. Smiling and laughing. Hugging everyone around him. Full of optimism. He told me he was *born* to entertain others and that being different and dealing with life's obstacles are what made him who he is today. He wouldn't trade away any of it."

"He said that? Really?"

"Every word."

Gazing forward, Dusty's chin lifted and his back straightened. His jaw squared with what looked like dignity.

A satisfied grin crept across Sean's face. Ray Charles had indeed performed a concert in Lakeland, Colorado, last year. Sean, however, had never been offered a security job to work it, nor had he ever met the singer.

The car lurched into a pothole and shook Sean back into reality. He pulled out a pen and a piece of scratch paper from the glove box. He wrote down Lumbergh's work and home phone numbers at the top and then a note below them. He folded the note in half.

"Take this," he said, passing the note to Dusty. "When you get back home, keep calling those numbers until you get a hold of Chief Gary Lumbergh. When you do, read to him what's on the note."

"You want me to drop you off but not wait for you?"

"That's right. I don't want you mixed up in any more of this. And I'm serious about that."

Dusty hung a right onto Beach Bridge Road. As he drove forward, Sean glanced to the side mirror to verify again that they weren't being followed. He nearly let his eyes slide back to the windshield when he spotted a silver car make the same turn they just had. He squinted and leaned forward to get a better look through the mirror. His eyes widened when he made out a narrow grill and projector headlamps.

"Holy shit," he muttered, his pulse ticking up.

"What?" Dusty asked.

"There's a dirt path coming up. I saw it when we were here yesterday. It leads into the forest on the right. I'm guessing it comes out on the other side of the trees somewhere. It might even lead back to the highway. I want you to take it."

"What's going on?" Dusty asked. He glanced at the rearview mirror. "Is someone following us?"

"The silver car. It must have trailed you to the marina and waited outside the parking lot—on the street—until we came back out."

"What? How do you know?" asked Dusty. "The driver might just live in one of the houses down here."

"He may very well live down here," Sean said, thinking of Albano. He brought the revolver to his mouth and blew some dust off the muzzle. Out of habit, he checked the gun's action, despite having just loaded it minutes earlier. "But he's not just another guy out for a Sunday drive. That asshole in the Mercedes is the reason I'm riding shotgun in this car instead of still driving my rental."

"Mercedes?" Dusty said, surprised. He glared back into his rearview mirror. "Is that a Benz E-320?"

Sean's head snapped toward Dusty. "Yes! What do you know about it?"

Dusty nodded nervously. "I know whose it is."

"Whose?"

Dusty's eyes shifted upward. His tongue slid to the side of his mouth. "I want to say Previne? No! Prevenas! It's Prevenas."

"Why do I know that name?"

"He's a police detective from up in Myrtle Beach. He stopped by the trailer a few days ago. He thought Jack might have been behind some other burglary up there."

"That's right. Maria told me about him. He searched through you and your mom's trailer, didn't he?"

Dusty nodded. "He didn't find anything though."

Sean's face tightened. "You didn't think it was weird at the time that a police detective was driving a Mercedes Benz?"

Dusty shrugged. "I don't know. I guess not. I figured he was some kind of special cop or something. Like Michael Knight. He had a badge."

"Michael Knight?" Sean said with a barely concealed scoff. "As in *Knight Rider*? Did his Mercedes talk?"

"No! I just mean—"

"The badge. How good of a look did you get at it?"

"Not all that good of one. He flashed it. He was dressed nice. I guess I assumed—"

"Here's the road," Sean said, raising his finger.

Dusty flipped on his signal and carefully pulled off onto the dirt. Sean watched in his mirror as the Mercedes slowed down, seemingly unsure of whether or not to follow. "You don't think he's really a detective?"

"No, I don't. Keep going at this speed. Don't let on that we're paying any attention to him. Take us into those trees."

The Mercedes nearly came to a stop at the road, the driver's hesitation to follow clear. From Sean's angle, he could now make out some of the body damage he had caused to the car's rear and part of its side. "Come on," Sean whispered, egging on the driver to follow. "Grow a pair."

Dusty kept his speed as Sean had instructed. He began humming a song that Sean paid little attention to until he recognized it as the theme from *Mission Impossible*.

"Dusty," Sean said sternly.

Dusty stopped humming. He followed the lumpy road in between families of tall, thin pine trees. The pines were very different from the ones Sean had grown up with in the mountains of Colorado. Rather than resembling a cone, where the branches were longer at the bottom and narrow at the top, these trunks were largely bare, the bark scaly and reddish brown. Only toward the top did their branches spread out, joining with others to block out the sun. The scarcity of low branches let Sean keep an eye on the street, where the Mercedes had all but stopped, until the sheer number of trunks began to hinder his view.

Dusty opened his mouth to speak, but Sean spoke instead. "Keep going."

Far enough away now that Sean was sure the driver of the Mercedes couldn't see in through their back window, Sean unbuckled his belt, twisted around, and watched the car. Just as it was about to disappear behind a staggered wall of trunks, he saw the Mercedes edge onto the dirt road. The corners of Sean's lips curved up.

He spun forward, his eyes darting along the landscape in front of them. Several yards ahead on the left side of the road was a grouping of dense bushes at least six feet tall. They were particularly thick at their base, next to the mangled roots of an overturned pine that rested on its side.

"Ease up on the gas a bit. Slow us down, but I don't want him seeing brake lights. I'm going to bail." Sean gripped the gun tightly in his right hand. With his left he grabbed onto the door handle.

"Bail? You're going to jump out of the car?" Dusty asked with wide eyes.

"Yes."

A sly grin formed on Dusty's face and he began humming the *Mission Impossible* theme again.

"Once I'm out, pick up speed and keep going," Sean ordered over the humming. "Don't come back. Don't even look back. Find the highway and get home. Call those numbers I gave you and give that message to Chief Lumbergh."

"What about you?" Dusty sang out the question to the melody of the song; the transition was remarkably seamless.

"I'll be fine," Sean answered.

He pressed his head to the window, eyes scouring the ground ahead on the right, looking for a patch of earth that was free of rocks and other natural debris. When he spotted one, he found himself joining in with Dusty's infectious tune.

"Dun-dun-dun-da-dada, dun-dun-dun-da-dada, dun-dun-dun-da-dada," the men strummed in unison, both wearing subtle grins. Dusty finally let out a deep, resounding laugh.

A second later, Sean took a breath, flung open his door, and lunged forward. His shoulder hit the ground hard as his flip-flops flew off and his gun got knocked from his hand, but he kept rolling counter-clockwise to flow with the momentum. It was a trick he'd learned from an old episode of *Spenser: For Hire*.

When he came to a halt, he wiped dirt from his mouth with the back of his arm. He crawled forward and grabbed his gun from the ground. With his other hand, he snatched up one flip-flop. He couldn't find the other; it must have ended up on the floorboard of Dusty's car.

Keeping his head low, he bolted for the bushes, taking a moment to glance down the road at the Datsun. A surge of acceleration had shut the vehicle's passenger door. A cloud of dust rose up from the car's rear tires as it rounded a bend.

Sean reached the bushes and knelt behind them, facing the road. He was confident he hadn't been seen. He tossed the flip-flop behind him and planted one hand on the ground. The other hand held his gun, which he pointed toward the road. He breathed heavily until he could hear the hum of the Mercedes engine. His right shoulder ached and when he glanced at it, he saw that he had reopened the cut from the yacht.

The car slowly approached from behind the mesh of brush leaves and branches. Sean stood up. With clenched teeth, spread nostrils, and blood running down his shoulder, he boldly walked toward the car, arms out in front of him with the gun. His sites locked on their target.

He squeezed the trigger and the echo of the gun's blast and the crunch of the windshield on the passenger side spread through the forest. Sean swung his arms toward the driver. The stunned man inside had slammed on the brakes and was frantically trying to turn the steering wheel.

Sean stood almost directly in front of the car. "Put it in park!" he yelled. "Put it in park now, or you're dead! Let me see your hands!"

He knew the driver wouldn't dare try and run him over. Sean had the gun pointed directly at him at a range from which he couldn't miss. If the Mercedes lunged forward, Sean wouldn't hesitate to pull the trigger.

There was a decent view of the driver through the glass. He had a thin face, with short, silver hair and long sideburns. Fearful eyes. A half-open mouth.

"Okay!" the man shouted, his eyes glued to Sean. His voice was muted from behind the windows. "I'm putting it in park! Don't shoot!"

When the man's right hand lowered from the wheel, Sean rushed to the side door, gun still trained on him. He wanted to make certain the man wasn't reaching for anything other than the transmission. Sean latched onto the door handle and yanked it open.

"Take it easy, take it easy!" the man pleaded, his voice no longer hindered. The car went to a louder idle, and the man's hand slid off of the gear-shift to join his other hand in the air.

Sean grabbed onto the collar of the man's gray, short-sleeved shirt. The man started to say something, but with a grunt, Sean yanked him outside of the car like a rag doll. He then shoved him chest-first to the dirt and grass.

"Ah, fuck!" the man grunted. He cried out when Sean's knee dug into the swell of his back. His legs kicked the ground.

Sean shoved his gun back into the waistline of his pants. With his pursuer subdued, he quickly frisked the man, starting at his armpits and working his way down his jeans to the ankles. He found no firearms.

"No gun?" he asked mockingly as he slid his hands under the man's ribs to double check. "That seems awfully odd for a policeman, *Detective Prevenas*."

He dug his hand into the man's back pocket and pried out his wallet. Keeping him pinned to the ground with his knee, he rifled through it, looking for a driver's license.

"Sean!" the man growled, turning his head in the dirt to try and look his restrainer in the eye. "Give me a minute . . . to explain." His face twisted in discomfort.

"Shut up!" Sean took his focus off of the wallet just long enough to slap the man across the back of his head. "You got that shit you stole from my room in your car somewhere?"

When he found the license, he saw "North Carolina" written at the top. To the left was the picture of the man squirming beneath him. At the bottom was a name that stole Sean's breath.

"Jack Slate?" he read, face contorted. "What the hell is this?" He tossed the wallet and license aside and reached again for his gun. He climbed off of the man, rolled him onto his back, and pointed the pistol directly at his face. "Who are you?" he roared.

The man let out a cough and slowly propped himself up on his elbows. His chest heaved in and out as sweat beaded then streamed down his forehead. It slid down the stubble along his jaw. He said nothing, but his eyes began to reveal a level of scrutiny that Sean found eerie.

Growing angrier, he was about to repeat the question. Then he noticed a circular bulge in a pocket on the front of the man's shirt. Chewing tobacco. Sean raised his gaze and read something more in the man's eyes. It was as if whatever fear he had seen in them just seconds earlier was slowly being drained out and replaced with what he could only describe as guilt. The man's dark, wiry eyebrows lowered closer to his hazel irises. He pursed his lips, the creases in his forehead deepening.

In that moment, Sean felt an inexplicable sense of familiarity. He had seen that expression before—not one similar to it, as worn by someone else, but displayed across that same face. He somehow knew the man but couldn't place from where or when.

The answer came crashing down on him like a tidal wave. It deprived him of air and thrashed his soul against rocks and earth until he could no longer see straight. Sean stumbled backwards, landing on his rear and hitting the back of his head on the door of the Mercedes. It slammed shut behind him. He kept his gun pointed at the man as his hands shook and his heart thundered.

Sean now understood why the man lying on a cold, steel bed at the coroner's office hadn't bore much of a resemblance to his father. That man *wasn't* his father.

His father was sitting on a patch of grass directly across from him, gazing at him with eyes that were beginning to well up from a lifetime of secrets.

Chapter 25

Sean struggled to find the words to say to the ghost who sat staring at him. His father's resurrection had to be some sick joke concocted by God himself. When his chest tightened to the point where he could no longer breathe, he forced himself to gasp and take in new air. His eyes remained on his father's.

"Why don't you put the gun down, Sean," his father said calmly, raising his hands to imply he wasn't a threat. "I'm not going to hurt you."

Sean's eyes narrowed. His face twisted into a sneer. "That's a hell of a thing for you to say to me," he growled. "I should shoot you right now, you son of a bitch."

Jack lowered his hands and scooted himself backward a few inches on his butt. "Why? Why would you shoot me, Sean?"

"Why?" Sean shouted, his upper body lurching forward and his hand gripping the gun tighter. "Because you won't stay dead!"

Jack swallowed, his eyes widening with fear. He spoke quickly. "We need to talk this out, okay? You don't understand what's going on here. We'll talk about this."

"You're damn right I don't understand," Sean snarled. He pulled himself to his feet, keeping his gun trained on his father. His legs felt clumsy, so he propped himself against the side of the Mercedes. "Who's the dead man? Huh? The man I saw at the morgue. The man who got himself all shot up."

"Okay. Just calm down," Jack pleaded, controlling his breathing.

"His name is . . ." He hesitated for a moment. "Well, his name is Prevenas. Lloyd Prevenas. We were in the army together way back."

"Prevenas? That's the name that *you've* been using."

"I know, I know. It was some stupid 'dose of one's own medicine' bullshit. I needed a name for when I talked to his family, and that's the first one that came to mind. I knew they knew him as Jack Slate."

The gears in Sean's mind labored to make sense of what was being said. The significance of the different names wasn't immediately clear, but the relationship between the men was.

"That's why he had your tattoo on his shoulder," Sean blurted out. "You served together. You. Him. Zed."

Jack carefully nodded. "And other guys, too."

"Who the hell is Jack Slate then?" demanded Sean, his heart blasting.

His father began to climb to his feet, placing his hands on the ground for support.

"No! You keep your ass down and answer my question!"

Jack nodded in concession, returning to the dirt. His joints popped as he did. "I'm Jack Slate. I changed my name after . . . after I left Winston."

Over the years, Sean had dreamed of his father returning to Winston and acknowledging the abandonment of his family. In those dreams, his father would drop to his knees and beg for forgiveness, promising that he was back with the family for good and that he would never leave again. It was like a scene from a soap opera. That moment of admission had finally come in the real world, among silent, hovering pines in a patch of unfamiliar South Carolina woods. Only it had come without any apology, stated as mere afterthought. His father's apathy infuriated him, but he bit his lip and continued to listen.

"Then a few years ago, I ran into my old buddy Lloyd," Jack continued. "At a carwash, of all places. A fucking carwash up in North Carolina. That's where I live now; I'm an auto mechanic there, specializing in foreign cars." He paused for a moment, seeming to wait for Sean to express some interest in the mention of his career.

Sean did react, just not in the way Jack was probably expecting. "The Mercedes isn't even yours, is it? Borrowed it from your garage, I bet. A customer's car."

Jack exhaled and nodded. "So Lloyd was passing through on the interstate. The son of a bitch recognizes me. After all of those years, he recognizes me. He walks right up to me and shouts out, 'Jack Hansen!'" A half-smile creased his mouth as he recalled the memory. His eyes then glazed over, and a sigh dropped from his mouth. "He was the first person from my past I'd seen in—"

"Thirty years," Sean interrupted, his eyes sharp.

"Yeah," Jack said after a moment. The smile had disappeared. "Something like that. So . . . I invite him back to my place. We get a few beers in us, and I tell him that I'm not Hansen anymore. That I'm Jack Slate. I tell him about, you know, about starting over." His eyes slid up to Sean.

Sean hoped the full extent of his hatred was being communicated through his glare. "Keep talking," he muttered through clenched teeth, fighting back the urge to advance the conversation with his fists. After all this time, he needed to hear his father's explanation to its conclusion.

"So, yeah. Lloyd's totally fascinated with how I changed my name and how I took on a new identity. He's asking me all kinds of questions about the process, half acting like he's not even buying my story. So, being an idiot, I end up showing him some of the paperwork. I kept it in a big wooden chest along with some valuables, some cash, and what few belongings I still owned from the old days, back in Winston and before."

"The chest that's now in my motel room—the one you stole from," Sean said.

"I didn't steal anything," Jack said matter-of-factly. "It's my stuff. It was stolen from me by Lloyd—who, as it turned out, had a history of taking things that didn't belong to him. When I woke up that morning, hungover with a knot on my head, I found that the asshole had made off with it all—the whole goddamned chest and everything in it. Money, documents, heirlooms, that gun you're holding on me right now—"

"Those old plates with the celebrities," Sean interjected.

"Yeah," Jack said, lowering his head. "Those, too. I didn't know until just a few days ago that Lloyd had also taken my identity. I thought he'd just wanted my stuff. I guess the allure of starting over was too much for him to pass up. He had everything he needed—the papers, the social security number."

"So you found him," said Sean. "And now he's dead. Did you help get him killed? Are you part of this somehow?"

Jack scoffed. "Of course I didn't kill him. Are you kidding? I saw his name—*my* name—turn up in a newspaper, saying that he'd been murdered."

Sean turned his gaze away from his father, giving himself a break from his face. He rubbed his chin with his shoulder as he processed the story. "You're telling me you drove down here from North Carolina just to get your shit back? The stuff in that chest?"

A nervous chuckle fell from Jack's mouth. He seemed to recognize how absurd his explanation sounded. "Yeah," he said, shaking his head and pursing his lips. "After reading about the case, I posed as a Myrtle Beach detective to get inside Lloyd's trailer and look around for what he'd taken. I didn't find hardly any of it. None of the important stuff anyway. I saw that Lloyd's girlfriend was getting his stuff together, so I hung out for a couple of days and followed the family around. I followed the girl—her daughter, I guess—to a storage shed. Some guys there loaded the chest into her truck. She then led me to you. I never thought word would get back to Winston about this. I never thought you'd come out here."

Sean shook his head in disgust. "You're full of so much shit," he said, his eyes becoming glossy.

Jack's face turned quizzical.

"What could have been so fucking important among your things that you would have gone to all that trouble?"

"It doesn't matter, Sean."

"It does matter! Why are you here right now? Why did you follow me here? Is it this gun you came for?" Sean quickly shuffled it around his hand and held the grip out in front of him. "Because you can have it! I've got one just like it at home, remember? You taught me to shoot with it right before you left! 'Load, align the sights, take a deep breath, and squeeze that trigger.' Do you remember?" Years of torment bubbled over.

"I remember," murmured Jack, lowering his head. "And I didn't come for the gun."

Sean clenched the top half of the pistol in his hand and stomped toward his father. He raised the weapon high in the air as if he was prepared to strike a blow. Jack scrambled backwards on his arms and heels, stumbled and fell back to his butt, crying out for Sean to stop.

Sean halted when he was within a few inches of his father. He panted, chest heaving painfully, eyes ablaze. His body shook and it took every inch of restraint he could muster to keep himself from bashing in his father's face.

"Sean!" Jack shouted. "I'm sorry, okay? I'm sorry!"

His face now beet red, Sean snarled and spun around, hurling the gun into the forest. He dropped to a knee and placed his hand over his face. It felt as if the trees around him were spinning. When he finally closed his eyes, they stopped.

"I was curious . . . curious about you," said Jack. "I was on my way out of town just now. The undercarriage of the car was all fucked up after what happened in that alley and on the bridge. Fluids were leaking everywhere. It needed some repairs before I could drive back up to North Carolina. That's what kept me here an extra day. Mercedes parts don't grow on trees."

Sean shook his head, unable to bring himself to look at this father.

Jack kept talking. "I recognized the green Datsun that I'd seen in front of Prevenas's trailer. Through the car window, I saw you riding shotgun. It was just for a second, but I knew it was you. I turned around and followed you . . . here."

"That night," said Sean. "That night on the bridge. You pointed a gun at me."

"That wasn't a gun, Sean," Jack said with a sigh. "It was a candy bar. I was holding it like a gun to scare you off. To get you to stop chasing me."

In the distance, there was a roar of a car engine. Sean wondered in the back of his mind if Dusty had defied his instructions and was now returning.

"Sean," said Jack. His voice was closer now. "I did a really shitty thing all of those years ago, and there's not a day that goes by that I don't regret what I did to her."

"Her," Sean whispered. "Mom?"

"Diana."

Sean's face soured. His eyes shot open and he turned his head to Jack, who was now kneeling just a couple of feet away. Sean's hands tightened into fists as he leaped to his feet. "Diana? *Just* Diana? Jesus!" Saliva flew from his mouth.

Jack pulled himself up to his feet and began backing away.

"What did I do?" Sean shouted. "What did I do that was so damn horrible that you left your whole family and the only fucking remorse you have is for your daughter?"

The sound of the car engine grew louder and more aggressive as Jack's mouth opened. "My God," he gasped, his face stretched in puzzlement. "Dolores never told you why I left? Oh Christ. All of these years? *Zed* never told you?"

"Uncle Zed's dead!" Sean yelled. "What is it? What were they supposed to have told me?"

"He's dead?" Jack said with a gulp. "Oh, God."

"Like you give a fuck!" Sean yelled. "Now tell me, what did I do?"

"Sean, it wasn't your fault I left. It was never your fault . . . It was Zed's!"

The bluster of the engine was now so great that it could no longer be neglected. Sean realized that it wasn't coming from the direction Dusty had left in. It was approaching from Beach Bridge Road. When Sean managed to pull his eyes from Jack, he saw a dark Cadillac tearing its way along the dirt road directly toward them.

"Shit!" Sean reached for the back of his pants, searching for his gun, then remembered chucking it into the woods.

"What's going on?" yelled Jack, his head snapping back and forth between Sean and the quickly approaching car. He looked off-balance, unsure of what to do. "Who is that?"

"No more bullshit! Are you a part of this?" Sean shouted. He pointed a finger at his father, a vein bulging at the center of his forehead. "Prevenas's death? Schofield's? *Any* of it?"

The look of confusion on Jack's face convinced Sean that he wasn't. The Mercedes was still running, but with the Cadillac already nearly on top of them, Sean knew they didn't have time to get inside and escape.

"Come on!" Sean barked, motioning Jack toward him with his hand. Sean was already slogging his bare-footed way toward some trees.

Jack followed him around to the other side of the Mercedes and they took off into the woods. The trees didn't provide much visual cover—not with their bare trunks and wide gaps between them. Still, they were just dense enough to keep the Cadillac from driving between them and running the two down. Sean searched the forest floor for the gun as they trounced over shrubs and tall grass. He didn't find it, and when he heard the slam of car doors, he stopped looking.

Jack was moving slowly—too slowly. He was already breathing heavily, no longer the spry man Sean had remembered from his youth. Now close to seventy, Jack's lanky body trudged along gingerly, as if one false step could send him crumbling to the ground in a heap of bones. Sean shouted for him to hurry, but words couldn't fix what thirty years had taken away.

Titus Blake emerged from a pair of pines a ways behind them dressed in a black polo shirt and khaki pants. A stray ray of sunlight reflected off his bald head. When his neck angled in Sean's direction, the two men's eyes met. Blake's arm rose. He was holding a long-barreled pistol.

"Get down!" Sean shouted at Jack, who was a good ten yards behind him.

Sean went to the ground. So did his father. A pop was heard, and a bullet whizzed over their heads. The shot had been muffled by a silencer. Blake shouted out something and another man answered him. There were at least two of them in pursuit.

"Don't shoot!" cried Jack, his voice bouncing off of the trees. His hands emerged from behind blades of tall grass. "I'm not any part of this! Don't shoot!"

Sean sneered at his father's spinelessness. He stayed on his stomach and crawled through dirt and scrub until he found a broken off tree limb resting on its side. It was roughly five feet long and three inches in diameter at its thickest point. He grabbed the end that didn't have dead pine needles sprouting from twigs. It gripped nicely in his hand, just like an axe.

Through the grass and weeds, Sean watched Jack's face glaring back at him with petrified eyes. He was lying still with his hands in the air, breathing hard. Sean held his finger to his mouth. Jack shook his head no, but Sean ignored him and began negotiating his way along the ground to try and get to the side of their pursuers.

"Please!" Jack shouted to their assailants. "I give up! I don't know what this is about, and I don't want to know! I just want to leave!"

After a moment, Blake yelled, "We won't shoot ya! Where's the man you're with? Where's Coleman?"

Sean didn't dare raise his head above the grass. He knew he'd be spotted quickly if he did. Instead, he listened to Blake as the thug continued to press his father for answers. Sean heard someone else approaching from the south, and he lay perfectly still, clenching the tree branch. He prepared to lunge to his knees and swing it like an axe the moment the pursuer was within reach.

"Coleman's hiding over there in the grass!" Jack shouted. "He's trying to sneak up behind you! We're unarmed. All he has is a branch!"

Sean couldn't believe what he had just heard, even coming from a man who had proven long ago that he wasn't worth the cost of his own casket. It was his father's second most horrid act of family treason.

"Mr. Blake, I see him!" shouted a voice Sean didn't recognize. It was very close by. "Right there!"

Sean sunk flat to the ground, his very soul oozing out of his body. He rolled over onto his back and let the branch slide from his grip. As aggressive footsteps and the sounds of moving brush grew in volume, he gazed in defeat at the blue sky above. A thin, white contrail from a jet was its only blemish, framed by lush tree tops and the bitter taste of betrayal.

Titus Blake's shadowy face bled with contempt when it entered Sean's view. It was soon eclipsed with the muzzle of Blake's gun. Sean said nothing. His eyes focused on what was left of the sky's grace until the quick snap of Blake's shoe heel eclipsed everything.

Chapter 26

"What the hell's going on? Who are these guys?" Sean heard a young woman's voice shout as he roused into consciousness.

"Shut up!" a man snapped. It sounded like Albano. "Make yourself useful and close the blinds and curtains."

Sean squinted from the glare of overbearing sunlight that poured in through a large, fuzzy window. The brightness deepened the pain throbbing across his skull. His knees and bare feet were being dragged along a glossy hardwood floor. Two men were pulling him, a pair of hands wrapped under each of his arms. The metallic taste of blood swished in his mouth, some spilling from his lips and onto his shirt.

"Careful!" said Albano, seeming to talk to a different person now. "Did anyone see you?" There was a brief snapping sound, and the sunlight was quickly extinguished.

"No," answered Blake from directly beside Sean. He was out of breath and struggling with Sean's weight. "No one was on the street. We parked the Mercedes on the side of the house, under the dogwood."

"What about the Datsun? And the fat guy driving it?"

"Don't know where it went. He was gone before we got there. Must have left through the forest. He wouldn't have seen us. I'll get Madigan t'run the plate and find out who he is."

A reflexive chuckle echoed up from Sean's chest, drawing silence from the men who likely still believed he was out cold. "Officer

McDaggin," Sean mumbled, his head facing the floor. "You're telling me . . . that Quammen trusts that southern-fried shithead to run errands for you guys?"

When no one responded, Sean sighed. "Or is Quammen clean?" When his question was again met with silence, he realized that Madigan was as high up as the conspiracy went. "Shit."

In unison, probably at the direction of Albano, the hands wrapped around Sean's arms suddenly let go. He crashed hard to the floor, his head bouncing off of wood. He winced, gathered his breath, and rolled onto his side. There was an immediate hard kick to the ribs. Then another. The third commanded a wicked cough up from his lungs, and blood splattered the floor.

"Hold on," said Albano. The assault ended. "Who are you?"

At first, Sean thought Albano was playing games with him, pretending to have forgotten their previous meeting—his way of demonstrating Sean's triviality. Sean soon realized the question had not been posed to him, but someone else.

"I'm no one," he heard his father answer. "I'm from out of town. I was just passing through. I was lost and thought this young man here could give me directions. I don't know what business you men have with each other, but—"

"Shut up!" snarled Blake.

Sean grimaced at his father's dodgy performance.

Blake continued. "His driver's license says his name's Jack Slate. From North Carolina." He paused for a moment, as if letting his words settle with Albano. "What do ya make a'that?"

A few seconds ticked by before Albano somberly answered, "I don't know."

As Sean's eyes adjusted, he peeled his head up off the floor and looked upward. The first pair of eyes he saw peering back at him belonged to the Goddess. She was standing across a patch of carpet. Her wavy hair covered her shoulders, and she was clad in a white robe, her tan legs stemming out from under it. Her arms were crossed in front of her stomach like a nervous child, and her face was white with fear.

"So you *are* alive?" Sean said to her, eliciting some confusion from her face.

Both Albano and Blake's heads snapped toward Sean as if they'd been struck with the same round-house punch. Sean's words had apparently hit a nerve—a sharp one. The two began communicating in whispers and a shared, serious demeanor.

Blake was holding his pistol aimed at the floor. Sean had a better view of it now. It was a nine millimeter with a silencer—most certainly the same gun that had fired a bullet into the shoulder of the late Lloyd Prevenas before Schofield had finished him off.

Albano was dressed in a white polo shirt, similar in style to Blake's though he didn't wear it as well, and a pair of red and white checkered shorts. The same pair of binoculars he'd held other day was dangling from a strap around his neck.

Sean's mind pieced together what had likely happened. Albano must have seen him and Dusty through the binoculars from an upstairs window and feared a visit from the authorities after what had happened the previous night. When he saw the Datsun head off into forest, he must have sent his men out after it.

If Albano had been in contact with Officer Madigan that morning, Sean realized, he would have known that Sean hadn't called into the Pawleys Island PD. What they couldn't have known was that he hadn't contacted *any* law enforcement agency other than his brother-in-law. No one was coming to Albano's home.

A different police force would have certainly responded to the bodies at the marina by now, but it would take time to establish a link back to Albano, especially with Sean having taken Schofield's wallet, and with it his identification.

"Go upstairs," Albano finally said, his intense eyes targeting the Goddess. He removed the binoculars from around his neck and handed them to her. "Watch out the window. If anyone pulls up to the gate, yell down."

She reluctantly took the binoculars, biting her lip. "I didn't sign on for this," she complained before briskly walking across the room.

The Goddess crossed in front of Jack, who was standing next to a man with a beat-up face who pointed a gun at his shoulder. The man, who Sean had never seen before, had to be the same person the cab driver had described as being with Schofield at the marina last night. That meant he was also the man inside the yacht's cabin with Blake.

Sean glanced around the room, surveying his surroundings as the Goddess quickly worked her way up a staircase along the back wall. She turned back once toward Sean, her eyes uneasy, before disappearing.

To Sean's left, in front of a half-dozen leather suitcases that looked ready for transport, was an elaborate dining room with a refined wooden table and four chairs in cherry finish. They stood on a large Persian rug that edged a lofty China cabinet on one side. A large vase of red flowers sat at the center of the table underneath a fancy chandelier. Albano was leaning against the back of one of the chairs as he quietly discussed something with Blake, whose turquoise eyes kept darting between him and Sean.

To Sean's right was a living room. His father and the man with the bruised face stood there. Two leather couches, a plush recliner, and a couple more cushioned chairs rested on a thick carpet. They formed a rectangle around a low-sitting, odd-shaped table that looked more like a conversation piece than a useful piece of furniture. A monotone oil painting of a European street alley hung above it.

A long row of closed curtains spread all the way across the back wall of the living room. Sean guessed that behind them was the lengthy sequence of windows and the French doors he had seen the other day while clinging to the neighbors' stone wall. He tried to remember the layout of the backyard property. He had trouble picturing the full landscape, but recalled where the patio and pool were.

Take a seat," said Albano, his eyes shifting to the man with the beat-up face.

The man spun one of the living room chairs around and shoved Jack into it. Jack, caught unaware, fell back into the deep cushion, his feet flinging up in the air for a moment before dropping back to the carpet. He looked terrified, his body shaking and his eyes darting back and forth between the different players. Sean almost felt sorry for him, but the betrayal in the forest wouldn't quite let him.

"How about everyone pull up a chair," said Albano, extending his arm out before him as if he were entertaining guests. "Except you," he said, turning to Sean. "You stay on the floor. I don't want you bleeding on my carpet."

Sean played it cool, pulling himself up to a seated position on the floor and resting his back against a short but solid wood cabinet. His eyes wandered over to the staircase. At its base was a wall mirror. His own reflection stared back at him. His face was a mess of dried blood, though it was thickest on his upper lip and chin. He also noticed that the cabinet behind him had a full water pitcher on its marble top. It looked to be made out of glass, its waterline crowded with ice and lemon slices.

Albano's men snagged some of the chairs from the dining room table. Blake set one right behind his boss, who carefully lowered himself onto it. Albano's face winced after he let himself drop the last couple of inches.

"Good work, butler," said Sean.

Blake swung his head and glared fire through Sean, emphasizing the gun in his hand.

"You're a real badass with that gun, aren't you?" taunted Sean. "Without it, all you've got are those pretty eyes of yours staring daggers at me."

Blake flared his nostrils and stepped forward.

"Take a seat," Albano said calmly to Blake. "We'll all discuss this matter like gentleman." A confident smile curled across his lips.

Blake reluctantly sat down, his eyes and gun still pointed at Sean.

"We'll start," Albano began, his gaze gliding across the attendees as if he were browsing through produce at a grocery store. They finally settled on Sean. "With you. What was it you said to my wife a moment ago? About her being alive?"

Sean ignored the question. "Why don't you start with the tourist over there?" he said, rubbing crystallizing blood from his mouth with the back of his forearm. "He's the guy just passing through."

Albano's eyes narrowed. His grin soured but didn't quite disappear. He obviously didn't appreciate being talked back to, but part of him seemed to respect Sean's gall to do so. His head angled toward Jack, who swallowed nervously. "Jack Slate was the name of a man who—well, let's say he met an unfortunate demise not so far from here. I find it very curious that you share his name."

Jack tightly clenched the ends of his armrests, his nails digging into the material. He shifted around as if he had ants in his pants, his eyes bouncing between Sean and Albano. His head looked ready to split from the pressure.

When Jack said nothing, the man with the bruised face delivered him a whack on the back of the head.

"I thought I knew the other Slate—the dead guy," Jack blurted out. "I thought he was an old cousin. I hadn't seen him in a while. I read about his death in a paper up north and came down to offer my condolences."

Sean fought back the urge to laugh. Instead, he glued his eyes to the audience. He wasn't sure where his father was going with the story but knew it was being done in the interest of detaching himself from the dire situation in which he'd found himself. It was apparent from the blank expressions Jack received that the others weren't buying it.

"Did ya?" asked Blake, rubbing the side of his chin with his gun to address an itch before aiming it back at Sean.

"Did I what?" Jack asked nervously.

"Pay your condolences."

"Well, no. You see, it wasn't him. I had thought it was my cousin, but—"

"You have the same first name as your cousin?" asked the man with the bruised face, his eyes narrowed.

"Yes, actually. It's a family name. The name of our late grandfather."

Sean marveled at his father's improvisational skills—how he'd managed to fabricate such a story out of thin air. Maybe craftiness was a required quality for anyone hoping to keep their discarded past a secret.

The grin across Albano's face didn't waver. He finally spoke up. "You came down from North Carolina to pay your respects to the family of your cousin . . . whose name is the same as yours. Only, the deceased individual *wasn't* your cousin, and his son shot a bullet through your windshield. And all of this happened, by some strange coincidence, right across the street from this house."

Albano slid his gaze over to Sean, presumably gauging his reaction. Sean kept his face deadpan, offering neither acknowledgement nor dissent.

"I, I confused him," Jack sputtered. "I didn't introduce myself well, and I think he got the wrong idea, and that's why he pulled a gun on me. Listen, I don't know who you men are, or why it's strange that this little incident went down close to your home—and it's a lovely home, by the way. I clearly made a very bad mistake, and—"

Albano's grin disappeared. He nodded to the man with the bruised face. The man quickly stood up, grabbed Jack by the hair, and slammed the side of his pistol into the center of his face.

Jack cried out in pain. Sean quickly lunged to his knees, reflexively ready to intervene, but he restrained himself when Blake stood up with his gun pointed. Teeth clenched and his heart racing, Sean turned to Albano. He was grinning again, amused at having drawn a reaction out of Sean.

"The blood," Albano said suddenly.

Blake retrieved a handkerchief from his back pocket and walked over to Jack, keeping his eyes and gun on Sean. He tossed the handkerchief onto Jack's lap.

"Make sure none gets on the furniture or carpet," Albano followed up.

Jack's tearing eyes glared through Sean, pleading silently for help as he held the wadded handkerchief to his face. Sean turned his attention back to Albano, staring icily at him. Blake sat down.

"That's a pretty intense look you're giving me," snickered Albano. "And over the welfare of a complete stranger. You must be quite the humanitarian, Mr. Coleman."

Sean said nothing.

Albano's face seemed to stiffen with thought before he turned back to Jack. "Lower the handkerchief."

The man with the bruises reached over and grabbed Jack's wrist, carefully lowering the hand holding the handkerchief from Jack's face. He kept it there, ready to catch any stray drops of blood.

"What do you think, Mr. Blake?" said Albano. "Do you think these two are really strangers?"

Blake leaned forward in his chair, his mesmeric eyes suddenly beaming as if he had just been asked to perform a talent in which he took great pride. He closely scrutinized Jack's face, then turned to Sean, doing the same. A smirk flashed across his features. "Both have hazel eyes. Similar hairline. Jaw lines are roughly the same shape. Shoulders hang at the same angle. Skin tone—"

"Are you guys sizing us up for a double date?" Sean quipped.

The man with the bruised face fought back a smile, squaring his jaw when Blake turned toward him with a disapproving scowl.

Blake's nostrils flared in anger. He focused his attention back on Sean. He said coldly, "I'd say these two are blood relatives."

Albano nodded. "Yes."

Just then, subtle footsteps could be heard coming down the stairs. Everyone turned to see the Goddess, now dressed in a short navy dress with thin shoulder straps that showed off her tight, tan body. She wore sunglasses and a white hat with a large rim that looked like the type one would wear to the Kentucky Derby. She was without the binoculars.

"Where are you going?" demanded Albano. "Get up there and watch!"

"I'm going to go out," she answered, pretending to ignore the troubling scene that was playing out around her. "Go out and be seen, remember?" There was nervousness in her voice.

"Not now," said Albano. "Upstairs!"

She defied the order, throwing the small strap of a purse over her shoulder and heading toward the same hallway Sean had been dragged down earlier. The high heels of her shoes now snapped against the hardwood.

"Stop!" Albano snarled. "Turn your ass around, go back upstairs, and close the fucking door!"

Blake fidgeted in his chair, glancing over at his boss for direction.

The Goddess finally stopped just as she was about to skirt around Sean. She spun toward the men, pouting, with a hand on her hips. Though she was trying to make herself look self-assured, Sean was close enough to see her lower lip quivering. He didn't know what it meant, but he recognized an opportunity that he couldn't pass up.

The second she puckered her mouth again to speak, he lunged to his feet and wrapped his arm around her chest. He yanked her body in front of his like a shield. The Goddess screamed, dropping her purse. Her hat swung to the floor. Blake and the man with the bruised faced leapt to their feet. Their arms shot forward, targeting Sean in the sights of their guns. Albano barely registered a reaction. He just sat there staring.

Sean lifted the Goddess up in the air so her head would give his cover. Her feet kicked wildly as she shrieked and struggled to break free. Her shoes landed somewhere off to the side. With his right arm pinning her against his chest, he grabbed the water pitcher next to him and smashed it over the edge of the cabinet top. Glass shards and water exploded into the air. The ice sounded like a hailstorm as it fell to the floor. Sean held what was left of the pitcher—a glass handle with jagged edges—directly at the Goddess's throat.

"Oh, God!" she whimpered. She stopped struggling. Her feet dangled loosely.

"You're gonna let us out of here, old man," warned Sean. "Or I'll jack up your prize here."

He didn't want to harm the Goddess, but he needed the others to believe that he would if he and his father had any chance of getting out of the house alive. To his shock, the grin returned to Albano's face—this time taking on a more sinister curve.

"Please don't kill me," pled the Goddess, a tear rolling down her cheek. "I'm not his wife. I'm not one of these people."

"Shut up!" shouted Blake, keeping his aim steady.

"What are you talking about?" Sean muttered, jostling the Goddess from side to side to keep the men from lining up a clean shot.

"I've only known these men a week. Please! I'm being paid to be here."

"Not another word!" Blake roared.

Sean's eyes went to his father, who looked even more confused than he did.

Albano's arm rose. His fingers were spread as he turned his head to Blake, urging discretion. "Edward," he said calmly. "Please place your gun against the temple of Mr. Slate's head."

"I'm serious!" Sean shouted as the man with the bruised face followed Albano's order. Jack's eyes pleaded to Sean for help. "I'll cut her throat!"

"God, please!" the Goddess whimpered. "They just wanted me to stay here and swim in the ocean and lay in the sun for a few days. I'm a goddamned stripper! I'm nobody!"

Sean's stomach tightened. "At Sunshine's? Do you work at Sunshine's?"

"Yes," she sobbed.

Sean glared at his father, then at Albano.

Albano turned to his men. "I believe Mr. Coleman is beginning to recognize the futility of his offensive, gentlemen," he said with a chortle. He swiveled back to Sean. "I can assure you that Mr. Blake here has absolutely no qualms with killing strippers. In fact, I've been left with the impression that he, well, rather enjoys it."

"Strippers already hate themselves," Blake said. "All of 'em. The way I see it, it's a mercy killing." A sneer crossed his face.

Sean's jaw stiffened. "Maria?" His hand shook.

"Maria's dead?" The Goddess groaned. "Oh my God." Her body went completely limp in Sean's arm.

"Don't ya worry, my brutha," Blake mocked. "It was a peaceful death, on her own terms. She just needed a little urgin' from Mr. Smith and Wesson here."

"Why?" Sean growled.

Blake's upper teeth slid across his lower lip. He opened his mouth to speak, but Albano cut him off.

"Because the dear girl had found herself in the unfortunate, astonishingly unlucky position of knowing everyone," said Albano. "Jack Slate. Sean Coleman. That woman you're holding in front of you right now. And she wasn't tight-lipped about your family two nights ago at Sunshine's. She was just one casual conversation away from figuring out everything."

Sean shook his head slowly, The Goddess's hair brushing against his lips. He carefully lowered her back to the floor, and when Blake motioned him with his head, Sean let the pitcher's broken handle drop from his hand as well. Edward then removed his gun from Jack's head and placed it back on Sean.

Albano's lips pursed. Crow's feet formed at the corners of his eyes. He opened his mouth to speak, but held his tongue, seemingly weighing some dialogue in his mind. He finally spoke. "You really have no idea what you've gotten yourself into, do you?"

"Explain it to me," Sean said, his mind struggling to slide the pieces of the puzzle into place.

Albano placed his hands on his thighs and leaned forward a bit in his chair. His eyes drooped after he took a deep breath. "So much death. It wasn't supposed to happen this way, you know. It shouldn't have happened this way."

Blake's eyes left Sean for a moment, resting on Albano.

"But your goddamned family," Albano continued, his voice now trembling with anger. "You. Before that, your blasted father. Breaking into my home. Stealing from me. From me! And seeing . . ." He stopped himself when his face began to turn red. He appeared to be forcing himself to breathe, his eyes momentarily adrift.

"Seeing you kill your wife?" Sean prompted.

Both Albano's and Blake's eyes darted up to meet Sean's. Their anxiety acknowledged that he'd guessed right.

"You murdered your wife that night—here in this house," Sean continued as a broader picture came into focus. "The *real* goddess. Jack Slate broke in to burglarize your home, never dreaming he'd end up witnessing a homicide."

Albano and Blake said nothing. The man named Edward looked at them but received verification from neither.

"But not just *one* murder," pressed Sean. "Two. Your pool boy,

Bobby—a man who was such a loner that no one's even noticed he's missing yet."

The room remained tensely silent.

"With him you caught a break," Sean said. "No one cared about him. Your wife was a different story. She was the kind of person that grabbed people's attention. Your neighbors had watched her outside every day over the summer, going through her routine. Swimming out to the yacht. Laying out by the pool. If the routine suddenly ended, people would notice. People would talk."

Albano nodded, his eyes firm. "Please continue, Mr. Coleman. You appear to be on a roll."

Sean complied. "So you happened to come across a look-alike. Hell. Maybe you even noticed her earlier this summer. You or one of your men was out one night, getting their rocks off at Sunshine's, and noticed the crazy resemblance. I'm guessing it was Blake here, since he's got an eye for detail, and he probably couldn't get a woman to touch him without paying for it."

"Mother f—" Blake began, but stopped when Albano flashed him a disapproving glare.

Sean's eyes widened. "Yeah, it *was* you, Blake. And you were there at the strip joint on Friday night, too, weren't you—when Maria came into work after she left me at the restaurant? That's when you overheard her talking to someone about me, about the conversation she had with the son of her mother's boyfriend who'd been murdered. You then followed her home when her shift ended."

Albano kept his eyes on Blake, a clear warning not to react.

"Maria's stripper friend here must be a dead-ringer for your wife, Albano, because the dirty old man next door sure as hell can't tell the difference. Suspicion avoided. Mission accomplished."

Albano shifted his eyes off Blake and back to Sean.

"Yeah," Sean said. "You borrowed goddess number two here from the strip joint—offered her an irresistible payday to lounge around in a bikini with a pair of sunglasses, and go through the motions—no questions asked. But there is one question left: Why? Why kill your wife and Bobby?" Sean nodded. "But that answer's not all that hard to figure out, is it? Young, hot woman. Old, decrepit man. Young, strapping pool boy."

"Let me shoot him!" begged Blake, incensed. "Him. Her. The other asshole."

"Please, no!" plead the stripper, her hands back out in front of her.

"Not yet," Albano said firmly, crossing his arms in front of his chest. "You're right, Mr. Coleman. Bobby was indeed a fine-looking young man who caught my wife's eye. He was hardly the first. He was, however, the last." He chuckled before taking a breath and continuing. "Tell me, Mr. Coleman. In nature, have you ever seen an animal trying to have sex with a dead mate?"

The words brought tightness to Sean's stomach. "Yeah," he replied, the conversation with Toby springing to mind. It felt so long ago. "Grasshoppers."

"Ah! Grasshoppers! Very good!" said Albano, excited. His attention turned to Blake. "Mr. Coleman might actually appreciate this metaphor. Tell me," he said to Sean, "why do you think they do that?"

"Instinct," Sean said. "They don't know any better."

"Precisely!" said Albano. "Instinct. They have no idea they're getting it on with a corpse. They're just doing what comes naturally with a prone body. *That* was Bobby's problem. He didn't know he was mounting a dead woman. My wife's fate had already been sealed, Mr. Coleman. Her sins had stacked up over months and months. Bobby knew I was a powerful man, and I suspect he knew what I was capable of. But he couldn't keep himself from doing what came natural, could he?" He shook his head, grinning. "You should have seen the look on his face when the three of us walked in on them . . . in my bed. It was magnificent! My wife was screaming and pleading, but Bobby—he was a like a deer in the headlights. He couldn't seem to process it. *Any* of it—until bam! A bullet right through his head!"

"You sick fuck," Jack said with a gasp, drawing the room's attention. "You sick, sick fuck." His eyes were dazed. He'd perhaps even surprised himself with the words that left his mouth, succumbing to the futility of his situation. He swallowed and fell silent.

Albano chuckled and turned back to Sean. "That should have been the end of it, you know. It would have been squeaky clean . . . and I mean that in the most literal sense. Tarps already under the bed in case blood came through the mattress. Our unwitting stunt-double here already lined up for her first early-morning swim." His eyes shifted to the stripper. "And then all of a sudden, lo and behold, some gentleman whom I've never met suddenly busts out of a closet in the hallway and races downstairs like an apparition. You can imagine our surprise."

"Jack Slate," Sean said.

"Yes, we'll call him 'Jack Slate the First,'" replied Albano, "since it's a surprisingly common name." He gestured his arm to Jack, who peered up at the rest of the room through wilted eyes. "We know that Jack Slate the First was the Kent's pool cleaner. We know that he was an acquaintance of Bobby. And we're pretty confident that it was Bobby who'd let it slip that I keep large sums of cash on hand in a safe down the hall."

Sean took a quick accounting of the room. His father's face was as white as a sheet, the blood dark red on his nose, his hair glistening with sweat. The gunmen were anxious, fidgety, waiting on their boss's instructions. The girl in front of him was sobbing, already resigned to a gruesome fate.

"Why did you drag me into this?" she suddenly cried out. "Why did you need *me*? Why didn't you just tell your neighbors that your wife flew back early to New Jersey?" Tears flooded from her eyes.

"Because she wasn't supposed to go missing here," said Sean, speaking the words as they entered his head. "Not in Pawleys Island. Not in South Carolina. Not as far as the authorities would be concerned anyway." He nodded to the group of leather suitcases by the table behind Albano. "New Jersey police would begin looking into her disappearance a few days from now, after he and you flew back up there. A record of an airline ticket in her name. A scanned boarding pass. Lots of cameras and security guards at the airport to take notice of a hot, young woman at his side. No one would ever think to search for her anywhere near Pawleys Island. They'd be searching up north, where she would be reported missing, and they'd find nothing. No evidence. No body. Nothing."

The room went mum again. Albano's eyes were vacant. Seconds ticked by before Blake finally spoke up.

"Mr. Albano . . ."

"Shut up, Titus!" Albano snarled, his teeth suddenly showing. "Mr. Coleman, I must admit that I'm impressed. But I do have one last question for you—one that I'm curious if you can answer: Why are you still alive? Why haven't I told my men to shoot right through that cheap whore—and believe me, she *is* cheap—and put a bullet right through your fucking head, just like I did with your father? I assure you that my fixation with cleanliness *does* have its limits!" His chest heaved in and out and his hands clenched into fists.

Sean said nothing at first. He finally let himself breathe. "You didn't kill my father," he said, turning to watch his father's face contort from the stopping of his heart. "My father died a long time ago."

Jack glared back with despondent eyes. He looked as though he wanted to say something but couldn't bring himself to.

Sean turned back to Albano. "You haven't killed me because you're a man who covers all of his bases. You're wondering who I've talked to—who knows what I know. You've got McDaggin running interference for you with the local police, but—"

"Madigan," Edward unexpectedly broke in.

All faces turned to him.

Edward shrugged his shoulders with a nervous grin. His lips

quickly flattened, and his eyes went timid. "His name is Madigan," he muttered.

After reproaching Edward with his glare, Blake belted out, "Madigan doesn't know dick!" There was clear spite in his tone. "That cracker took a $40 bribe on a $100 ticket last month, and now we slip him a few more bills whenever we need some info. No questions asked. He ain't smart enough ta run interference for no one. He ain't one of us!"

"Enough!" Albano shouted, his jaw tensing.

Sean continued. "Right now, you're wondering if in about ten seconds, county sheriff deputies are going to bust through your gate and knock down your door."

Albano stared back bitterly. Sean couldn't get a read on what he was thinking until he chortled abruptly. It evolved into a belly laugh, with Albano leaning forward in his chair and loudly clapping his hands together. He beamed from ear to ear, a sight that drew tepid grins from both Blake and Edward. Jack's hopeless gaze drifted off into space. The stripper crumbled to her knees, her hands holding her face.

"Mr. Coleman," Albano gleamed. "If you had talked to anyone, we would have heard—"

The loud chiming of the doorbell echoed off the walls of the house. Its sound held in the air as if it were a song from a chapel.

Everyone froze. Smiles disappeared. Faces turned serious. The stripper removed her hands from her face and lifted her head.

Jack glared at Sean, his eyes loaded with questions.

Chapter 27

"Whut yo' reckonin' he's skipped town?" asked Officer Madigan, jostling around in the driver's seat of the police cruiser. He was having trouble getting comfortable as he drove.

Quammen stared straight ahead through the windshield, deep in thought. "I don't know," he finally answered. "He could be scared and hiding out somewhere. If the night clerk's right, and he never came back to the motel last night, he might think we've got an eye on the place. Or maybe none of that shit he left inside is worth coming back for."

"Yo' reckon he knows we're on t'him? Thet we knows he was at th' marina?"

Quammen sighed. "I hope not. I think we put on a pretty good act back at the Bouche's trailer. If Coleman contacts them, he should think we're only looking at him for what happened at the strip joint. Maybe that will convince him it's okay to talk to us." He shook his head. "Damn, I was hoping Bouche was going to lead us right to him this morning. The way he was acting on that phone call. But when he walked into that store and walked out with those goddamned balloons . . ." He shook his head.

Madigan grinned, his crooked yellow teeth like kernels of corn. "A man's gotta make a livin' somehow."

"Yeah, well, you'd think he would have taken the day off work. Stayed at home with his mom and mourned. She was a wreck, but he was acting like he'd won the lottery when that call came in."

"People deal wif death in diffrunt ways, ah suppose," said Madigan, lifting his chin.

Quammen couldn't help but smirk. "That was pretty damned profound, Madigan," he said. "You should write for Hallmark."

Madigan snorted, glancing at his boss. "Yo' knows me. Allwus lookin' fo' other methods of income. This hyar job don't pay shit." He held Quammen's gaze for a few extra seconds before turning his attention back to the road.

Quammen rubbed his forehead with the back of his knuckle. "None of this makes sense."

"Whut yo' mean?"

"Well, let's run through it again." Quammen collected his thoughts before continuing. "We know from the report up north that last night, Coleman showed up at the strip joint where Maria Ortíz worked. He got in a fight—his second in two nights. This time, unfortunately, no two people have the same story of what happened or who all was involved, but we do know that Coleman left with the bouncer's gun. He didn't shoot anyone. He didn't appear drunk. He just left. Multiple witnesses agree on that, and because the bouncer wants his gun back, he handed over the serial number to the responding officers."

Madigan nodded his head.

Quammen continued. "Several hours later, that *same* gun—the 38 Special—turns up at the marina down south, along with two dead bodies. A woman on her boat, and a man on the beach."

"It makes sense t'me," said Madigan, digging his finger into his ear. "Coleman foun', o' thunk he foun', th' man who killed his pappy, an' killed him. Revenge. Then he kills a witness ta it."

Quammen sighed and shook his head. "On paper that might make sense, and we'll know more once we've got a name on the dead man, but you weren't there at the coroner's office that day. From what he said, and from what Warner said he'd said about his father, Coleman wasn't looking for revenge. That man had already been dead to him. For years. Hell, Coleman was more upset over Ortíz's suicide, and he barely knew her. This feels like something else."

"An' Coleman's brother-in-law still hasn't heard fum him?" asked Madigan.

"I don't know. Lumbergh hasn't returned my calls." Quammen winced and pounded his fist against the panel of his door. "Dammit, I should have taken Coleman into custody after he punched out that guy at the Wicked Scallop that first night he got here!"

"Why didn't yo'?"

"Everyone in there eating said that the asshole had it coming. Some loudmouth, begging to get hit. I wasn't going to toss Coleman behind bars for that—not when he was only here for his father's body."

The loud screech of tires peeling on pavement sounded off in the distance.

"Whut th' hell?" Madigan blurted, his voice raising an octave.

When Quammen turned toward his officer, he saw him gazing wide-eyed and open-mouthed into the rearview mirror. The police chief pivoted in his seat and looked over his shoulder. Through the back window he saw a lime-green car rapidly approaching, erratically weaving in and out of traffic.

"Thet guy flew right outta th' fo'est!" said Madigan. "He nearly hit thet red pickup!"

"Jesus, is that a Datsun?" said Quammen, narrowing his eyes. "That looks like Bouche's car. Slow down."

Madigan volleyed his attention between mirrors and eased on the gas. The policemen watched as the Datsun switched lanes and approached them quickly. Its headlights flashed and its horn wailed.

"Pull over," ordered Quammen.

Madigan flipped on his blinker and eased the cruiser onto the shoulder of the road, applying his brakes until the vehicle came to a stop.

"Whut in th' hell does he want?" asked Madigan.

The Datsun whipped onto the shoulder behind them, its driver not applying the brakes until the last second. The scream of rubber again filled the air, and Quammen clenched his body to brace for impact. The Datsun came to a tense halt just inches from the cruiser's rear bumper.

"Sweet dammit!" Madigan shouted, his hands in a death grip on the steering wheel.

The Datsun's door swung open, and Dusty dashed out of the driver's seat, waving his arms in a panic. "Help!" he screamed, his face anguished.

Quammen bit his lip, unbuckled his seatbelt, and exited his car. He stumbled when his feet met uneven ground, but he maintained his balance.

"Guys! Thank God! Guys!" Dusty shouted. His hair was wet with sweat as he slid his thick legs between the cars' bumpers.

"Mr. Bouche!" Quammen exclaimed with his hands out in front of him, urging calmness. "What are you doing?"

Madigan waited for a car to pass on the road before opening his door, hoisting himself from the driver's seat, and climbing out of the vehicle.

Dusty was desperately out of breath. When he reached Quammen, he slowed to a stop and leaned over to brace his hands on his knees. Sucking in wind, he gasped, "He told me to keep driving. To not look back . . . I didn't listen."

"Who?" asked Quammen, placing his hand on Dusty's broad shoulder. "What are you talking about?"

"Sean. He got out of . . . the car. I wanted . . . I wanted to see what he was going to do . . . to the fake detective." Dusty's face was beet red. "I hid. I watched from behind some trees."

"Sean? You know where Sean is?" Quammen asked intently.

Dusty nodded, his mouth wide for a few seconds before he continued. "Some guys pulled up. They had guns. They grabbed

Sean and the detective. Sean wasn't moving. They drove them to a house on Beach Bridge Road."

Quammen's eyes widened. He glanced over at Madigan to see his officer's mouth dangling open.

The police chief turned his attention back to Dusty. "What house?"

Chapter 28

"**E**ddie?" Blake said, keeping his voice low and his gun pinned to Sean. "Tell me ya locked the gate after ya took care of the car."

The goon swallowed. His eyes turned timid when they went to his mentor. "I . . . I don't remember." His own gun was still pointed at Jack.

Blake's eyes closed. He tilted his head and slid his tongue inside his cheek before he glared right through Edward, who turned away. His attention went back to Jack.

"Everyone remain calm," said Albano, carefully scanning the room. "For all we know, it's some Girl Scout selling cookies." He gripped the armrests of his chair and clenched his jaw as he slowly pulled himself to his feet. Blake assisted him.

"Yeah," Sean said, his eyes watching Albano like a hawk. "Make sure you order me a box of Thin Mints."

Albano ignored him. "Get them out of sight," he said to Blake.

Blake nodded and approached Sean, his gun aimed at Sean's face. He stood just a couple of feet away. Sean thought for the briefest of moments about grabbing for the gun. He worried, however, that the move would result in Edward firing on Jack. It wasn't worth the risk. His father might have already been dead to him, but he wasn't going to contribute to his literal murder.

"Get over here," Blake said, barely opening his mouth, jerking his pistol in the direction of the living room.

Sean glared at him for a second before complying. Negotiating his bare feet around the broken glass from the pitcher, he slowly made his way over to Jack and Edward. He felt the muzzle of the gun tracking each of his movements. When he heard the Goddess let out a squeal, he twisted to see Blake still glaring at him. Keeping his gun on Sean, Blake's other hand was wrapped around a fistful of the Goddess's hair. He dragged her along the floor by it.

Sean noticed her right hand was fisted, as if he she was concealing something in it. He scanned the floor for the sharp pitcher handle he'd dropped earlier. He didn't see it.

"Sit in the chair. The red one," ordered Blake, nodding to the one stationed a few feet from Jack.

Sean carefully turned and sat down in it, sinking into the cushion as he watched Blake yank the Goddess onto the carpet. He shoved her down on her back next to Sean's feet.

Albano adjusted his shirt with his hands, composing himself. "Anyone says a word, they get shot." He sidestepped the remains of the broken pitcher and began a slow trek down the hallway that led to the front of the house.

Chapter 29

Standing in front of a pewter-colored, wrought iron front door with a design reminiscent of ocean waves, Quammen eagerly waited. He tapped his foot on the stamped concrete slab beneath him and turned down the volume of his side-radio when static blared out of it.

"Come on," he groaned impatiently.

"Ah doesn't reckon we sh'd haf come up hyar, ta th' door," said Madigan nervously.

"Why not?" Quammen asked, turning to his officer.

"Th' gate was closed."

"Yeah, but it wasn't locked. It's fine."

"Ah reckon Bouche is jerkin' us aroun'," Madigan said, swallowing. "Ah mean, as enny fool kin plainly see, we knows the guy's not playin' wif a full deck."

Quammen nodded, turning back to the door. "Oh, he's off, no doubt about that. And I'm sure he exaggerated the hell out of what he saw. I've talked to him a few times now, and you heard him back at the trailer. He says a lot of weird shit. Dramatic. He fancies himself some kind of Broadway actor. I'm half expecting him to be belting out a musical number by the time we get back to the car."

When Madigan didn't react with an expected chuckle, Quammen's eyes moved back on him. He found his officer tugging at his collar with his finger. A bead of sweat rolled down the side of his pale face.

"Are you all right?" Quammen asked. "You look sick."

"Ah's fine. Ah jest reckon we might be want ta git a warrant."

Quammen shook his head. "Bouche isn't the kind of guy whose eye-witness account is going to get us a search warrant. Let's just check this out. It's likely nothing. I doubt Coleman's here."

"Do yo' reckon he's makin' it all up?"

"I don't know," Quammen said, shaking his head a bit. "What's bothering me is that this isn't some random house he pointed us to. I've been here before."

"When we were he'pin' canvass th' area af'er Slate's hide warshed up?"

"Yeah. I took this house and a few others along the street. Some old guy lives here. He had a well-dressed, bald, black guy with him. Business associate, maybe."

Madigan's head swiveled toward his boss. "Bouche said—"

"I know," Quammen said. He turned and glanced at the dark Cadillac parked beside a cement fountain behind them. "He said that one of the guys who grabbed Coleman was black and bald."

Madigan's shoulders sank. He let out a meek groan that puzzled Quammen.

"Just stay sharp, okay?" said Quammen. "Keep your eyes and ears open. Like I said, this is probably nothing, but it could always be something."

Quammen was about to ring the doorbell a second time but lowered his hand when he noticed some subtle motion on the other side of a pane of frosted glass along the door. His hand rubbed up against his holstered pistol. He glanced at Madigan when he heard the release of a deadbolt. The officer's face was shriveled up as if he'd just sucked on a lemon.

The door opened slowly and the elderly man that Quammen had met nearly a week ago emerged from around its edge. The man's thick eyebrows arched when he saw the two uniformed men standing before him.

"Officers," the man greeted after a second or two. He was clad in a collared, short-sleeved shirt and long shorts, looking relaxed. "Can I help you?"

"Mr. Albano, isn't it?" Quammen asked. "We met last Monday. I asked you some questions about the body that had washed ashore, over by the bridge."

"Ah yes. I remember," said Albano, grinning. "Have you made any progress on the case?"

"Some," answered Quammen. "Not enough. But that's not why we're here."

"Oh?"

"Well," Quammen began, trying to choose his words carefully. "We received a report. A report of a man being taken and held here . . . against his will." He watched Albano's eyes carefully, searching for any hint of panic in his reaction. He saw none. The corners of the old man's mouth curled and his eyes shifted between Quammen and Madigan.

"You must be joking," Albano said with a chuckle. "Who told you that?"

"Is there anyone inside the house but you?" asked Quammen, ignoring his question.

"No. I've been here by myself all morning. Catching up on some reading, you know." He placed his hands on his hips. When his eyes shifted back to Madigan, wrinkles of irritation formed along the loose skin of his face.

"The African-American gentleman," Quammen continued. "The guy who was here with you on Monday. Do you know where he is?"

"He left yesterday," Albano answered matter-of-factly. "He does some accounting work for me, up in Mendham. I thought it would be good for him to spend a few days here in the sun with my wife and me, but he's gone now." His eyes narrowed. "What's going on here? Why do you need to talk to him?"

"That's not his car out front—the Cadillac?" Quammen asked, bobbing his chin to the side.

"No. It's *my* car."

Quammen nodded. After a few seconds, he spoke again. "Do you mind if we come inside and take a look around?"

"I most certainly do mind," said Albano, pursing his lips and folding his arms in front of his chest. "This is turning into harassment! Do you have a warrant?"

"No," Madigan quickly answered, drawing a disapproving scowl from Quammen. "No we don't."

Albano smiled in satisfaction. "Then I'm going to have to ask you both to leave my property."

Quammen continued glaring at Madigan, unsure of why his officer had decided to interject himself into the inquiry. Madigan's eyes stayed on Albano, unwilling to acknowledge his boss's scorn.

"Good day, Chief Quammen," Albano added. "Good day, Officer McDaggin."

Quammen had been about to tip his head in farewell, but his body tensed as if electrified when he heard the second name. "What?" Quammen held his eyes steady on Albano. "What did you just call him?" His heart pounded.

Albano's eyes tightened. "Officer McDaggin. It's right there on his badge."

"No," said Quammen. "His badge says Madigan. I've only heard one other person call him McDaggin."

Albano scoffed, took a step back, and began to close the door.

"Sean Coleman!" Quammen abruptly shouted, the volume of his voice prompting both Albano and Madigan to recoil. "This is Chief Quammen! Are you inside this house? Do you need assistance?"

"You're mad," said Albano, his eyes burning through the chief. He slammed the door shut, rattling a steel porch light that hung above the doorbell.

Multiple locks secured before muffled retreating footsteps dissipated. Madigan released a breath and turned to leave, but Quammen snagged him by the arm.

"Wait," said Quammen, listening. He placed his ear up to the door for several seconds but heard nothing. No calls for help. No talking of any kind.

Quammen finally left the cement porch, angrily guiding his officer with him onto the stone driveway. "Why the hell did you tell him so quickly that we didn't have a warrant? We could have danced around that."

"We *don't* haf one, Chief," Madigan said, shrugging his shoulders. He didn't make eye contact, preferring to stare sullenly at the ground. "Yo' lissened ta whut thet man had ta say, an' yo' still don't reckon Bouche is full of shit?"

"Hold up," said Quammen, slowing his pace. His head was tilted toward the ground.

Squinting, he took another couple of steps forward before lowering to one knee. With an index finger, he shoved a small, round stone from the driveway onto its side. Half of it was covered with a sticky red substance.

"Is this blood?" His eyes traced the area. He found another stone with a similar blemish about a foot and a half away, in the direction of the Cadillac. When his eyes rose up to the grill of the car, he noticed its New Jersey plates. "Mendham."

"Whut's thet, Chief?" asked Madigan, leaning over his shoulder.

"These guys are from New Jersey."

"So?"

"Remember that rare bullet that was pulled out of Slate's body. The kind Warner said is only sold in two states? One of them is Jersey."

Madigan snorted. "A lot of people fum Jersey vacashun down this hyar way, Chief."

The piercing scream of a woman suddenly sounded out from somewhere inside the house. Quammen's head spun toward the door as he leapt to his feet. He and Madigan shot each other a quick look before they both drew their firearms. With his pulse racing, Quammen ran toward the door. Madigan was close behind.

Quammen checked the door, even knowing it was already locked.

A man yelled from inside the house. A second later, there was the pop of gunfire.

"Shit! I'm gonna take down the door!" Quammen shouted. "Cover me!"

"Yeah!" he heard his officer say.

Quammen took a step back and prepared to send a hard stomp in just below the knob. As he was about to launch forward, his skull took a heavy blow from behind. He crashed to the cement. His teeth felt loose and his vision was floating as his head pulsed with pain.

"Dammit," he heard Madigan mutter. There was regret in his tone. Conflict.

Quammen no longer felt his gun in his hand. When he spotted the pistol leaning up against the door in front of him, he reached forward. He was immediately struck a second time across on the head. He went down flat on his chest, blacking out.

Chapter 30

Until Sean heard his name echoing down the hallway, he hadn't known who Albano was conversing with at the front door. Somehow Quammen had found his way there. Somehow he suspected Sean was inside and in trouble. But suspicions were clearly all Quammen had, otherwise the police chief would have entered the home by now.

Blake stared at Sean, pointing his gun at his forehead with one hand while holding a finger to his mouth with the other. His piercing blue eyes refused to blink. Sean held his stare, unflinching.

Edward and Jack were in a similar pose. The only one not trapped between crosshairs was the Goddess. She was still cowering on the floor beside Sean's feet. Her hair, frazzled after its rough treatment, covered most of her face, though Sean could see dark triangles below her eyes from her tears and mascara. She looked like a punk-rock singer. With one hand covering her mouth, the other was still a fist around the glass handle. She was holding it so tightly that blood had trickled from between her fingers and onto the carpet.

He knew that any sudden movement would be met with a bullet in his head. He also understood that if he did nothing, the same would be his fate. Albano and his men were responsible for multiple murders. They weren't going to let any of their captives go free to tell the police what they knew. They had no intention of living out the rest of their days in a maximum security prison.

Right outside the house was an armed police officer. Quammen didn't know what was happening inside, but he was the best chance any of them had of surviving. Sean couldn't let him leave.

He slowly turned his head toward his father, careful enough with the movement not to spook Blake into thinking he was going on an offensive—not yet. Jack looked as though he was on the verge of hyperventilation. His face was pale and his glassy eyes were large and glued to Sean. He knew the stakes as well, and it looked like he was counting on his son to do something about it.

When Blake and Edward turned their attention to the sound of the door slamming shut at the front of the house, Sean mouthed the word "Cochise" to his father. He prayed Jack would remember it as the war cry the two had used so many years ago to launch their double-team attacks on Diana. When Jack's eyes sobered and he subtly nodded, Sean knew he was onboard.

Sean clenched a fist with his right hand, took in a deep breath as every muscle in his body tensed, and silently counted to three. By two, his plan went astray.

Without warning, the Goddess snarled and swung her arm as if throwing a discus, plunging the jagged glass in her hand into Blake's inner thigh. She howled savagely—teeth showing and nostrils stretched wide as she sunk the glass deep into his flesh.

Blake howled and his body buckled as if he'd just taken a jolt of electricity. His eyes bulged and he whipped his gun to aim at her. She threw herself to her back and raised her arms in front of her face, turning away. Blake pulled the trigger just as Sean's fist sent a wicked right-cross to his mouth.

The gun went off. Blake's head snapped to the side and he stumbled off balance. Sean tackled him to the floor. A louder gunshot sounded off from across the room. Out of the corner of his eye, Sean saw his father and Edward grappling against the back wall for Edward's gun. One of their elbows crashed through the glass of the blind-drawn window behind them. Shards fell to the floor.

"Quammen!" Sean bellowed, catching Blake's incoming arm in his grip.

The veins along Blake's head swelled with intensity as he fought against Sean's strength and leverage. He twisted his wrist and tried to target Sean as best he could with the gun, but each time he pulled the trigger, the bullet whizzed past Sean's head, lodging in the ceiling. Blake kicked and flailed like a trapped animal as Sean fought to wrestle him down to the floor. Sean's hand was in an unrelenting death grip on Blake's trigger arm.

He almost had Blake's wrist pinned to the floor when he heard his father cry, "Grab the gun!"

Sean swung his head to see the Goddess scrambling along the floor on her hands and knees toward Edward's pistol. Jack had managed to knock it from the gunman's grip. Edward was now leveling Jack with wicked lefts and rights across his face, every one of them connecting. Jack had his hands twisted firmly into Edward's shirt, using the drag of his own body weight to keep his foe from retrieving the firearm. Jack was hanging on like a pit bull, wrapped up with his assailant as blood streamed out of his nose and mouth.

Sean hadn't held any respect for his father for thirty years. It had been that long since he had felt a hint of pride in the man who'd abandoned him. But for that second or two, he felt both. The fervor ended when he felt a sharp heat plunge into his stomach just below the ribcage.

His eyes widened, mouth gaping as he looked to see Blake's free hand tremble as it clasped the dark handle of a switchblade. The opposite end was firmly embedded in Sean. He didn't know where Blake had worn the weapon and it didn't matter at that moment. The damage was done.

He clenched his jaw, snorted like an injured dog, and landed another punch across Blake's face. It lacked the strength of the first one, but it caught him clean enough to knock him flat to his back.

The blade slid out of Sean's flesh, drawing with it a loud moan. He toppled backwards, falling off of Blake and down to his back.

He could barely breathe and his arms began to quiver. For a few seconds, his vision tunneled, but he willed himself awake and the darkness passed. He had to stop the bleeding. He covered his hand over the wound and applied pressure as best he could. Warm blood oozed from between his fingers, and he felt something digging into his back.

When he raised his head from the floor, he saw a sadistic sneer on Blake's battered face. The thug propped himself up on an elbow as blood shined off his lower lip. He aimed his gun at Sean's face.

Sean tried to speak, to call to the others for help, but the best he could muster was a strained groan. He glared steadily at the man who was about to take his life.

A flash of movement in his peripheral vision coincided with Blake pulling the trigger. The muffled pop of the silencer seemed to slow down time. Sean's view was eclipsed by a gray figure leaping between them. The weight of a man crashed down across his torso.

Sean gasped and cringed from the pressure as a pair of anguished eyes at the center of a badly beaten face now glared back at him from just inches away. They were the eyes of his father.

"No!" Sean groaned.

The side of Jack's head was resting on his chest. Labored breath crawled out of his mouth and pressed against Sean's chin. He had thrown himself between Sean's body and Blake's gun. He had taken the bullet meant to end Sean's life. It was a sacrifice many fathers would have made for their sons, but not one Sean would have ever dreamt of from his.

Jack's eyes began to swim. The corners of his lips twisted upward, as if he were lost in some endearing memory from long ago. Blood streamed from his nose and mouth.

"No," Sean gasped, his head shaking. He pried his hands from between his wound and his father's chest, and wrapped his arms around his father's shoulders.

Over the sound of Jack's wheezing, Sean heard the Goddess cry out in pain.

"Shut up, bitch!" Edward snarled. The goon had regained control.

Her voice reduced to a stuttering whimper. Footsteps shuffled along the wooden floor toward Sean.

From over Jack's shoulder, Sean saw Blake's head rise. He was standing up straight, hovering above them. His penetrating eyes were that of a scavenger, a vulture staring down at the prey it was about to devour.

Sean's eyes went back to Jack. He was now grinning at Sean the way a proud father would at the wondrous, life-changing sight of his first son being born. The familiar scent of tobacco Sean remembered from his youth floated up from his father's shirt.

"Dad," Sean whispered, holding his father. He rested his bloody hand on the back of Jack's head.

"Sean," Jack gasped. "I'm ... sorry. Should ... never ... have left."

"It's all right . . . It's okay," whispered Sean, his eyes wet.

In the seconds that drifted by, thirty years of bitterness and resentment fled from Sean's soul as if drawn out through an exorcism. A tear rolled down the side of his face. The wound in his stomach no longer hurt. All he could feel was something solid and sharp pressing against his back, between him and the floor.

"Your . . . sis-s-ster," Jack slurred. "Tell her . . ."

"I'll tell her, Dad."

Blake stood silently, watching and listening, glaring down at them. The right corner of his mouth quirked up into a hint of a grin, as he admired his handiwork.

"Could," Jack continued, his face tightening. His eyes closed. "Could have never . . . been so lucky . . . to have a son . . . like you."

The words dragged Sean's heart down to his wounded stomach. He held onto his father as he felt one last long breath empty from his lungs.

Chapter 31

Blake's chest heaved in and out as he lifted his gun to Sean's face.

Sean glared back without fear. "I'm gonna kill you," he said. Adrenaline and rage burned through his body.

Blake quickly pulled the trigger. Nothing happened. He pulled it a second time. Only a click. "Fuck," he barked, digging into his pocket.

"Blake!" came Albano's loud voice from down the hallway.

Blake's eyes shot toward the entrance of the house. "What?"

"The situation. Is it under control?"

"Yeah," he said, glancing back down at Sean for a moment. "It's under control."

"Good. Get over here. Now!"

His face contorted in irritation, Blake yanked his hand back out of his pocket. If he was looking for more ammunition, he didn't find it. "Stay here," Blake ordered Edward. "Watch them."

"But I—"

"Just do it, asshole!" Blake yelled, his patience expended. He hobbled down the hallway, the sound of his uneven footsteps echoing off the walls.

Sean carefully—and painfully—leaned to the side, supporting his father's head until the rest of his body slid to the floor. He looked at Jack's face one last time, burning the image into his mind. He wouldn't look at him again until things were over.

There was blood everywhere: on Sean, on his father, on the floor. Sean couldn't tell how much of it was his. A lot of it belonged to his father and Blake. Sean pressed his hand back over his stomach and applied pressure again, wincing from the pain. The blade had left a deep wound and had sent his body into some form of shock, but he felt as though the pressure he was now applying was keeping him from bleeding out and losing consciousness. He hoped he'd have enough strength to do what he needed to do.

"Where is it?" he heard Edward ask under his breath. It wasn't clear if he was posing the question to the Goddess or to himself, but there was anxiety in his voice.

"I don't know," she whined. "*You* kicked it! *You* find it!"

Sean looked at them. The Goddess was lying on her stomach on the floor with her head angled toward him. Edward was hunched down behind her with his knee in her back as his hands held her wrists together. His head was jerking back and forth like a weather vane in a tornado, searching for something. It was then that Sean noticed the man held no gun.

Sean realized what was digging into his back—Edward's pistol, kicked by Edward himself during the scuffle. The weapon couldn't have been closer in proximity, but Sean couldn't grab it without reaching behind him. He wasn't sure he'd be able to pull it off before Edward figured out what he was doing.

At the other end of the house, Sean could hear a panicked discussion between Albano, Blake, and a man whose voice he couldn't place at first. When a couple of unintelligible statements grew higher in volume than the other two, however, he realized the third man was Madigan. Absent was Quammen's voice. He hoped the police chief wasn't dead.

He wondered if Madigan was a tighter part of Albano's inner circle than Blake had let on. Either that or the officer had recognized an opportunity to put down Quammen in front of his sugar daddy and walk away with a big payday. Whatever the scenario, things were far from under control. Madigan's voice was emotional and growing louder.

Sean subtly slid his back in a slight circular motion along the floor, gritting his teeth against the pain as he got a feel for the positioning of the gun. When he'd convinced himself that the handle was pointed toward his legs, he stopped, panting. His eyes shifted to Edward. The thug was staring directly at him.

"What are you doing?" Edward demanded.

The Goddess was staring at him, too.

"Got . . . glass in my back," Sean grunted, slurring his words to make himself seem in even worse shape than he was.

"Good," said Edward, his eyes going back to the floor to continue scanning for his gun.

"Got to turn to . . . side. It's killing me."

"That glass isn't what's going to kill you today, asshole," Edward said dismissively.

Sean sighed laboriously. "Rolling over."

Edward didn't protest when Sean began rotating his body ninety degrees toward him, onto his side. With all the blood on the floor and his slow movements, Sean hoped Edward assumed he was going to keel over at any moment. Edward was intent on searching for his gun but didn't move away from the Goddess.

The gun was now uncovered and obscured from Edward's view by Sean's large body. All Sean needed to do was reach behind him and grab it. When he saw rattlesnake-like intensity in the Goddess's eyes, he knew that she understood what he was planning. She had either guessed or knew the gun was kicked his way during the melee but had written off him having enough life left to use it. He saw renewed hope in her face.

She suddenly began bucking and twisting her body along the floor, pulling Edward off-balance and drawing his full attention back to her. He sneered and yanked up on her arms to regain control, oblivious to Sean's movements.

Sean flung an arm behind him, groaning from the pain of his wound, as his fingers fumbled along the floor until they found metal.

His hand latched onto the gun handle and he swung it in front of him.

Edward's eyes grew wide, his focus back on Sean. Mouth gaping, he dropped the Goddess and leapt to his feet. He bolted toward Sean, going for the gun.

Sean's quivering index finger found the trigger. He squeezed.

The shot rang out, and Edward's body seized up as the bullet entered his chest. He bellowed a sick, inhuman sound from lips in a perfect "O," stumbling over his own feet as his hands fumbled across his torso. The Goddess watched for a moment in shock before darting toward Sean, scrambling across the floor on her knees to join him.

With wandering eyes, Edward turned his body away from Sean and lumbered to the back wall. He grabbed the curtains and yanked, pulling a panel and its supporting rod down to the floor. A pair of French doors were exposed and sunlight flooded through, lighting up the room.

With the Goddess's help, Sean pulled himself up to his hands and knees. His leg rubbed up against his father's as he twisted around him. With one hand covering his gut, he used his other to point the gun toward the hallway. He was expecting the other men in the house to emerge to investigate the sound of the shot, but he neither saw nor heard them anymore.

Edward was no longer a threat, though he still had some will left in his body. He pulled down on the door handle. When it released, the hinges moaned and Edward fell forward. He collapsed in the doorway to a score of ocean surf that now swept inside the house along with a breeze.

"Go out the back," Sean told the Goddess. "Don't look back. Just run. Get down to the beach and call for help. I won't let them stop you."

A stray tear slid out of the corner of her eye. "What about you?"

He bit his lip from a painful spasm that spread from his wound to his ribs. "I'm not in any shape to run," he muttered. "And I'm not done here."

"They'll kill you," she whispered, her glistening eyes tugging at him.

Sean nodded. "Or they'll die trying."

Chapter 32

Sean knelt at the end of the hallway, his eyes blinking rapidly as he fought to push down the most recent bout of dizziness. He watched for movement until he could no longer hear the Goddess's vigorous footsteps above the sound of distant waves and the screech of seagulls.

She had begged him to join her, pleaded with him to escape through the courtyard to safety. Maybe, even in his condition, the two would have fared better than Lloyd Prevenas had the night the burglar witnessed a double murder. But personal safety wasn't what was driving Sean—a reckoning was.

He hadn't come to South Carolina looking to avenge the death of his father, but that's how he was going to leave it, in one way or another. Jack, Maria, Schofield, and even Prevenas—none of them deserved what had happened to them. They all died because evil men had committed evil acts, and those men were so consumed with escaping punishment that they let nothing stand in their way—nothing.

The long mirror on the wall revealed Sean to himself again. He wasn't the same man he'd been even minutes earlier. His father's blood was smeared across his face. His eyes burned with vengeance. His being was filled with darkness.

He carefully edged his way down the hallway, his back leaving a blood trail on the wall as he slid along it. On the opposite wall hung several framed photos of men in business suits, posing together. In some of the shots, they were standing outside on newly turned earth, holding shovels in their hands—apparently groundbreaking ceremonies. The shovels' blades were even with their cocky, grinning faces. Sean was certain that a younger Albano was standing somewhere among them, but he wasn't concerned with the baron's past—only what Sean intended to make of his future.

He kept one hand pushed on his wound, ready to move it up to his gun if needed. The floor started to creak with each new step, fueling the bitter flow of adrenaline that surged through his body.

The front door was wide open, swaying in the light breeze that streamed past Sean toward the open door at the back. Just outside of the entryway, laying facedown across the front step, was Quammen. The thick part in his hair along the center of his scalp identified him. His gun looked to be missing from his side-holster. So was his radio. There was blood on the back of his head at the center of a matted patch of hair. He was either dead or unconscious, compliments—Sean assumed—of his corrupt officer.

Madigan, however, was nowhere in sight. Neither were Albano and Blake. They hadn't come back down the hallway. Either they had fled outside when they heard gunshots or were waiting to ambush him in the room just to the right side of the entrance. The room's opening had no door. Sean watched it closely, ready to react if a gun emerged from it.

Blake had to have reloaded by now, and Madigan was surely armed as well. Sean may have been walking into a trap, but he felt no reservations with continuing forward. Things were going to end.

Sean's gaze shot back and forth from the front door to the side room's entrance, watching for shadows or any sudden movement. He could now see into part of the room where a tall white bookcase hosted a series of leather-bound books and hardback novels. He slowed and leaned forward. Next to the bookcase, he saw prestigious-looking plaques hanging at eye level. The room appeared to be a study.

If he went right up to the doorway, he'd be an easy target for anyone waiting inside the room or outside in the driveway. He stayed against the wall behind him, carefully skirting along it. He took his hand off his wound and doubled up his grip on the gun to help steady his aim. He controlled his breathing.

"Sean Coleman!" a frantic voice suddenly shouted out from inside the study.

Sean's eyes bulged. He flattened against the wall and stretched his arms out tight, his finger tense on the gun's trigger.

"Ah doesn't wan ta be part of this hyar enny mo'e!" It was Madigan. The pitch of his voice was high and panicked. "They told me ta stay in hyar an' shootcha when yo' walked outside. Ah doesn't wan t'be do'n' thet!" He sounded scared out of his mind.

"Then don't, asshole!" Sean shouted back. "Get your ass out here, now! Arms in the air and lay on your stomach!"

"Ah didn't knows these min were murderers!" Madigan yelled. "Ah took money fum them, dawgone it! Ah panicked an' ah hit th' chief! Ah did wrong!"

"McDaggin, if you don't get out here right now, I swear to God I'm going to come in there and shoot your ass!"

Sean waited and listened, hearing only what sounded like faint sobbing. But the officer wasn't budging. Sean slowly moved further down the wall, brushing past a tall, leafy potted plant. He stayed out of the line of fire through the front door, taking in a wider view of the interior of the study.

The corner of a thick redwood desk presented itself. There was a tall chair behind it and another rich Persian rug spread across the floor. When Sean saw a large hand extended in the air, he lurched left to the edge of the front doorway, adrenaline allowing him to ignore the sharp pain in his gut. He aimed his gun at Madigan who was standing with both arms in the air, his legs together and tears rolling down his red face. There was no one else visible in the room.

Madigan's spread fingers were empty and trembling. His mouth gaped open, moving as if he was trying to say something but couldn't.

He was a frothing mess, his face twisted so sharply that he looked as if he was having a stroke.

"Walk out here! Slowly!" Sean ordered. "Keep your hands in the air!"

Madigan didn't move.

Sean noticed that the officer's gun wasn't in its holster—or on the desk or floor. He was unarmed. As Sean opened his mouth to demand an explanation, a pair of dark arms swung out from behind the sides of the officer's wide waist. Each hand was holding a pistol.

Sean lunged to the side, falling through the front doorway just as a barrage of gunfire poured through the house. Splintered wood and shards of drywall exploded through the air as he spilled on top of Quammen.

Managing to keep hold of his gun, he rolled off of Quammen. Keeping his momentum, he hooked his free arm around the police chief's torso and rolled the man's dead weight across the cement patio until the two of them crashed through short shrubs and crumbled onto gravel. Sean lay there panting, vision tunneling again as pain threatened to send him under.

In a haze, he heard Madigan cry out from inside the house. "No, no, no!" His pleas were followed by a single gunshot, then a loud thud.

Sean knew the officer had chosen to hedge his bets on the bribes he'd taken from Albano. Madigan had the opportunity for a much bigger payday in helping the old man evade murder charges. By seizing on that opportunity, however, he'd paid with his life. With Albano's house of cards crumbling to the ground around them, Madigan's only remaining value had been as a human shield. And that worth had just expired.

Blake had to know the game was over. Any hopes of him and Albano covering up their trail and avoiding prison had been shredded to pieces. Gunshots had echoed through open doors and across the neighborhood. Police officers were down. The Goddess was probably already on the beach, screaming for help. Sirens from county or neighboring authorities would likely be zooming down Beach Bridge Road within minutes.

Albano was still absent, but Blake was Sean's more immediate concern. He'd come out of the house with guns blazing before he'd be taken alive. He was now a man with nothing to lose, even more dangerous than before.

Sean would have been smart to just get out of his way, but that wasn't going to happen. It was brutally personal—more personal than the matter that had brought him there, and more personal than what his father had done thirty years earlier. Blake had killed his dad. And he would pay for that with his life.

Allowing himself two deep breaths, Sean braced himself as he rose slowly to one knee and trained his gun on the front door, putting his body between it and Quammen. He swallowed and fought back the urge to cough. When his vision began to blur again, he dropped his eyes to his gut. Blood was steadily draining out of it. He covered the spot again with his hand. "Dammit."

A dull pop sounded, and brick and mortar exploded out from the wall of the house, dumping across Sean's head. He ducked lower behind a shrub, his eyes searching for the shooter. The bullet hadn't come from inside. It wasn't Blake.

Sean swung his arm across the driveway, his eyes blinking as he struggled to maintain his focus. When he spotted what looked like an arm sticking out of the passenger window of the Cadillac, he fired two shots through its windshield. Glass crunched and a man howled in pain. The arm disappeared inside the car, but something had fallen from it to the ground.

It had to be Albano inside the vehicle. He'd been hiding there, waiting for Blake to finish off Sean. When that didn't happen, and Sean had made it outside, Albano couldn't bring himself to pass up a clear shot. Luckily, Albano had bad aim.

The object that had fallen to the ground had to be a gun—Blake's gun with the silencer, judging by the sound of the shot it had made. Blake must have had the two officers' pistols.

Sean watched the Cadillac wobble from the movements of its passenger. Albano was still alive and was probably lowering himself to the floorboard to avoid more gunfire. He may have still been a threat, but he wasn't the primary one.

"Come on out, Blake!" Sean yelled, directing his gun back at the doorway. It took every bit of effort he had to just hold the weapon straight. "Your boss needs you to make him a drink! He's feeling a bit parched!"

When there was no response, he feared Blake had left the house through another door. He searched back and forth between the entrance and the corner of the building behind him, praying the gunman wouldn't suddenly emerge from around it.

A moan rose up from Sean's side. Quammen was beginning to stir.

"Two Jack Slates!" Blake shouted from inside the house, near the entrance. "I don't know which one was ya daddy, but I killed one and ordered the kill on the other. I guess that makes *me* ya daddy now!"

Sean's eyebrows caved inwards. His nostrils flared in anger. Blake was confident—cocky even—that he was going to get out of the situation alive. Sean took his hand off his wound and reached behind him, shaking Quammen by the shoulder.

"Quammen. Wake your ass up," Sean grunted. Shaking Quammen made him feel lightheaded, and he returned his hand to his side, blinking furiously as sweat poured down his head.

He felt Quammen stir beside him and glanced just long enough to catch the chief's open, glassy eyes. The chief's eyelids flickered with uncertainty.

"What? What's happening?" Quammen slurred.

"No time to explain, Chief," Sean said, his eyes now back on the door. "Your officer's dead. The man who killed him and my father is inside and he's armed."

"Madigan?" Quammen said with a gasp. "What? He hit me."

"Yeah. He was an asshole. That doesn't change our situation. The man inside's going to try and drive out of here in that Cadillac. We're not going to let him."

"My gun," Quammen said, his hand fumbling along his holster. "I don't have it. My radio's gone, too."

"I know," Sean said impatiently, starting to nod but stopping when dizziness threatened to topple him. "There's a pistol next to that Cadillac on the ground. Passenger side. Albano's inside the car. He's injured. I don't know how badly. He might have another gun, but I doubt it."

"A shotgun!" Quammen said. "There's one in my car."

Sean shook his head, eyeing the distance between the house and the propped open front gate. "You'd never make it. He'd pick you off easy."

Blake's arm shot out from the open front door and fired off a round.

Sean heard it wiz by, just over their heads. He returned fire just as Blake's arm disappeared back inside the house.

Blake's head never broke the plane of the doorway. It was a blind shot. "Mr. Albano!" he yelled from inside. "Start the car!"

Albano said nothing. The car sat still.

Sean began to believe Albano was injured even worse than he'd thought. "Listen," Sean said, keeping his voice low so that only Quammen could hear him. "We're at a stalemate here, but it's not going to last much longer. Blake knows that reinforcements are on the way. The clock's ticking, but he's not going to leave his boss behind. Albano can buy their way out of the country. He's Blake's meal ticket."

"What are you saying?" asked Quammen, his words now coming out clearer.

"Can you shoot straight?"

"What?"

"Can you shoot straight? You're not seeing double from that whack on the head or anything, are you?"

"No."

"Good, because I'm seeing two of everything." Panting, Sean begrudgingly shoved his pistol into Quammen's hands.

The chief fumbled with it for a second, unprepared for the handoff, but he quickly took control of the weapon and pointed it toward the front door.

Sean swore under his breath and ducked behind the chief, who moved to fill in the position Sean had just vacated. Sean hated giving up the weapon he'd intended to kill Blake with, but his eyes were swimming and his reflexes were dulling. Still, he had no intention of subcontracting the fate of his father's murderer. His gaze floated up to the face of the house.

"Stay here," he said to Quammen. "You're too close to the building to be seen from the upper windows. He can't lay in a shot from inside without exposing himself. If he . . ."

Sean suddenly felt off-balance. The world tipped. He stretched his arm out and planted his hand on the ground.

"Sean?" Quammen said, watching the door.

"He's killed more people than you know, Quammen," Sean whispered, blinking. "When he comes out of that house, you shoot him. Don't hesitate. Just shoot."

Sean pulled himself to his feet, fighting lightheadedness, and leaning back against the house. He glanced down at the sight of his crimson-covered hand glued to his stomach. Multiple streams of blood crept through his fingers.

"What are you doing?" demanded Quammen. "Stay down!"

"I'll flush him toward you. Out of the house. Be ready."

Quammen snapped Sean a quick scowl before returning his attention to the door. "What the hell are you talking about?" he said. "You're hurt. Hurt bad. Get back down and stay put."

"No," Sean said, shaking his head. "Be ready. He's coming your way."

"Mr. Albano!" Blake yelled, failing again to get a reaction from his boss.

"He's still at the front door," Sean said. "Good."

Sean shook his head like a dog after a swim and then staggered his way through hedges, mulch, and exposed driplines until he reached the corner of the building. He pulled himself around it and hunched low when he saw a windowsill below tall glass. The window likely belonged to the study where Madigan was killed. Sean slid under it, wincing as his rubbery legs searched for solid footing.

Once past the window, Sean picked up his pace, slogging around a couple of palm trees and a dented air-conditioning unit that sat inside a narrow rock garden. When he glanced to his left, he saw the eight-foot stone wall that separated Albano's property from the Kent's. Beyond it was the Kent's house, standing on higher ground but partially obscured by trees.

By the time Sean reached the back corner of the home, his bare, bloodied feet were covered with leaves and gravel. He peered around the brick and saw the distinctive, white pillars from the other day. They sprouted up from the long, wooden porch. There, the wide-open French doors the Goddess had escaped through still swayed in the breeze, overlooking the concrete patio and swimming pool.

A dull knocking noise grabbed Sean's attention. He pressed his back flat against the building. His eyes and ears searched for the sound's source. It didn't seem to be coming from inside.

His gaze shifted up over the wall to the Kent's house. In one of the upper windows, he spotted some motion. Someone inside was knocking on the glass with their knuckles.

"Shit," he groaned, realizing through the fuzzy details of her face that it was Nicola, the Kent's young granddaughter.

Her face was blurred, but he made out a wide grin stretched below her nose. She seemed to realize she had grabbed his attention, because her hand rose high and swung in a friendly, enthusiastic wave.

The scene was surreal. The little girl hadn't a clue what was going on. She hadn't heard the shots, and her grandparents clearly hadn't either. Maybe it was the breeze, the sound of the ocean, or the property's low setting that had suppressed the ruckus of the small war-zone. Whatever the explanation, Sean began to wonder if more help was even coming. If not even the next door neighbor had heard the shots, all he had left was faith in a stripper he hardly knew.

Nicola's demeanor suddenly changed. Her hands went to her mouth and she backed up a step from the window. He knew she had finally taken note of the condition he was in—blood all over his clothes and body, his complexion white as a sheet. She lifted at the bottom of the window to try and open it. He waved off the effort, immediately regretting the expended energy, but Nicola was too focused on the window to notice.

When Sean heard a crash at the back of the house, he stuck his head around the corner. His heart stopped when he made out Blake's bald head poking out from between the back doors. Sean shrank behind the cover of the building. *Blake heard me? Did he see my shadow slide past a window?*

Sean steadied his breath the best he could. His eyes lifted back up to Nicola, who was still struggling with her window. If she were to get it open and shout something out, Blake would hear her, and Sean's position would be blown. He had no weapon to defend himself, and he doubted he could find quick cover if Blake came after him.

He shook his head vigorously at Nicola. The motion didn't get her attention but did prompt another spell of dizziness. He leaned forward, his eyes watering as he fought with his body to gather his bearings. He felt like he was going to vomit.

He swallowed the bile that filled his mouth and peeked around the corner again. Blake was still in the doorway, now hunched over and pulling at something along the porch. With one gun in hand and the other slid halfway down the back of his pants, Blake swore under his breath and dragged Edward's bloody, lifeless body a couple feet outside of the house. Blake then dropped to his knees, his back to Sean as he rifled through Edward's pants pockets.

At first Sean figured Blake was searching for more ammo, but when the henchman's arm recoiled, dangled from his fingers were keys. As sunlight reflected off them, Sean realized they were car keys.

They wouldn't have belonged to the Cadillac. An extra set wouldn't have done Blake any good if he couldn't get out the front door. They had to go with the Mercedes. When Sean had first been carried inside the house, he'd heard Blake say that he and Edward had parked Jack's car on the side of the house under a dogwood tree—the opposite side of the house that Sean was now on.

Sean swore to himself. He had counted on the notion that Blake wouldn't leave without his boss, but with Albano not responding from the Cadillac, Blake may have written him off as dead. With the Mercedes, Blake could tear around the corner to the driveway and make it through the open gate unscathed. Quammen might get off a lucky shot, but only if he would be willing to take it without knowing with certainty who was in the driver's seat behind the car's tinted windows.

"Sean!" Nicola's young voice cried out in the distance. "Are you okay?"

A chill shot through Sean's spine. He watched in horror as Blake's head craned in his direction. Sean ducked back behind the wall, convinced the thug hadn't seen him but had heard the girl.

Sean held his finger to his mouth and glared at Nicola through angry eyes. He shook his head and waved her away again. She seemed confused, unsure of how to interpret his mannerisms. When her head turned to the porch, she cowered and moved away from her window.

Sean's eyes bulged. His attention shot to the side where the large shadow of an approaching man dimmed the gravel along the ground. Blake was now just a couple feet away.

Without a second to spare, Sean could do nothing other than let the survival instinct determine his fate. With a clamped jaw and a face stretched with savagery, he lunged from around the corner and pounced on Blake.

Adrenaline exploded through Sean's veins as one hand latched onto Blake's raised gun arm and the other one wrapped around his throat. He drove his legs forward with every ounce of strength he could muster, growling until Blake's shoulders slammed into the raised edge of the porch. Blake cried out and his gun went off, filling the air with the taste of metal.

Sean arched his back and delivered a vicious headbutt across the bridge of Blake's nose, crushing it and sending a gush of blood across both of their faces. The gun fell from Blake's hand and onto the rocks. Sean's hands went to Blake's eyes, gouging them and forcing a howl that didn't sound human. Through his soul, Sean was bellowing out the names of Blake's victims, ending with his father.

The act of barbarism came to an abrupt halt when one of Blake's hands went to the deep cut on Sean's stomach, his fingers digging into the flesh. Sean wailed in agony and switched to a front face-lock, wrapping his forearm under Blake's chin and severing Blake's grip. He sent repeated knee-lifts into Blake's stomach.

Blake's body folded in half with each blow. Air spewed from his lips in violent coughs. Sean's eyes were falling in and out of focus, but they sharpened just long enough to spot Blake's second pistol wedged into the back of his pants. He pulled one of his arms from Blake's head and reached for the gun. Blake wrapped his own arm around Sean's thigh and pushed him backward to take him off balance. Sean hopped on one foot until he knew he was going down. He let Blake's head slip from his grip and fell to the gravel in a heap.

As Blake staggered to stay on his feet, Sean flipped to the side and reached for Blake's first gun on the ground just inches away.

The rush of endorphins through Sean's body was quickly petering out, but he managed to grab the pistol. By the time he swung around and pointed the gun forward, Blake was already lumbering his way up the hill of rocks, flowers, and shrubbery toward the patio. Blake reached back blindly for the gun in his pants, but Sean fired off a shot before he could pull it out.

Blake's head snapped to the side and his hand lifted to his ear. Sean had only grazed him. Blake kept moving, circling around to the opposite side of the patio and quickly disappearing from sight.

Sean groaned and rolled to his hand and knees. He pursued Blake, crawling to make it up the same small hill that Blake had scaled. When he reached the top, he tried to pull himself upright but collapsed back to his knees. He saw that Blake had already descended the other side of the patio. Gun in hand, he vanished around the other corner of the house. He didn't look back. He was focused on the Mercedes.

Sean clambered along the cement, trying to keep his gun pointed forward. He snarled and swore with effort, pushing forward until he reached the other side of the hill. He tumbled down through greenery, rock, and mulch, until he spilled to the bottom.

A high-pitched whistling in the distance tugged at Sean's attention for the briefest of moments before the crank of an ignition and the roar of an engine echoed out from the side of the building. Blake was already inside the car.

The grin Jack had worn in his dying breaths back in the house glowed through Sean's mind. He hadn't seen that smile in decades, not since a day or two before his father had left. It had come after a much younger Sean had exploded three beer bottles in rapid succession through the sights of the Colt Python—the gun his father left him.

After a long day of learning to shoot, Sean's steady hand had finally won his father's pride. And though Sean had vowed over the years to never again live for that man's regard, the memory of that day was now fueling him, taking the place of his spent adrenaline.

"Take a breath . . . steady yourself . . . squeeze," Sean mumbled through labored breath, recalling his father's instructions.

He climbed to his feet, swaying on wobbly legs. The whistling melody in the distance soon morphed into a fluctuating howl of what sounded like police sirens. Sean didn't know if they were real or the product of a hallucination from his body's loss of blood.

He swayed around the corner of the building with a tight grip on his gun. "Take a breath . . . steady yourself . . . squeeze."

The Mercedes came into focus.

The car was parked under the low-hanging branches of a tree with bright pink leaves. Through the glare of the windshield, Sean made out the outline of Blake's bald head and stout shoulders. Blake had one hand pressed against his ear as the other grasped the top of the steering wheel.

Sean raised his arm and fired off a round.

The driver's side mirror collapsed off the car. It swung around on loose wires as the Mercedes reversed.

"Didn't steady yourself," Sean slurred, channeling his father. "Didn't breathe." He trudged toward the car, keeping his gun pointed in front of him.

A hole punched through the windshield of the Mercedes, and something whizzed past Sean's head. Blake was firing back. Sean didn't flinch or move for cover. He kept his pace, continuing toward the car. He lowered his head under the vibrant leaves of the dogwood and shoved a deep gust of air from his lungs.

The car was turning its way around the corner of the building when Sean squeezed the trigger again. The driver side window shattered and Blake's voice barked from inside the car. What was left of the glass was red with blood. Dirt and gravel flew through the air as the car took a hard turn, escaping from view to the front of the building.

"Gotta keep it steady," Sean lectured himself over the rising volume of the sirens.

A loud crash vibrated the ground and shook Sean's legs. He plodded around the corner of the building and saw that Blake had backed right into the Cadillac. The Cadillac had been pushed into the fish fountain and a burst pipe was sending a thick arch of streaming water across the tops of both cars. The Mercedes's rear tires were still spinning, flinging gravel and debris toward the front tires. They stopped a second later.

Sean heard his name shouted by Quammen over the splash of water and the piercing sirens, but he kept his eyes focused on the window of the Mercedes. He saw something move inside. The door bumped open just a bit, and when a bloody hand holding a pistol busted through the remaining glass, Sean dropped to a knee and closed one eye.

"Steady," he said, squeezing the trigger.

The blast sounded and the driver's head snapped backward. The gun fell from his hand to the ground. Blake's crimson head dropped to the top of the door panel. The door swiveled open and his limp body slumped to the ground. With it came papers, wrappers, and other trash that Sean's father had let litter the inside of the car.

Sean kept his eyes on Blake until he was certain the man wasn't going to move again. He then submitted to the calls of his own body, toppling forward to his chest. The side of his face was now flush with the ground and his eyes floated in and out of darkness until he closed them to end the nuisance.

Above the continual splashing of water and screaming of sirens, Sean heard Quammen shouting out a well-rehearsed right to silence, presumably at Albano. A moment later, he heard Dusty's excited voice rambling about calling for help on a radio before demanding to know of Sean's whereabouts.

When Sean slid his weak eyes back open, he saw his father—young again with dark hair. He was wearing a smile, and Sean believed for a brief moment that he was witnessing a vision from the afterlife. When he saw the face of his sister, as a little girl, nestled directly under Jack's chin, he realized he was looking at a photograph. It had been carried by the breeze over from the Mercedes. Sean's eyes remained on the picture.

The photograph was large—probably an eight by ten. It wobbled against a chunk of cement that had broken free of the fountain, and it glowed with familiarity. Sean remembered it once hanging proudly in his childhood home.

Darkness swept in for a final time, warping the photo's image into a cruel portrayal of Sean as an outsider, one who was hopelessly tapping on the window of a world that wasn't his own.

Chapter 33

Two gravestones sat side by side at the base of a Colorado hillside, resting in the shade of a family of tall aspen trees with thinning yellow leaves and flaky white bark. Engraved words on their granite faces spoke of men who'd passed on before their time— men of the same blood, separated for decades but finally reunited.

Eight days had passed since the gunfire had ended in front of a posh Pawleys Island home, the lives of all involved forever changed.

Diana Lumbergh wept with her shoulders low and her hand over her face. Her police chief husband cradled their daughter in his arm as he spoke to the small group of people in attendance who'd gathered to pay their respects. Diana rested her other hand on the frail shoulder of her elderly mother, who sat in the wheelchair in front of her, emotionless in dark clothing.

Family friend Ron Oldhorse stood straight and quiet with his hallmark stoic demeanor. His long black hair was pulled tightly into a ponytail that draped down along the back of his leather vest. He held the hand of Joan Parker, whose eyes were trained on her son Toby standing on her other side. She bent to whisper words of comfort into Toby's ear, but her voice didn't loosen his shriveled face that shook with heartache.

When Oldhorse leaned in to say something as well, Toby pulled away from the two of them. Thick tears rolled down his red cheeks as he ran past the attendees. All heads followed him until he wrapped his arms around the large frame of a man dressed in a dark shirt and pants who stood apart from the rest.

"I feel so bad," Toby whispered through tears.

"It's okay," said Sean, cringing from the pressure the boy was unknowingly putting on his stitched-up stomach.

At the boy's sobbing, Chief Lumbergh halted speaking and looked from him to Sean.

Sean's eyes went around to the guests before he returned the boy's embrace. With his head high over Toby's shoulder, his gaze switched to the granite slabs that bore the names of his father and his uncle. "They're up in Heaven getting reacquainted," he assured the boy.

"At least you got to see him again, before he died," cried Toby, whose own father had abandoned him years ago.

Sean nodded.

Chief Lumbergh continued his eulogy, speaking of Jack Hansen's early days and his contributions to the town of Winston, along with his brother Zed. Lumbergh had always been an effective speaker, a good diplomat who could put the best face on a bad situation, when the circumstances called for it. Today was no exception. Dressed in a sharp suit and tie, he described Jack as a grandfather, among other things, and took a second to lift his arm a bit and present Ashley to the onlookers who managed a collective grin.

Ashley was napping peacefully against her father's chest, having recovered from a respiratory virus that had kept her parents at the hospital the day Sean couldn't get a hold of them.

Lumbergh wrapped up his speech, and the town pastor delivered a short sermon. Guests then approached Diana and Sean, extending their hands and offering their sympathies. Even Lumbergh's officer, Jefferson, who had long butted heads with Sean, was gracious and careful with his words. Jefferson's stout wife did the same, offering Sean a hug.

Over heads and around shoulders, Sean repeatedly peered at his mother, searching for any hint of awareness that might creep out from behind her tight, angled face. He saw none.

After the crowd thinned, Sean approached his sister. He offered to wheel their mother back down the dirt path to where their cars were parked.

"I'll catch up to you in a second," he said to Diana. "I just want to spend a couple of minutes here with Mom if that's okay."

Diana's eyes narrowed at the request.

"I'll bring her on down shortly. Don't worry," he said, waving her on.

She nodded and grabbed her husband's hand. They and their daughter started their descent down the path. Sean watched them until they fell out of earshot. He then turned and gripped the handles of his mother's wheelchair. The two stared straight ahead at the gravestones. A small chipmunk was now sitting on top of one of them, nibbling at something it held in its tiny hands.

"I always thought it was my fault that he left," Sean said to his mother, knowing she could hear his words though uncertain if she could process them. "No one ever came out and told me that. You didn't tell me that. But it was always there, hanging over the family like a storm cloud that wouldn't lift. The way he was with me before he left. The way you were with me after he left, for all those years. I was made to feel like an outsider—like a black sheep—long before I ever did anything bad enough with my life to earn it."

A gust of wind whisked across the two. Aspen leaves fluttered, some falling from branches and whirling to the ground. The scent of pine drifted past.

"You know, I asked myself a million times just what I had done wrong," Sean continued. "What could this little boy have done that was terrible enough to tear apart his family? And then one day, thirty years later, an unforeseen series of events leads me back to my father. And I finally get to ask him. I finally get to ask him why." He took a breath and swallowed before continuing. "And you know what he tells me? He tells me, 'Sean, it wasn't you. It was Zed.'"

His eyes lowered when the wheelchair felt slightly different, as if his mother's body had somehow managed to tense up.

"Zed," he repeated. "My uncle. The man who stuck around in Winston all those years before he died. Before he was killed. The man who you stopped talking to after Dad left." He took in a breath before continuing. "I had always assumed it was because he reminded you of Dad. Zed looked like him. He talked like him. I thought he'd become the object of your scorn simply because he was Dad's brother. But that wasn't it at all, was it?"

He released the wheelchair and circled around in front of his mother. He dropped to a knee so that he could stare directly into her eyes, the right one misplaced by her stroke.

"Jack Hansen took some things with him when he left Winston. Some of it was just shitty collectibles like those stupid plates that used to hang in our kitchen. But he took other things. He took documents and photographs that were so important to him that he came looking for them in Pawleys Island after they'd been stolen by his friend. Jack broke into my motel room and made off with them. They stayed in his car until he died." His jaw tightened almost painfully, his nose spreading open. "I was given the stuff from the car, while I was in the hospital out there, recovering from surgery. And guess what? You and I weren't in *any* of those photographs. None of them. All of them were of him and Diana . . . together."

Dolores's straight eye suddenly slid to him. He glared back, refusing to blink.

"*Why would that be?* I asked myself. I get why he wouldn't want to remember you—the way you two always fought, but if it was Zed's fault that he left, and not mine, why didn't he want to remember me?" He stood up and began pacing back and forth in front of his mother, taking a second to run his hand through his hair. "Diana's the one he called on the phone a couple of years ago, when she lived in Illinois. Not me, because he didn't feel as though he *needed* to. Diana's the one who he believed deserved an apology. Not me." His voice rose with anger. "And after he'd been shot—after he'd saved my life—he tells me that he could have never been lucky enough to have a son like me. What the hell was that supposed to mean?"

Down the hill, the Lumberghs's heads were turned up at Sean and his mother. The volume and tone of his conversation had grabbed their attention.

Sean bit his lip and waved to them, pretending that nothing was wrong. Diana waved back, the mistrust in her face unmistakable even from that distance.

He lowered himself back to a knee, staring right through his mother. He lowered his voice but not the intensity behind it. "One of the papers that Jack had in his car . . . it was an invoice from an old, old doctor's visit back in Winston—a doctor's visit by *you*, back before I was born, saying that you were over two months pregnant. The words 'two months' were circled over and over again with a pen, and so was the date of the visit at the top. They were circled and scribbled up so many times that whoever had done it had put holes right through the paper." He placed his hands on the armrests of the wheelchair and pulled his mother in closer. "That information really pissed someone off—so much that they abandoned their family because of it."

Dolores's eyes began to water. A tear slid down her cheek. Her lower lip began to quiver.

Sean spoke through his teeth. "Those dates were important because they somehow showed that Jack wasn't really my father. They showed that I was conceived at a time when he was either out of town or God knows what, but when he discovered that doctor's bill years later, he figured it out. Maybe he'd had some suspicions all along, but he suddenly had proof. He suddenly realized that only *one* of his children was actually his." He exhaled in frustration.

His mother's gaze fell to her lap.

"Yeah," he said, shaking his head. "Jack should have stuck around for her. He was an asshole for leaving. He was a coward. But in his weak, selfish mind, the betrayal was so sick and so personal that he just couldn't bring himself to own up to the one responsibility he still had. He abandoned it all: the woman who'd cheated on him . . . and his brother, who she'd slept with."

He raised his hands to his forehead and scratched at his scalp, growling under his breath. "You know, I sat in that hospital trying to figure out how Zed could have never told me over all those years—how he could have never just said, 'Sean, I'm your father!'" His voice shook. "And then it suddenly occurred to me. He never knew, did he? You had kept the truth from him, just like you had kept it from Jack for the first seven years of my life. You lied to both of them about who had gotten you pregnant, and you probably fed Zed some other line of shit about why his brother left and never talked to him—to any of us—again."

He gripped the armrests tighter. The wheelchair began to shake from his hold on it.

"You didn't want Zed to know. You wanted to deprive him of knowing that he had a son. You wanted to deprive his son of knowing that he had a father, alive and well and living in the same town . . . all of those years—all because you blamed Zed for Jack leaving. That was your bitter, bitter revenge. No, you didn't blame yourself. You blamed *him*. And though you never said it to me, and probably still wouldn't say it even if you could talk, you blamed me, too. Our family fell apart because I was born. It just took seven years before anyone else knew it."

He yanked his hands from the wheelchair and stood up straight, ignoring the pain along his stitches that flared from the sharp movement. With a tight fist, he glared down at the top of his mother's head.

Diana was now walking back up the hill toward them, her face tight and tilted with concern.

"I could have had a father," Sean growled, his chest heaving in and out as he stared at his mother. "What you did was evil. It was evil. And now . . . now I don't have a mother, either."

Diana was within a few feet of them, and Sean lifted his head to meet her gaze. He tried without success to slow down his breathing.

"What's going on?" she asked with confused eyes. She leaned down to her mother before lifting her head back up to Sean. "Are you okay?"

He nodded his head intensely, his face still fuming. "I'm thinking you'd better wheel her back to the car after all."

He turned and stormed past them. He made his way down the hill, his heavy footsteps commanding an eerie silence from the birds in the surrounding trees. When his sister called after him, her voice echoing off the forest, he ignored her. He could feel Chief Lumbergh, standing in front of his car with a blank face, watch the scene, still holding his daughter. He said nothing.

Sean whipped open the door of his Nova and climbed inside. He slammed the door shut and smashed his fist on the steering wheel. The engine revved after a twist of the ignition, and he tore off down the dirt road, sending a trail of dust and madness high into the air behind him.

———————

That evening, Sean didn't show up at the reception at his sister's house, and he ignored the repeated, obnoxious rings of the phone. Instead, he ended up at a local bar called O'Rafferty's at the center of town. There, he guzzled down his first drink of alcohol in over a year.

It was far from his last of the night.